MY GRANDFATHER, THE MASTER DETECTIVE

Masateru Konishi graduated from the Department of English and American Literature at Meiji University, and now works as a writer for TV and radio. He has previously written for the stage as well as a manga story; *My Grandfather, the Master Detective* is his debut novel. Partly based on his own experience of caring for his father with dementia, the book won the twenty-first edition of the prestigious 'This Mystery is Amazing!' Grand Prize.

Louise Heal Kawai has been a Japanese-English literary translator since 2006. Her first publication was Shoko Tendo's bestselling autobiography *Yakuza Moon*. She has gone on to translate a large number of crime fiction titles, including Seishi Yokomizo's *The Honjin Murders* and works by Soji Shimada and Seicho Matsumoto. Her literary translations include *Ms Ice Sandwich* by Mieko Kawakami and Hideo Yokoyama's *Seventeen*, which was a finalist in the 2018 Believer Book Awards, and longlisted for the 2019 Best Translated Book Award. She is also the translator of Sosuke Natsukawa's *The Cat Who Saved Books*. Louise comes from Manchester in the UK, and currently resides in Yokohama.

My Grandfather, the Master Detective

MASATERU KONISHI

Translated from the Japanese by Louise Heal Kawai

MACMILLAN

First published in the UK 2025 by Macmillan
an imprint of Pan Macmillan
The Smithson, 6 Briset Street, London EC1M 5NR
EU representative: Macmillan Publishers Ireland Ltd, 1st Floor,
The Liffey Trust Centre, 117–126 Sheriff Street Upper,
Dublin 1 D01 YC43
Associated companies throughout the world

ISBN 978-1-0350-3768-1 HB
ISBN 978-1-0350-3769-8 PB

Copyright © Masateru Konishi 2023 [2025]
Translation copyright © Louise Heal Kawai 2025

The right of Masateru Konishi to be identified as the
author of this work has been asserted in accordance
with the Copyright, Designs and Patents Act 1988.

Originally published 2023 in Japan as *Meitantei No Mama De Ite Vol. 1* by Takarajimasha Inc., Tokyo.
English language translation rights arranged with Takarajimasha Inc. through
The English Agency (Japan) Ltd and New River Literary Ltd.

All rights reserved. No part of this publication may be reproduced,
stored in a retrieval system, or transmitted, in any form, or by any means
(including, without limitation, electronic, mechanical, photocopying, recording
or otherwise) without the prior written permission of the publisher.

Pan Macmillan does not have any control over, or any responsibility for,
any author or third-party websites (including, without limitation, URLs,
emails and QR codes) referred to in or on this book.

1 3 5 7 9 8 6 4 2

A CIP catalogue record for this book is available from the British Library.

Typeset in Galliard by Six Red Marbles UK, Thetford, Norfolk
Printed and bound in the UK using 100% Renewable Electricity by CPI Group (UK) Ltd

This book is sold subject to the condition that it shall not, by way of
trade or otherwise, be lent, hired out, or otherwise circulated without
the publisher's prior consent in any form of binding or cover other than
that in which it is published and without a similar condition including this
condition being imposed on the subsequent purchaser. The publisher does not
authorize the use or reproduction of any part of this book in any manner
for the purpose of training artificial intelligence technologies or systems.
The publisher expressly reserves this book from the Text and Data Mining
exception in accordance with Article 4(3) of the European Union
Digital Single Market Directive 2019/790.

Visit **www.panmacmillan.com** to read more about
all our books and to buy them.

CONTENTS

I – *Those Little Scarlet Cells* 1

II – *The Izakaya Locked-Room Murder Mystery* 37

III – *The Vanishing Person at the Pool* 103

IV – *They Were Thirty-Three!* 169

V – *The Phantom Lady* 193

VI – *The Riddle of the Stalker* 265

Chapter 1:
Those Little Scarlet Cells

1

'A blue tiger dropped by this morning,' said Kaede's grandfather. 'I wonder how it managed to turn the knob. Must be amazingly adept with its paws.'

The fact that a tiger had been in his study, or even that its fur was blue, seemed far less puzzling to him than how it had managed to open the front door.

'Good thing you didn't get bitten,' Kaede remarked, careful to sound casual about it, but in truth her heart sank a little.

Here we go again . . .

Kaede only managed to make it out here to the Himonya district of Tokyo once a week, and when she did, generally found her grandfather asleep. But then, in the rare moments she caught him awake, all he'd talk about were his hallucinations, and she'd leave without having had any kind of meaningful conversation at all.

Nevertheless, she listened without complaint to his tale of the blue tiger, nodding along at the appropriate moments. She cherished the time she got to spend with her grandfather in the house she'd grown up in.

'And when the tiger went to leave . . .' Grandfather was saying, imitating the way it crossed its forelegs in front as it walked, 'it flashed me a big smile.'

'The tiger smiled?'

And now here I go again too . . .

Yet another far-fetched tale, and she found herself hanging on his every word. At first, she just pretended to listen, but her grandfather was such a skilled storyteller that she was completely drawn in to his alternate universe. And now he'd even got her believing that at any moment a blue tiger might leap out of one of the illustrated books on the shelf.

It seemed Grandfather had had his fill of talking. His eyelids began to close.

Kaede's grandfather spent all day in this room in his reclining chair. She had gone to the trouble of finding an extra-large one to suit his tall, skinny frame, but this had turned out to be a mistake, as now he was so comfortable he didn't budge from his spot.

A wooden walking stick, which he needed to get around,

Those Little Scarlet Cells

was propped up against the side table. The care manager who'd recommended it would complain that although he'd use it to go to the toilet, he never bothered with it whenever he was browsing his bookshelves. 'One of these days he's going to have a fall,' she'd sigh reproachfully.

Still reading books then, but how much is he really taking in . . . ?

The crammed bookshelves gave off a musty smell of old ink. Kaede was reminded of her beloved Jinbocho, the used-bookshop district in Tokyo.

As he dozed in his chair, Kaede observed her grandfather under the dappled sunlight from the window. The high bridge of his nose and deep crow's feet created shadows on a face that was surprisingly blemish-free for a seventy-one-year-old. These days his cheeks had hollowed out, but this served to accentuate his chiselled features. His long, thick hair, parted in the middle above his prominent forehead, was about 70 per cent white these days. The salt and pepper effect reminded Kaede of a Roman emperor's head engraved on a coin.

As his granddaughter, Kaede was biased but she knew he was an impressive-looking man.

He must have been popular with the ladies . . .

She retrieved the blanket that had slipped down and gently covered him back up.

After she finished cleaning her grandfather's room, she

sprayed the space with an antibacterial solution that had the fragrance of soap, careful not to let it into contact with any of the books. It was about time for the physiotherapist's visit.

This antibacterial spray wasn't only for cleaning purposes; her grandfather would often hallucinate that the room was filled with tiny insects, such as mosquitoes. At those times the spray doubled as a makeshift 'insecticide'.

All right then, Grandpa. I'll see you soon . . .

Over by the door was a dressing table with a mirror which had belonged to Kaede's grandmother. Rather than it having aged, Kaede preferred to think of it as having evolved through the years, its woodgrain accumulating layers of time, giving it a complex depth of colour. She took a hairbrush from the drawer of the dresser and quickly fixed her hair, stopping to compose her facial expression in the mirror.

Smile!

The solid oak door to the study had been replaced with sliding doors, in anticipation of the day her grandfather would be confined to a wheelchair. Kaede silently slid the door shut behind her and left the house.

2

Aboard a swaying Toyoko Line train, Kaede caught sight of her face in the window. It was expressionless. There was no hint of the carefully composed smile she'd worn for her visit.

Those Little Scarlet Cells

Twilight had fallen and the sky was streaked with faint pink lines like the traces of a lipstick kiss. It was early autumn and the cumulonimbus clouds of summer were gone; instead, the sky was filled with clouds of all different shapes. Memories of her grandfather flitted through Kaede's mind.

Twenty-three years earlier, when Kaede had been four . . .

She sat with him on the low, wooden *engawa* veranda as they watched the reddening sky. Grandfather's bright and wise eyes had dropped to his beloved granddaughter, secure in his lap.

'Kaede? See those clouds over there – what do you think they look like? See if you can make up a story using all three.'

In retrospect, she realized he was asking for a classic three-topic *rakugo* story. He'd been trying to give flight to her imagination. It was typical of her grandfather and his knack for nurturing creativity.

Kaede hadn't hesitated.

'That cloud there is a tiny little grandpa. That cloud is a squished grandpa. And then the biggest cloud of all is a big, fat grandpa, bigger than you.'

Grandfather's face broke into a huge grin.

'Well, you can't make a story out of that . . . or can we?'

And then, to Kaede's surprise and delight, he made up a fairy tale for her on the spot, entitled 'The Three Grandpas'. She didn't recall all the details, but she did remember the ending where greedy Big Fat Grandpa ate up all the cold medicine in the world, mistaking it for sugar, and although everyone teased him for it, he ended up living the longest life of all of them.

She guessed now that the story was meant as a lesson for her four-year-old self, who had hated the bitter taste of powdered medicine. But at the time, the way he told the tale was so entertaining that she had clapped her hands in delight.

'Oh wow. Kaede, look!'

When she had looked up at the sky again, only the big fat grandpa cloud remained; the tiny little grandpa and the squished grandpa had, quite literally, vanished into thin air.

Just like the end of the story.

Kaede had stared in amazement at the big fat grandpa cloud, and then her own grandfather's face.

Thinking back, she realized that he must have been keeping an eye on the cloud movement as he spun his tale. Had either the tiny little grandpa or the squished grandpa survived, then for sure the story would have taken quite a different turn.

'Hey, Grandpa! Tell me another story, or else . . .'

She'd reached up and tugged on the hair growing from the mole on his Adam's apple.

Kaede recalled how easily the hair had come out, which at the time made her burst into giggles.

Those Little Scarlet Cells

Maybe it was my fault . . . Did I pull the plug and drain Grandpa's mind?

It was only six months ago that Grandfather had started showing symptoms.

They'd gone for a walk together and Kaede noticed his stride had got shorter.

'Grandpa, are you putting on weight or something? Your feet can't seem to keep up with you.'

'Must be getting old,' he'd replied with a self-deprecating smile.

At first Kaede put it down to weight gain or, as he said, a simple case of ageing. At least that was what she wanted to believe.

However, the decline was fast. His hand shook when he drank his coffee, and whenever Kaede visited, she found him dozing in his study chair. His posture grew more hunched and his movements sluggish.

But then came the biggest shock of all. Kaede would never forget the day.

Late one night her phone rang. She rubbed her eyes, and picked up.

'Um . . . I'm with emergency medical services . . .'

The young man on the end of line seemed to be having trouble expressing what he wanted to say.

'Am I speaking to Kaede-san? Good. I see. We found your name on a note pinned to the wall . . . as an emergency contact. It seems that your grandfather called for an ambulance. And then . . . well, how can I put it . . . ?'

'What's happened?'

'He's saying that you're here, um . . . lying dead in a pool of blood.'

At his regular clinic, they said that it might be Parkinson's disease but they couldn't be sure, and recommended that he go to a major hospital. At the university hospital they did a full battery of tests, including a CT scan.

The young female doctor gave Kaede the diagnosis, despite the presence of her grandfather asleep in the seat next to her.

'Your grandfather has Lewy Body Dementia.'

It had been a struggle for Kaede to accept that her brilliant grandfather had been diagnosed with dementia at such an early age; he was only just into his seventies. However, after researching, she found that every one of his symptoms was consistent with the disease. She read that over 4.5 million people in Japan suffered from dementia, and that it wasn't one single condition; there were several different variations of the disease.

Dementia can be categorized into three main types.

Most commonly, there's Alzheimer's, accounting for about 70 per cent of patients. It's caused by the accumulation of a plaque on the brain. This plaque is created by the breakdown of a protein known as beta-amyloid 42. When people hear the word dementia, it's likely Alzheimer's that comes to mind first.

The second most common is vascular dementia, brought on by the after-effects of a stroke, and is the cause of 20 per cent of dementia cases.

Both of these types present with similar symptoms: memory loss that causes the patient to repeat the same thing over and over, and disorientation, where sense of time and/or place becomes hazy and the patient often ends up wandering around, confused.

And then there's Dementia with Lewy Bodies (DLB), commonly known as Lewy Body Dementia, affecting 10 per cent of the patient total.

This was Kaede's grandfather's diagnosis.

DLB wasn't named until 1995, making it one of the more recently discovered diseases in the long history of human illness. It has gained attention in recent years as 'the third dementia', with the race to understand its pathology underway in the medical field. There are a number of ongoing clinical trials.

Tiny, fried-egg-shaped crimson structures called Lewy bodies are consistently found on the brains and brainstems of DLB patients. These mini fried eggs cause symptoms such as tremors in the limbs and walking difficulties, often referred to as Parkinson's symptoms; or shouting out in one's sleep, known as REM sleep behaviour disorder. They also lead to states of drowsiness during the day, known as hypersomnia, and to spatial recognition impairment, where patients cannot perceive distances accurately.

However, the most distinctive symptom, and one that is unique to this variation of dementia, is the visual hallucinations. While the appearance of the hallucinations varies – some patients report seeing them in black and white, others in colour – the common denominator is that they are always described as 'vivid', 'graphic' or 'distinct'.

For example, upon waking in the morning and opening their eyes, a patient may see ten people standing in their room, silently staring at them. Or perhaps there's a giant snake coiled up on the dining table. Or sometimes a girl with pigtails will trail behind them all day long.

Fantastical visions are not uncommon either.

A pig marches briskly across the room on two legs.

A fairy leaps gracefully onto a plate.

And then of course there's the blue tiger that Kaede's grandfather claimed to see . . .

Oddly, in most cases, there's no accompanying auditory hallucination. These creatures that manifest themselves are purely visual illusions. In other words, they don't talk to the patient.

Human beings possess five senses, but it is believed that 90 per cent of the information we receive from the world around us is through sight. To the majority of DLB sufferers, these hallucinations are completely real. The most common expression used by patients is 'seeing is believing'. It's no easy task to convince them that something doesn't exist when they can see it with their own eyes.

When their friends or family use phrases such as 'there's nothing there' or 'that's impossible' or even 'pull yourself together' it's very common for the patient to get angry. This is one of the reasons why caring for DLB patients is so difficult.

In a handbook for caregivers, Kaede found the following advice:

If the patient tells you for example that they can see a giant insect or that they're scared, don't dismiss their fears with responses such as 'It's just your imagination' or 'You know it's because of your illness'. Be patient with them. Try clapping your hands and saying, 'Look! I scared it away. You'll be fine now.' Changing the topic of conversation is also effective.

That all made sense, Kaede thought.

Her grandfather had never in his life raised his voice to her, and she was determined not to get into an argument with him. For that reason, she always avoided discussing his illness with him. And when he talked about his hallucinations, she was careful not to deny their existence.

Making a patient aware that they have dementia is next to impossible. Even if it were possible, it would be too cruel.

But at the same time, Kaede couldn't help but feel an odd sense of unease. It was like doing a simple mathematical equation that should have divided evenly, but inexplicably left a remainder where there shouldn't be one . . . It was a feeling subtly different from the wishful thinking that her grandfather's dementia wouldn't develop further or that he would never lose his sharp mind.

But something's not quite right . . .

What was causing her feeling of unease? Kaede couldn't identify it.

3

A fifteen-minute bus ride from Gumyoji station in Yokohama brought Kaede back to her one-room apartment.

A book had arrived in the mail, a collection of essays by literary critic and mystery fiction connoisseur Takeshi Setogawa.

Those Little Scarlet Cells

The title page read: 1 April 1998, First Edition.

If Kaede remembered correctly, Setogawa had passed away shortly after its publication, at the age of fifty. In other words, this book had been his last work.

Under her grandfather's tutelage, Kaede had become an avid mystery fan. Eventually, she'd felt the need to branch out beyond reading novels and had begun delving into the essay collections by Setogawa that she found on her grandfather's bookshelves. She was completely blown away.

The literary critic would select a work and, with his unique perspective and quite natural brilliance, discuss its appeal. His essays, almost without exception, were more entertaining than the works themselves. For example, in a series of essays titled *A Pilgrimage of the Masterpieces*, he skewered the classic works of three iconic authors of the genre – Ellery Queen, Agatha Christie, and John Dickson Carr – daring to ask the question 'Are these true masterpieces?' His arguments were more logical, thrilling and flawless than the novels themselves. Yet, whether intentionally or not, Setogawa's deep love for these authors seeped from between the lines of his writing, leaving Kaede with a warm and fluffy feeling each time she read them.

This was the god who had turned Kaede into a fan of the classic Golden Age mystery.

Takeshi Setogawa. (Just whispering his name to herself made Kaede's heart flutter.)

Back in 1970 or so, the young Setogawa had been a central figure in the legendary Waseda Mystery Club, a university student circle that would go on to produce a whole slew of famous mystery writers and critics.

There used to be a cafe in Nishi-Waseda called Mon Chéri where, day after day, the students of the Waseda Mystery Club would froth in excitement over the latest mystery novels. At the centre of these discussions was always Setogawa, with his heavy eyebrows and striking facial features, smiling brightly.

And Kaede's own grandfather had been a core member of this same club.

Coffee and mystery novels went extremely well together.

The cafe's vertical sign that read *Speciality coffee: Mon Chéri* in three-dimensional white lettering on a blood-red background seemed inviting to nobody but the most dedicated mystery aficionados. Its dark, bitter coffee swirled with bubbles that seemed to conceal an unfathomable mystery. The yellow-tiled exterior was reminiscent of Gaston Leroux's *The Mystery of the Yellow Room*, and the echo of the actors' footsteps as they trod the boards in the tiny theatre right above could have come straight out of G. K. Chesterton's 'The Queer Feet' or Edogawa Ranpo's 'The Stalker in the Attic'.

But now Mon Chéri was gone; all Kaede could do was give free rein to her imagination. With Setogawa and her grandfather as regulars, that cafe must have radiated a vibrant energy, much like the iconic Tokiwa-so apartment building full of aspiring manga artists, or Mount Liang from the classic Chinese novel, *Water Margin.*

I wish I could have been there to hear the two of them debating classic mysteries . . .

The coffee shop no longer in existence, Kaede's imagination expanded to fill the gaps created by its absence.

Mon Chéri was no more, but there were still Setogawa's books. Kaede preferred to have her favourite books within easy reach, but since all her grandfather's books were meticulously preserved in translucent glassine covers, not a single page dog-eared, Kaede was hesitant to borrow any. Consequently, she had made the decision to purchase all of Setogawa's essays for herself.

Wonderful! It even has the original obi *wrapper band intact . . .*

Kaede was overjoyed to find that the book she'd just purchased was in mint condition. Truth be told, she would have preferred to collect brand-new copies of everything, but as this particular book was out of print, she'd had no choice but to buy a used copy from an online specialist bookshop.

With this volume, her Setogawa set was complete.

I wonder what it says about a twenty-seven-year-old woman that I'm this proud of my collection?

With a delighted grin on her face, and without bothering to sit down, she starting flipping through the book. As she did so, four small pieces of paper fluttered out from between the pages like ginkgo leaves in autumn, and landed softly on the carpet.

What's this?

Kaede carefully gathered up the papers and laid them out on the dining table. She stared at them a while. They were rectangles of various sizes.

Too many to be bookmarks . . . And the paper is too sturdy for them to be sticky notes . . .

They were clippings from a magazine or a newspaper.

And each was an obituary reporting the death of Takeshi Setogawa.

4

Taking advantage of the national holiday, Kaede set off for Meguro Ward. It was three days since she'd last visited her grandfather. He lived in a residential area, by Himonya Hachimangu Shrine, which housed the local guardian deity.

Grandfather's home was an unassuming two-storey wooden house that had fallen into some disrepair. Cherry tree and Japanese paper plant branches extended beyond the wall of the modest garden.

The wooden nameplate on the gatepost was beautifully

etched, the ink still vivid. It was in her grandfather's bold handwriting, familiar to Kaede since childhood. It is said that a nameplate is the face of a house, and Kaede reflected that perhaps the reason this rundown house still retained an air of dignity was thanks to her grandfather's skilful brushwork.

However, after she passed through the gate, it was a different story. The house's charm rapidly diminished. There had once been a sequence of smooth, rounded rocks creating a path to the front door, but since Grandfather's diagnosis these had been replaced with characterless concrete. The front door was long overdue for renovation, and its knob squeaked as Kaede turned it. Immediately she was assailed by the smell of antibacterial soap.

She was about to call out to see if the home helper was in, but stopped herself when she noticed there were no shoes in the *genkan* entranceway. It was likely that the helper had just left after finishing the cleaning and laundry.

Several new handrails had been installed along the hallway, essential for her grandfather to get around the house. There had been complicated procedures and paperwork to get through when applying to the local authorities for equipment like this, and the delays and excessive waiting times had meant that Kaede's grandfather, like many others, had ended up paying out of pocket for the installation.

Kaede took the door on the left into the living room.

Her eyes went straight to the house's main supporting pillar, its sheen long gone. There was a series of horizontal pencil marks on it, recording the height of her mother while she was growing up, and of Kaede too, the only grandchild. Although the numbers and dates had almost faded to nothing, her grandfather's master penmanship was unmistakeable. But she felt her chest contract in pain when she saw one of the handrails bolted straight through the middle of the lettering.

She noticed that several white T-shirts had been hung up to dry by the window.

Oh no. That was careless of the home helper.

It was advised not to hang laundry to dry indoors, because DLB patients might mistake the clothes for people. White T-shirts were the worst for this, because they were like a blank canvas for the patients' most intense hallucinations.

Kaede had read that for similar reasons paintings with human subjects and family photographs should be kept out of sight. This had prompted her to stash all the framed photos from her grandfather's desk in the back of a drawer.

She hurried over to the window and had just begun to take the T-shirts off the hangers, when she heard her grandfather's voice behind her.

'I'm sorry. Sanae hung those up to dry. Are they not properly clean?'

Those Little Scarlet Cells

Grandfather walked across the living room, coffee cup in hand, and sat down on the bed. The upstairs bedroom had already been converted into a storage room, so now his movements were limited to this living room, where his bed was located, and the study, next to it at the far end of the hallway.

Judging by his steady gait, he seemed to be doing much better than on Kaede's previous visit. One common characteristic of Lewy Body Dementia was significant fluctuations in the day-to-day physical condition of patients.

'No, I was just trying to straighten out the creases,' Kaede replied, giving up and leaving the T-shirts where they were. 'So, it was Mum who came by today, not the home helper?'

'Yes, she was in a bit of a hurry because she had to get back to work. It's a pity – you just missed her.'

Kaede felt relieved.

It's better that way . . .

. . . at least today, when she needed to bring up such an important topic with her grandfather. It was rare these days to see him in such good health.

'Sanae's coffee tastes good even when it's gone cold,' remarked her grandfather with a smile, readjusting himself on the bed. With a slightly trembling hand he lifted his cup to his lips and took a sip before continuing.

'No danger of spilling it today. I'm in pretty good shape,

even though I say so myself . . . I'd like to ask you something. It's just a hunch though . . .'

He took another sip of coffee and then looked Kaede straight in the eyes.

'You have something important to discuss with me, don't you? I can tell just by looking at your expression.'

Kaede felt a bit like crying. As usual he avoided using the third person to refer to himself ('Grandpa can tell') the way most grandparents did when talking with a grandchild. It was one of his endearing quirks.

She saw that those clear, brown eyes with their gentle gaze were alert. It felt as if her beloved Grandpa from long ago was back with her; there was no hint of drowsiness and his speech was lucid. She realized that, out of concern for his health, she'd avoided any serious conversation for about six months.

Now was the moment to ask. She gathered her courage.

'Yes, actually, there is something I want to ask you.'

'What is it?'

'Grandpa . . .'

She struggled to hold back her tears.

'Grandpa . . . you know, don't you – that you're ill? That you've been seeing things that aren't there? You already know that, don't you?'

She couldn't do it. Her voice was beginning to wobble.

'But because you didn't want to worry me . . .'

The tears began to fall. She had promised herself she wouldn't cry.

'Because you didn't want to worry me, you've been pretending not to know.'

Her grandfather wore the same gentle smile as he took another sip of coffee. Then, with the greatest care, he placed the cup on the dining table by the bed.

'Yes, Kaede, you're correct. I have Lewy Body Dementia.'

Her instincts had been right.

Her grandfather's irises were iridescent, like fine glasswork, with a depth that pulled you in. Yes, that was it – they were still alive with the same light of intelligence that had always been there. And that, Kaede now recognized, was the true source of the unease that she had been feeling.

Over the next couple of days, Kaede dug deeper into the subject of Dementia with Lewy Bodies.

She discovered that among DLB patients there could be significant differences in the decline of memory and spatial recognition, depending on where in the brain the Lewy bodies developed.

Some patients were constantly fearful of their hallucinations, while others got used to them very easily. The intensity of symptoms varied greatly from patient to patient.

There were also numerous reports that when the balance of medications was perfectly managed, the visual hallucinations could disappear completely, as if a fog had lifted. In fact, depending on their physical condition, there were days when patients might show no signs of cognitive decline at all.

What surprised Kaede the most was learning that many DLB patients were fully aware that the images they saw were not real, but rather a product of the illness. There were those who took an extremely positive approach to the situation, looking forward to whatever hallucinations the day might bring; some even made a hobby out of sketching them.

However, there was still a lack of scientific understanding in the field of DLB, which led to many misconceptions, even in the medical field. There were plenty of doctors who would jump to a diagnosis of progressive dementia simply due to these vivid hallucinations, without properly considering the full range of possibilities.

The onset of DLB did not necessarily mean mental decline. When Kaede learned this, her own sense of unease lifted like a fog.

'Well, besides these Parkinson's-like symptoms . . .' Kaede's grandfather had said, glancing down at the slight quiver in his hand, 'I noticed a long time ago that my mental state was far from what you'd call normal. For example, when I look at those bookshelves, I see the kind of intricate engravings that a skilled carpenter would carve into a *mikoshi* festival float. But when I try to trace them with my fingers, there's no texture to suggest it's been carved at all – the wood is perfectly smooth. So, which should I trust, my sight or my touch? Well, it makes no sense to assume someone snuck in at night and created intricate carvings the whole length of that wall without my noticing. Who in their right mind would break into an old man's room just to engrave a bookshelf? This unfortunately led me to the conclusion that it's my sense of touch I need to trust. I can't rely on my sight any more.'

Kaede had listened silently, unable to find the words to respond.

'So, then I wondered: what was the cause of this anomaly? My computer's down so I can't use that to investigate. I thought about searching on my smartphone, but as you can see, my hands are too unsteady. But more significantly, after I saw you lying dead on the floor and called an ambulance, your mother confiscated my phone, so I had no way to access the internet at all.'

Grandfather had pouted, but there was a devilish twinkle in his eye.

'I convinced the helper to call me one of those wheelchair-accessible taxis, and I took a trip to the library. It took me the whole day to investigate because my eyes would go blurry staring at all those words, but in the end, I knew what disease I was suffering from. Incidentally, you know how Hercule Poirot is always talking about his "little grey cells"?'

He smiled ruefully.

'Well, it turns out that in my case, due to the reddish-orange appearance of those Lewy bodies scattered throughout my brain, I have "little scarlet cells".'

'Wait . . .' Kaede heard her own voice begin to crack. 'Then why did you make a point of telling me all about your hallucinations if you already knew they weren't real?'

'Well, you see . . .'

Grandfather hesitated a moment.

'It's because while I was telling you about them, your facial expressions would change so much. You'd look surprised, or you'd smile. But most importantly, you'd speak, responding to the stories. And that was how I could be sure that you were really there.'

'Huh? What are you talking about? I'll always be right there for you, Grandpa.'

'Let me put it another way. I once turned to you and told you that I was afraid that I didn't have very much longer to live, and . . . how can I put it . . . ? I dislike that term *shukatsu*; planning for the end of life has a very unpleasant ring to it . . . Anyway, I had a conversation with you where I was completely honest about how I envisaged living out the rest of my life. At the time I thought I was in excellent shape, perfectly lucid. I remember thinking, "Now's the right moment to express these thoughts." I must have talked for about an hour. But for some reason, you sat there listening to my whole speech in total silence, expressionless. And then . . .'

Grandfather paused and dropped his gaze.

'You vanished before my eyes. You were a hallucination.'

Perhaps it was the memory combined with the taste of his dark-roasted coffee, but a look of bitterness flashed across his face.

'I can't imagine anything more miserable than that. At that point I resolved never to bring up the subject of my illness unless you mentioned it first. Even if it meant you thought I was a senile old man who couldn't hold a decent conversation any more. There was nothing else for it.'

Grandpa . . .

She whispered the word in her heart.

Grandpa . . .

Her grandfather who couldn't bring himself to – or rather didn't dare to – talk to his granddaughter about preparing for the end of his life.

How had she not noticed how much pain he was in?

He saw hallucinations clear as life, and frequently. Along with memory loss, he also suffered from occasional impaired consciousness. His movements were slow and laboured due to Parkinson's-like symptoms.

And yet his mind was still as sharp as ever.

5

School was out at the nearby Christian-run preschool.

Kaede could hear the children singing what sounded like a nursery rhyme as they passed by the house. Their slightly off-pitch singing was adorable. Even the lines on Grandpa's face naturally relaxed.

It was autumn, when the evening sun seemed to plunge like a pebble into a well. But today there was still time before the sun set.

'Grandpa, I've got something I want to show you.'

Kaede took the collection of essays by Takeshi Setogawa out of her black bag.

If Grandpa had been napping in his chair as usual, she would have draped the freshly laundered blanket she had brought over him, then sat beside him reading for a while.

But perhaps with Grandpa alert the way he is right now . . .

Grandfather took his rimless reading glasses from the pocket of his gown and placed them on the high bridge of his nose. Even then, he still had to hold the book at quite a distance to make it out.

Those Little Scarlet Cells

'This is Setogawa's last work!' he said, deeply moved. 'You didn't need to buy it; I would have given you my copy.'

Kaede smiled to herself.

No way. I'd never have taken your precious book . . .

'I'm pretty sure it's out of print,' Grandfather added. 'I'm surprised you managed to get a copy.'

'Well, these days they have speciality stores online for used books, so you can get hold of rare books fairly easily. Anyway, I found these tucked inside.'

Kaede opened the book and took out the four obituary clippings, placing them on the table.

TAKESHI SETOGAWA, PROMINENT MYSTERY NOVEL AND FILM CRITIC, PASSES AWAY

THE PASSING OF SETOGAWA; HIS TALENT WILL BE SORELY MISSED

AN ERA OF MULTILAYERED CRITICISM – THE LEGACY OF SETOGAWA

SETOGAWA TALKED OF A JOYOUS UNION OF MYSTERY AND FILM

Grandfather glanced over the headlines.

'Yes, I read them all at the time,' he said, a tinge of sorrow in his voice. 'Two other newspapers also ran articles. Of course, I've kept them all in my scrapbook.'

Kaede found herself once again impressed by her

grandfather's memory. Although the disease had caused him to forget many recent events, when it came to the past, the drawers of his mind seemed to slide right open.

'Grandpa, I think we've got an everyday-life mystery to solve here.'

'Is that so?' he remarked. 'Something like, "Who placed these clippings inside this book, and for what purpose?"'

'Exactly. For a start, using four newspaper clippings as bookmarks is a bit excessive, don't you think? And obituaries in place of sticky notes? Weirdly inappropriate, right?'

'Hmm, reminds me of a Harry Kemelman story,' Grandfather said, taking off his glasses.

Kemelman's famous short story 'The Nine Mile Walk' was a mystery of pure logic in which the single line, 'A nine-mile walk is no joke, especially in the rain,' overheard outside a pub, leads to the solution of a murder case from the previous day.

'Kaede, pass me a cigarette, would you?'

There was something rhythmic about his request, almost incantatory.

Kaede retrieved a blue box of cigarettes from the drawer of the writing desk. Gauloises, a French brand. They weren't particularly expensive, but not easy to find either. Kaede always bought them from a famous tobacconist's – a tiny shop in the second-hand-bookshop district of Jinbocho.

'I'd appreciate it if you could light it for me. Yes, that's

Those Little Scarlet Cells

it. My hands tremble a bit, so I avoid imbibing when I'm alone.'

Grandfather would often say 'imbibe' or 'drink' a cigarette rather than 'smoke'. It was a holdover from a bygone era when cigarettes weren't considered a vice, and were instead an accepted luxury item like alcohol. Even when he was young, he only 'drank' a few a week; now he rarely partook. Kaede believed he should be allowed to indulge in this one small pleasure.

As Grandfather drank in his cigarette, an expression of quiet bliss passed across his face.

Kaede didn't mind the smell of Gauloises, but she cracked the window slightly, afraid the drying T-shirts might absorb the smoke. Grandfather slowly exhaled.

'Right then . . .' he said, his voice alive with anticipation. It was as if the cigarette had flipped some kind of switch in his brain. 'What kind of tale can you weave from this evidence?'

Kaede's pulse quickened. Her grandfather had always referred to these kinds of hypotheses as 'tales' to 'weave'.

He was back. This was her old Grandpa.

'Here's what I've come up with . . .'

She did her best not to get too excited, sharing a couple of theories that she'd been carefully piecing together in her head.

'Tale Number One: the person who put the obituaries

inside the book was its original owner. He or she wanted to share with other Setogawa fans the overwhelming sense of emptiness they'd felt at his death, so they put the articles inside the book for the buyer to find.'

She glanced at her grandfather, who nodded as if she had just voiced his own thoughts.

Presenting her 'tales' to him usually made her nervous; today, however, she only felt joy.

Just like the old days . . .

'Um . . . Tale Number Two . . .' she announced, forcing herself to focus. 'The owner of a used bookshop put the clippings in the book. He or she is a fan of Setogawa. Decades after its original publication, an order comes in for the last book Setogawa ever wrote. Thrilled, they include these obituaries as a gift to a fellow enthusiast – namely me – despite never having met me.'

Kaede's throat felt dry, surely from the excitement at engaging with Grandpa this way.

'What do you think?' she asked eagerly. 'That's what I've come up with so far.'

'Hmm. Not bad, I suppose. Both stories have a certain logic about them, neither are too far-fetched. But you know there are serious inconsistencies in both.'

'Are there?'

Kaede bit her lip.

'Let's start with Tale One. Why would someone who is

Those Little Scarlet Cells

such a diehard fan of Setogawa as to cut out and keep his obituaries sell his or her precious copy of this book? The author's last ever published work no less? Anyone with a normal sense of attachment would have kept the book, along with the cuttings, as part of their personal collection.'

Kaede could only agree.

'You're right. From a book lover's perspective, that theory is difficult to accept.'

'The second tale is more plausible than the first. But there are still inconsistencies. If the bookseller included those obituaries out of generosity, then why didn't they include even a short note? They took the trouble to place those cuttings between the pages, so why didn't they write something like, "I'm so happy this book is going to a fellow fan. I've taken the liberty of including a few cuttings to commemorate Setogawa's death." Why did he or she make so little effort? In short . . .'

Grandpa's conclusion was characteristically blunt.

'Both Tale One and Tale Two are fundamentally flawed. Which means there must be another explanation. We'll call it Tale X.'

'All right,' said Kaede, her voice a little hoarse. 'Can you weave Tale X for me?'

Grandpa didn't respond right away. He clung to the shrinking Gauloise between his thumb and forefinger as if it pained him to part with it, then finally exhaled the last of its smoke.

His eyes began, ever so slowly, and yet surely, to close. Kaede was afraid he was falling asleep. But she needn't have worried. They suddenly snapped back open.

'I'm seeing a picture now!' he pronounced. 'I'm sorry to say that the man who previously owned that book is already deceased.'

'What?'

'Take a look over there. Can't you see the face of a man at peace?'

Oh, he's hallucinating . . .

And yet, Kaede's intuition told her that this hallucination was grounded in logic.

'Here's our Tale X: before he passed away, this man kept copies of the obituaries of Takeshi Setogawa between the pages of this book. Perhaps it was a memorial to his beloved writer, or some kind of mourning ritual. His widow, having no idea how much the book had meant to her late husband, packed it up with the rest of his book collection and dropped them off at a used bookshop.'

That had to be it!

It was the perfect tale. No gaps in logic, no inconsistencies.

But Kaede decided to press her grandfather further.

Those Little Scarlet Cells

'How can you be sure that the previous owner was a man? It could just as easily have been a woman.'

'No, it couldn't,' Grandfather replied simply. 'When a spouse dies it's the wife who can control her grief enough to behave in a composed and practical manner. A husband would be completely useless. I know, because it happened to me.'

He looked down at the floor.

'When your grandmother passed away, I couldn't function at all.'

Kaede pictured her late grandmother's kind face.

There was a lingering silence.

Then Grandfather shifted gears and laughed with delight.

'See?' he said, staring intently into the floating cloud of cigarette smoke. 'Right now, the book's owner is sitting there at a table in Mon Chéri, deep in conversation with the great Takeshi Setogawa himself! They'll be talking mysteries until the wee hours.'

Another hallucination. But there was something oddly beguiling about this one. Kaede held her breath as she listened.

'It's all just as it used to be. The cedarwood walls steeped in the aroma of coffee, and now the scent of a brand-new mystery is about to be added to the mix. At the counter, the owner is absorbed in a game of shogi with a university student. What's this? The part-timer just scrambled to his feet. What's going on . . . ?'

A grave look crossed his face a moment, but his features soon relaxed.

'Ah, no wonder he's flustered. Ellery Queen and Agatha Christie just showed up. And what do we have here? Somehow John Dickson Carr has joined the discussion too. It's turned into a tea party with the three greatest mystery writers of all time. Or perhaps, as Queen was actually a collaboration between two authors, it would be more correct to refer to them as the "Big Four". Christie has asked to borrow the kitchen a moment to brew a pot of her favourite tea and serve up a Devonshire cream tea, much to the delight of Setogawa and the rest. Carr, of course, is sitting staring at the teapot, probably coming up with a brand-new poison trick. It's amazing – everyone seems to be having such a wonderful time.'

What is this? What's going on, Grandpa?

Was it a manifestation of her grandfather's kindness, needing to find a happy ending to his tale? Tears spilled from Kaede's eyes again, but this time they were warmed by the smile on her face.

What Grandpa is seeing is real . . .

She had absolutely no evidence of that, but she knew she was right.

With a tiny sizzle, the cigarette end tumbled into the

water in the bottom of the ashtray. A soft autumn breeze blew through the open window, ruffling the T-shirts on their hanging rod.

Grandpa turned towards the T-shirts and bowed several times.

'Are you from the senior citizens' association? Thank you all for coming.'

And as the Gauloise finally fizzled out, Grandfather slipped back into the grip of dementia.

Chapter 2:
The Izakaya Locked-Room Murder Mystery

1

Public elementary school teachers were technically civil servants, so how come she never got to leave at five p.m.? Kaede reflected ruefully, as the staffroom clock struck six.

Her mind wandered from the test papers she was marking to her grandfather's latest mysterious hallucinations.

How had he done that?

What kind of thought process had led him to see a 'picture' otherwise known as the truth?

What if . . .

Kaede's red pen came to a halt.

Her grandfather was extremely intelligent and had accumulated a massive amount of knowledge over the years. What if his hallucinations were a manifestation of the logical conclusions that his mind had come to? What if he had become able to make a conscious effort to see them? And the smoke that rose from his Gauloise was a fog that blurred his view of the real world, but at the same time made it easier to see his 'pictures'?

Of course, it's just a theory. Or wait . . . should I say 'tale'?

Kaede grinned, lowering her head so the other teachers wouldn't notice. She'd remembered something.

Her grandfather had a favourite saying: 'Everything that happens in the world is a story.'

As far back as she could remember, her grandfather had been the local primary school principal.

When Kaede became a pupil at his school, she discovered that her grandfather had a nickname: 'Principal Window Wiper'. He was also the most popular teacher in the school.

Apart from at graduation or other ceremonies, nobody had ever seen him wear a suit. He was to be found with his shirt sleeves rolled up, cleaning the windows in the hallway, watering the flowers in the schoolyard or scrubbing the toilet bowls in the bathrooms. His arms were slender, yet well defined, like someone with a background in martial arts, although he was far from the typical sports teacher type.

The Izakaya Locked-Room Murder Mystery

Whenever he passed by a child, he would address them by name and ask them what book they were reading at the time. Kaede was amazed that he seemed to know the name of every pupil in school, but she was really blown away that he was always familiar with their favourite books, and loved to get into passionate discussions about the appeal of their stories.

At graduation, he would hand every child a book along with their certificate, choosing the genre to match their personality. He handed out everything from serious literary works through mysteries, science fiction or manga.

Once he gifted a child a horror-themed video game. Grandfather was a steadfast believer that even games played a valuable part in shaping a person's character. He firmly believed that children needed stories that made their hearts race – the thrill of a mystery, or tales so terrifying that they were kept awake at night. This was how sensitivity and creativity were nurtured.

As it turned out, Grandfather's vision was spot on. That child went on to start a video game company, producing one hit game after another.

Kaede would never forget the unconventional address her grandfather had made at her own graduation ceremony. From his pocket he'd whipped out a book and begun to read with great theatricality.

'There's a word you don't hear much any more,' he

began in a startling baritone that would have made an opera singer proud. Children and parents alike listened in amazement to the principal's impromptu dramatic reading.

'. . . not spoken seriously, anyway. It's out of style, and you're supposed to smile when you say it. You know what the word is?'

Kaede's grandfather paused a moment to scan the audience, before concluding in that rich baritone:

'It's "adventure".'

For a full minute, he stood in silence, waiting for the murmurs throughout the auditorium to die down. Then he resumed in his customary cheerful tone.

'That was a famous line from the mystery novel *Assault on a Queen* by Jack Finney. It's a word that feels old, yet at the same time new. A word that stirs something inside everyone. When you hear it, you can't help but feel a sense of excitement – that nine-letter word, "adventure". Oh, and to those of you who were just thinking, "Hey, doesn't it have eight letters?" – you need to work harder on your spelling.'

There was an outbreak of giggling in the auditorium. Grandfather waited for it to die down, then assumed a serious expression.

'To all of you graduating here today, it's not an infinite future that awaits you. Everything is finite. Things come to an end. Youth is a weapon that will rust away before you

The Izakaya Locked-Room Murder Mystery

know it. If you want to grab that future you've been dreaming of, then go have an adventure. That's all. Thank you.'

Kaede's adventure was to follow in her intrepid grandfather's footsteps and become a primary school teacher.

And how could I forget . . .

Her own graduation gift had been a collection of science fiction stories by Robert F. Young, *The Dandelion Girl*. The title story, as its name suggested, featured a girl with hair the colour of a dandelion, and was a bittersweet tale of love that crossed time and space.

Even now Kaede could recite all the famous lines from the story, including, '*Day before yesterday I saw a rabbit . . .*'

Having inherited her mother's light chestnut-coloured hair, Kaede always felt that she had something in common with Dandelion Girl. But she suspected that her grandfather chose that particular book because he wanted his only granddaughter to have a beautiful romance one day.

Sorry, Grandpa, my love life never seems to work out . . .

As for *The Dandelion Girl*'s influence on Kaede . . . Well, she'd grown up loving flowers, that was about it. She smiled to herself again, this time more wryly.

'Kaede-sensei, what are you grinning about?'

The voice came from right above her. Startled, she turned

to see Iwata-sensei, a male colleague of around the same age. He had a plate in his hand.

'I know – you must have caught a whiff of these delicious treats.'

'No, not at all,' Kaede mumbled, hurriedly grabbing her red pen, and getting back to her marking.

It was already early autumn, but Iwata was still in short-sleeves. She supposed it was because he wanted to show off his muscular arms for the maximum possible number of days a year.

'Here, I tried my hand at a new recipe today – *gateau au chocolat*. It might be too sweet for you, though.'

'Wow. Looks delicious. Don't mind if I do!'

Iwata's hobbies were cooking and baking. You'd probably never have guessed it from his rather macho, sporty appearance.

Kaede took a bite and the cake melted gloriously on her tongue. As always, it was a little too sweet, but she felt rejuvenated by the pleasant flavour. The kids must have loved it.

'Thank you. Amazing as ever.'

Iwata's face crinkled into a massive grin and he scratched his head in embarrassment as he made his way back across to his own desk, directly opposite Kaede's. His naturally curly hair was adorable – he always looked as if he had just stepped out of a hair salon. She suspected he might have a bit of a crush on her.

The Izakaya Locked-Room Murder Mystery

Without doubt, he was a good person, but while she appreciated his open and cheerful nature, it was all a bit too much for her. Kaede was more of an introspective type, prone to overthinking. She always felt overshadowed by Iwata's dazzling personality, which everyone else seemed to find appealing.

Over the years, Kaede's female friends had offered her several pieces of 'constructive' criticism.

'Kaede, you're so cute, why do you insist on using such difficult vocabulary all the time? Can't you be a bit more casual? You'd get on much better with everyone.'

Of course, some of the criticism was more malicious than constructive.

'Why don't you read books on your phone like everyone else? Honestly, reading paperbacks these days is just pretentious. Are you trying to make some sort of statement?'

Other girls would tease her for her lack of fashion sense.

'Why do you always wear dark clothes? Your hair's that lovely bright shade. Don't you think you should try some brighter colours to match? Oh well, sure, of course you're free to wear what you like . . .'

Kaede could never come up with a response to these criticisms. She'd wonder if she was too mature for a woman in her twenties. In the end, she'd developed a bit of a complex, which kept her from having any kind of love life. Was it because she read too much? Was she some kind of book junkie? No . . . if she was honest with herself, it was due to *that incident* . . . That was what was preventing her from having a normal dating life, or even socializing like a normal adult. Maybe she was just like her grandfather after all – most confident talking to children.

'Kaede-sensei? Are you listening?'

'Oh, sorry.'

From the desk across the island, Iwata had been trying to talk to her.

'I was just lost in thought . . . What were you saying, again?'

Iwata looked a little put out.

'Didn't you catch any of it? Seriously, you're going to make me tell this scary story all over again?'

'Scary story . . . ?'

'That's what I'm talking about. You remember that izakaya we went to about a year back? Haruno, on the north side of Himonya?'

'Yes, of course I remember.'

How could she forget? Back then, that little neighbourhood bar was her grandfather's favourite haunt, and Kaede had picked it because she knew she'd feel uncomfortable drinking alone with Iwata. She remembered that night all too clearly – Iwata got drunk and passed out on the table, so she'd joined her grandfather at the counter for a leisurely drink.

The Izakaya Locked-Room Murder Mystery

'So last night,' Iwata said, his expression serious, 'there was a murder.'

Someone was killed at her grandfather's favourite izakaya?

According to Iwata, a man he knew back in high school happened to be there during the incident.

'I just got a text from him asking me to meet him for a drink. Do you want to come along?'

'Huh? Won't he be surprised if I show up?'

'Don't worry about that. You know I played baseball in high school, right?'

'That's the first I've heard of it.'

'Oh, is it? Well, with baseball club, no matter how many years have passed since high school, you still have to do whatever a senior member tells you to. He's a couple of years younger than me, so there'll be no problem showing up with you. There's just one thing . . .'

'What?'

'The guy's got quite a few issues of his own. How can I put it? He's pretty eccentric.'

2

Kaede arrived five minutes early at the little Italian restaurant that had been designed to look like a log house. As she scanned the Nordic pinewood interior, it crossed her mind that it resembled the interior of Mon Chéri. The place was cosy; besides the counter seats there were only two tables. A young couple sat at the far table, drinking wine, and the nearer one had a reserved sign. This must be the right place.

On one side of the reserved table, paperback in hand, sat a person with unusually thick, straight hair, cut in a chin-length bob style, a stark contrast to Iwata's curly locks. It was impossible to tell the person's gender, but as their loose-fitting blue shirt was buttoned left over right, she guessed probably male. The feminine hairstyle obscured most of their face, neat ends falling in perfect alignment with a sharply sculpted jawline. She noticed how long and slender their fingers were.

Gathering her courage, Kaede spoke up, although she was normally very uncomfortable in these types of situations. Still, she reminded herself, she was probably the older one here.

'Um, are you Iwata-sensei's old schoolfriend?'

'Yes,' replied the bob-haired man, without meeting Kaede's eyes. He picked up his phone from the table and gave it a quick tap with his long, slender ring finger.

'There are still four minutes and twenty-five seconds until our agreed meeting time. I'll just finish reading this first.'

For the next approximately four minutes Kaede sat in silence, listening to the bob-haired man turning pages.

The Izakaya Locked-Room Murder Mystery

Strangely, she didn't feel any irritation at being ignored – perhaps it was because of the delicate way he handled the book, taking the greatest care not to damage its pages.

The owl in the wall clock gave a soft hoot, announcing eight o'clock.

With a flourish, the bob-haired man swept the hair back from his face. It was all rather theatrical, Kaede thought. But it drew her attention to his slim, elegant nose.

'Nice to meet you. Please call me by my given name. It's written with the characters for "season" – Shiki.'

'Shiki-san. Nice to meet you too.'

Guess I should use my first name too, she thought.

'One character, combining tree and wind. Kaede, meaning maple, its leaves so beautiful in the autumn.'

Shiki snorted.

'Was that a poem?'

Kaede was taken aback.

'I mean, I get it. You were kind of manipulated into it by the way I did it, but do people normally start talking about the beauty of autumn leaves in their self-introduction? You must think you're pretty hot, comparing yourself to autumn foliage.'

'No, that's not what I . . .'

Kaede tried to force herself to smile but she was sure she just looked awkward.

What is it with this guy?

Well, maybe I'll forgive him because of those impossibly long eyelashes . . .

But if she was honest with herself, she didn't have the guts to think of a smart comeback. If he'd been one of her young pupils she'd have been throwing zingers, but right now she couldn't come up with a single witty retort.

'More importantly, Iwata-senpai's late,' Shiki complained, using the honorific term *senpai* for an older colleague. 'I can't believe someone would plan drinks and then not turn up on time.'

'True. But he did say he was swamped at work.'

The waiter came over.

Bob-haired guy – no, Shiki – knew how to deal with the situation.

'We're waiting for one more person, so we'll order then . . . No, you know what, we'll have two beers. You can handle beer, right? You already forced me to handle that weird poem of yours.'

'Wha—?'

What a thing to say . . .

But Kaede just hung her head, frustrated at herself for suppressing her feelings.

'Yes, if it's just one glass.'

'Bring us a caprese salad and the prosciutto platter. We'll order the rest when the other person gets here . . . Thank you.'

The Izakaya Locked-Room Murder Mystery

'Um, excuse me?'

'What is it?'

With another forced smile, Kaede finally spoke up.

'I'd appreciate it if you'd ask my opinion before ordering for me.'

Shiki continued to avoid her gaze, but this time chuckled softly to himself.

'Maybe you haven't realized it, but you've been eyeing the caprese salad on the next table. At least twice – no, three times now.'

Huh? Unbelievable . . .

Kaede felt her face turning red.

'Come on, don't blush. If anything, I'm sure the tomatoes, mozzarella and basil leaves are far more embarrassed at being stared at like that.'

'Then what about the prosciutto platter?'

'That's what I feel like eating. You have a problem with that?'

'No.'

Just as she felt her face redden even further, Shiki made a small exclamation of surprise and pointed to the slim volume with an oil painting on the cover that was peeking out of Kaede's pocket.

'What's this? Master of the Locked-Room Mystery, John Dickson Carr?' he asked loudly. 'Stylish in a retro kind of way.'

Oh, finally something I can talk about . . .

'Yes, it's *The Four False Weapons*. I'm nearly at the end, and it's pretty good.'

'What?'

Shiki looked genuinely astonished.

'You're not just showing it off as a fashion statement, then? You're really reading it? One of Carr's early works in this day and age? No offence, but with your modern style . . . I'm sorry. I mean it as a compliment.'

'Hmm, I'm not quite sure what you're getting at.'

'Ah, the beers are here!' he said quickly.

'Don't you think it would be polite to wait for Iwata-sensei to get here before we toast? Anyway—'

I'm getting a little worked up here, what am I doing talking this much with a guy I just met?

'So, tell me,' Kaede persisted, 'what's so wrong with reading Carr?'

'No, no, there's nothing wrong with Carr.'

Shiki scratched the side of his prominent nose.

'I'm just surprised that you can stand reading one of those translated classic locked-room mysteries.'

'And what's that supposed to mean?'

'If I listed all the reasons, we'd be here all night, but I'll give you the short version. For a start, the setting is outdated. Realistically, who builds a grand mansion with multiple rooms on a remote desert island? Frankly, I'd be

The Izakaya Locked-Room Murder Mystery

more afraid of starving to death than of being the victim of a serial murderer.

'Next, the characters are stereotypes to the point of caricature, not to mention extremely old-fashioned. One of the suspects is a retired military man who is still always addressed as "Colonel", and he has a stunning blonde wife, young enough to be his daughter. You can't help but worry that he's going to end up murdered by this wife.

'And then, the Japanese translation feels so antiquated. Every time an elderly character makes an entrance, they inevitably start off with something like, "I barely survived two world wars." It's supposed to be set in London, but out of nowhere it feels as if we're in Okayama or Hiroshima. And another problem, which is a recurring issue with translated works – it's hard to keep track of character names. It's a total drag to try to keep the full names of every member of "the Fortescue family" straight in your head. When Imhotep's daughter, "Renisenb", makes an appearance, it just doesn't stick. The more elaborate the name, the more artificial the whole thing feels. And instead of giving them some complicated surname, why don't they just stick to given names, or even nicknames? Or better still, how about just using "Grandmother" or "Brother" and leave it at that?

'The point is, these classic murder mysteries are an artificial construct to begin with, and translation only adds further layers of artificiality to the story. I like to call them Matryoshka Doll Mysteries.'

Wow, he's not shy about sharing his opinions . . .

It was true that these old, foreign murder mysteries tended to show their age with their dated settings and characters. Kaede recalled that the late critic Takeshi Setogawa had written about the antiquated style of Carr's writing. And yet, like Setogawa himself, she had an unwavering affection for the works of Carr and his contemporaries.

Reading a good book was like gently running a hand over finely crafted wooden furniture. And older translations had their own unique depth and richness, reflecting the age in which they were written.

Kaede wanted to argue her case, but she had always disliked confrontation. She decided instead to redirect the conversation.

'So – Shiki, was it? – what kind of mysteries do you read?'

'I only read works by Japanese authors,' he declared. 'No other country has as many awards for new or up-and-coming writers in the mystery genre. If plot or characterization is weak, the work gets weeded out at the early stage, and this naturally leads to an overall improvement in quality. And obviously the tragedy of a poor-quality translation can be totally avoided. The diversity of sub-genres on offer is staggering – I'd call it a true explosion of creativity. I think we can safely say that globally Japan has become the leading power in the mystery genre.'

'Isn't that just your personal preference? Or dare I say bias?'

'Huh? Come on, I've given you a solid argument here. Let's not reduce it to a matter of mere taste.'

Wow, he's quite something. One of those 'argument for argument's sake' types . . .

Kaede shrugged in response.

'Aha! There it is!' Shiki announced.

'Eh? There what is?' said Kaede, confused.

'Right then, you shrugged your shoulders. Normally, Japanese women don't make that gesture when they're confused. What are you – some wealthy lady of leisure, vacationing at a resort in the South of France? You've been reading so much Agatha Christie that the shoulder shrug has become second nature to you. I call that Matryoshka Mystery Syndrome.'

You totally made that up right now!

Very uncharacteristically for her, Kaede was on the point of losing her temper, when she heard a voice behind her.

'That's enough!'

It was Iwata. He turned to Kaede.

'I told you this guy was a prize weirdo, didn't I?'

Kaede took a deep breath.

Calm down. Smile . . .

'It's all good – I'm a bit of a weirdo myself,' she said. 'But, Iwata-sensei, may I just say one thing to your junior here?'

How many years had it been since she had stood up to a person she had just met – a man no less? Gathering her courage, Kaede turned to look Shiki full in the face.

'The Fortescue family is from *A Pocket Full of Rye*. And Renisenb, daughter of Imhotep, is a character in *Death Comes as the End*. Sounds like you read more Agatha Christie than you like to make out.'

'Hey, Kaede?'

Kaede noticed that since they'd started ordering wine by the decanter, Iwata had dropped the honorific 'sensei' when addressing her. She decided to let it go.

'You know what's funny about this guy? All the time he was playing baseball he'd say he wanted to be an umpire or a coach. There was even a time he claimed he wanted to join the cheerleading squad. And somehow he's ended up a struggling stage actor. Doesn't make a lot of sense, does it?'

An actor . . . actually, that does kind of make sense . . .

'And get this, he has a super weird outlook on life too. Hey, what was it again?'

Shiki grinned like a little kid.

The Izakaya Locked-Room Murder Mystery

'Well, Kaede-sensei, I believe that everything that happens in life is a story.'

Kaede was startled. It was déjà-vu. Or should she say 'Shiki-vu'? Irritating to hear it from this guy, but it still resonated with her.

'There was this famous Japanese actor who said right before he passed away, "Everything that's happening right now is exactly as it should be." I interpret this as meaning "every event is part of a story, and every story has a happy ending". I've decided that in my own life I'm going to try to dive into as many of these stories with their happy endings as I can, no matter how shallow the water.'

Shiki brushed his long hair out of his eyes for the umpteenth time, but the gesture didn't irritate Kaede as much any more.

Seeing the spaghetti bolognese arrive, Iwata rubbed his hands together in anticipation.

'This dish is what the restaurant is known for. Doesn't it make you want to talk about the *Cooking Papa* manga? I've got the entire series at home.'

'Every volume?' Kaede said with a laugh. Shiki let out a chuckle at the same time.

After the main course of veal Milanese, cappuccinos were served. It was the perfect moment for a change of topic, and fortunately, Iwata, who normally couldn't hold his alcohol, hadn't got too drunk yet.

'Is it OK if we talk about the case now?' Shiki asked.

The murder had happened at a traditional izakaya in the capital city; therefore, under normal circumstances, it would have been all over the news, but due to some major football game featuring the Japanese national team, it had only been given a small mention in the newspapers, and caused barely a blip on the online news sites.

'Also, maybe it just hasn't blown up yet. It only happened yesterday,' Shiki confided, leaning in closer to his dinner companions. 'The police haven't released a detailed statement yet.'

The couple at the other table had already left, so they were the only customers in the place. Still, as if afraid someone – perhaps the kitchen staff – might overhear, Shiki deliberately lowered his voice.

'But this was a murder all right, and I guess you're wondering why I wanted to talk about it. Well . . . it's because a friend of mine has got mixed up in it.'

Iwata picked up where Shiki had left off.

'That's right, Kaede-sensei.'

The moment the cappuccino had touched his lips, he was back to calling her 'sensei'.

The type who doesn't flirt unless he can blame it on alcohol . . .

That kind of awkwardness wasn't without its appeal, but still . . .

The Izakaya Locked-Room Murder Mystery

'When Shiki asked me for my help with the case, you were sitting right across from me, and I remembered you were a mystery buff. That's why I invited you along.'

Shiki sent a rough layout of the izakaya that he'd made with an image generator app to both their phones.

'First, take a look at this. It's a basic floor plan of Haruno. Just like this restaurant here, there are only two tables, and then a few counter seats, mostly occupied by regulars. It's a cosy little bar.'

Kaede looked at the image.

'Yeah, I've been there a few times, and this is about right.'

Haruno was located in an old traditional stand-alone house, a few minutes beyond Meguro-dori, the street that cut through northern Himonya. Despite being described as a dining izakaya, it wasn't the kind of upscale place that the average person would hesitate to enter. It was run by a cheerful woman in her forties, whose customary outfit was casual jeans. The atmosphere was laidback and the prices on the hand-drawn menu board over the counter reflected that. The little individual dishes served were surprisingly sophisticated, and the owner's famous *nimono* stew dishes were all excellent for the price. Kaede pictured the owner's bright complexion and warm smile, along with her spotless white apron.

'It's just the right size. Plus, they've got a great selection of local sake,' Iwata added.

Listen to you trying to sound like a connoisseur. As if you didn't pass out last time before we even got to the sake . . .

But Kaede kept the thought to herself. Instead, she turned to Shiki.

'These labels A to M, they're the customers?'

'Exactly. On the left – the west side – at Table ① there was a group of four people. Two men and two women, probably on their way home from work. Those are A through D. On the east side at Table ② were four members of my theatre troupe, including me – four men, E to H. And as I recall, all the counter seats were occupied by male customers too. In other words, the place was packed. The owner runs the place by herself, so she must have been kept busy that evening. Is everything clear so far?'

Kaede and Iwata nodded.

'Now, the person here at Table ② marked F is none other than yours truly. The TV in the corner behind me was showing that football match, so most of the customers were there to drink and watch the game. In that sense, as there weren't so many food orders coming in, the owner might have had a little breathing room.'

'Got it,' said Kaede. 'The izakaya had turned into a sports bar for the evening.'

'Exactly. To be honest, I couldn't care less about football, and I was getting fed up with the "Go Nippon!" chants that kept breaking out. I mean, could the players even hear

Izkaya Restaurant Floor Plan

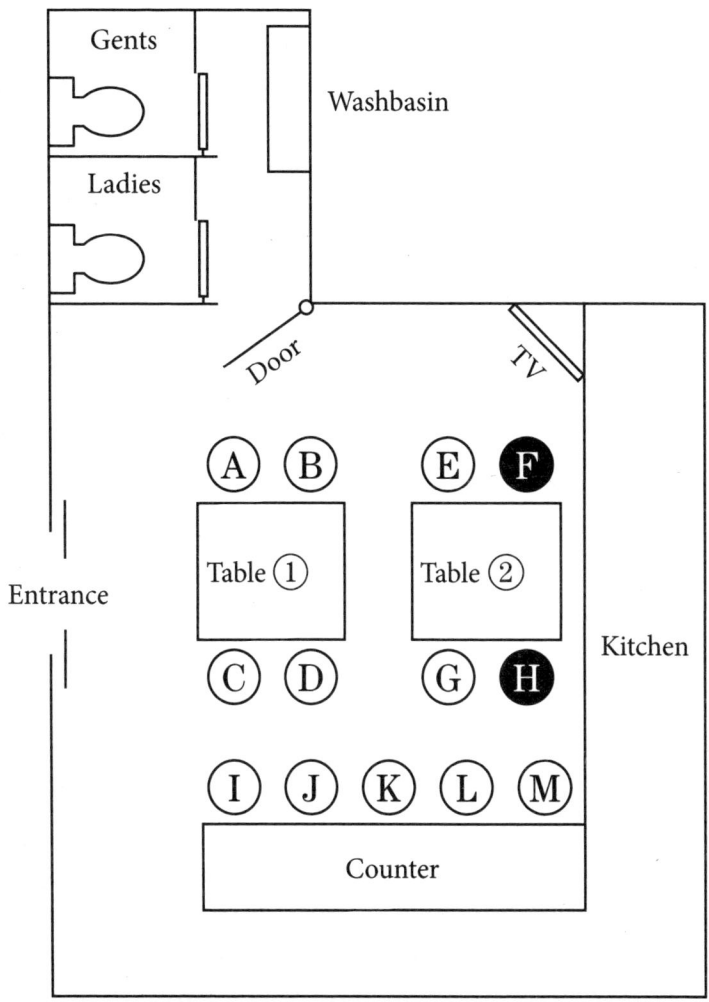

them? No! So, what's the point? I admit it made me feel like rebelling, and a couple of times I took advantage of the chaos to yell out, "Go Saudi Arabia!"'

Iwata looked annoyed.

'That's not the point,' he said sternly. 'Fans' cheers matter. It doesn't make a difference if they're in the stadium or not, the support reaches the team. The players feed off it.'

'Huh. You're saying that the cheers of some random dude chowing down on grilled salmon at a random Tokyo pub travel all the way to the National Stadium? If that was true, Japan would have won the World Cup ten times over by now.'

Iwata's expression instantly darkened.

'You're kidding me, right? That's coming from a former baseball player? You're into theatre now; doesn't that mean you need to learn empathy? What if you have to play the role of a football supporter who wanted to go to the game but couldn't, and tries to find a way to cheer for his team? Everything you said just now is in total contradiction to that character.'

It was a valid point.

There was an awkward silence. Then to Kaede's surprise Shiki jumped up from his seat and bowed deeply.

'I'm very sorry. One of my theatre buddies might be mixed up in all this and it's put me a bit on edge. Please, let me get the dinner to make up for it.'

The Izakaya Locked-Room Murder Mystery

'What? No, don't worry about it. I'm not letting my junior pay for me.'

Flustered, Iwata scratched at his curly mop of hair.

'Look, I might have overreacted. Sit down, sit down. I'll let it slide this once.'

Kaede had never been a member of any kind of sports club. As she watched from the sidelines, she was strangely envious of their relationship.

'To get back to the topic,' Shiki continued, 'this next part is something I confirmed later by watching the sports news . . . It was ten minutes to ten and the second half had just started. The score was tied at 3–3. At this point, the Japanese team unleashed three incredible back-to-back assaults on goal. The first was a powerful mid-range shot that blew past several defenders; next a corner kick aimed right at the goal; and finally, following a foul, a direct free kick taken from the perfect spot. Unfortunately, none of these found the back of the net. They were either blocked by the goalkeeper's excellent defending or hit the crossbar. But this extended attack had everyone in the place on their feet, completely caught up in the excitement.'

'Yeah, those ten minutes were intense. Even you must have joined in, right?'

'Nah. I was the only one still seated. I was eating nuts.'

'That's not the definition of "everyone in the place on their feet",' Iwata sighed.

'But I do remember the commentary: "Japan has just unleashed three killer shots. It's already after ten in the evening, and the whole country is still glued to their seats." That stuck with me because it was right after he said this that I checked my watch and it was exactly 10 p.m., and the opposing team finally regained control of the ball. I remember the atmosphere calmed down a little; everyone must have been tired from all the cheering. Now, this is when it happened. Sitting across from me was a member of my theatre troupe, a guy around the same age, and who happened to be a regular at that izakaya. Let's call him H for now. Anyway, he went to the toilet, and returned to his seat about three minutes later. What happened next is important, so I'm going to re-enact the scene for you.'

Shiki's expression turned serious, and Kaede hurriedly interjected.

'Hold on a second, Shiki-san. Is it OK if I record this?'

With Shiki's consent, she placed her phone on the table and started the voice memo app. She had a gut feeling that she was going to need her grandfather's help with this one.

'Ready? All right . . .'

Shiki switched into full-on actor mode and began retelling the story.

'*H returns from the toilet and lights a cigarette. From across the table, I ask – or rather F asks him, "Is the toilet free?"*

The Izakaya Locked-Room Murder Mystery

H replies, "Ah, yes, go ahead. It's free."

F gets up and heads towards the toilets. He passes the Ladies and goes to open the door of the Gents beyond, but for some reason the door is stuck. He notices that the latch-style lock is engaged from the inside. He knocks to check if it's occupied, but no one returns his knock. Then he glances down at the ground and lets out a startled cry.

"Aagh!"

Why does F – do I – cry out like that? Because a red liquid, unmistakeably blood, is seeping out from under the toilet door.

"Is everything OK in there? Did something happen?" he calls out but there's no response.

F clambers up onto the washbasin opposite to peer over the top of the door. He sees a thin, middle-aged man with a shaved head, tattoos, and piercings in both ears. He's sitting slumped forward on the toilet seat, a knife-like object sticking out of his back, and blood spurting from the wound. The floor is already covered in blood. The middle-aged man's satin bomber jacket is drenched in blood, but he isn't moving.

That was when I bec—F became certain. This man was already dead. And he had been murdered right here, just moments earlier.

Cut!'

Kaede was silent, her hand over her mouth. She hadn't imagined that Shiki would be the one to discover the body.

What's more . . . if the victim had been stabbed in the back that meant it couldn't be suicide; it was surely murder.

Iwata appeared to be hearing this for the first time too. He was as silent as Kaede, his arms folded. After a long silence, he finally spoke.

'What happened next? I suppose you called the police?'

'Yes . . . Well, before that, I did my best not to cause a scene. I slipped past the counter and into the kitchen. The owner was at the prep table, resting her chin in her hand and writing a note for the menu board to let the customers know she'd run out of offal stew or something. But when she saw the state I was in, she dropped her marker pen and tore up the paper. Maybe the panic on my face threw her off and she messed up the lettering. I urged her to call the police, but you could tell she was in shock. Her voice was usually so strong, but I tell you it was trembling. After she hung up, she just kind of collapsed right there on the floor.'

'Poor thing,' said Kaede.

She knew how hard-working and kind-hearted the owner was, and she could well imagine the scene.

'Three patrol cars showed up and temporarily cordoned off the area. They started questioning people right away. Now this next part is crucial, so pay careful attention.'

Kaede and Iwata leaned further in, totally absorbed.

The Izakaya Locked-Room Murder Mystery

'*The plainclothes cop asks, "Prior to the discovery of the body and the ensuing disturbance, did anyone observe someone heading in the direction of the toilets?"*

The customers seated at Table ① with its clear view of the toilets at the back give their statements.

Male customer C: "Well, up until around 9.30 p.m. loads of people were going in and out, but after that . . . I'm drawing a blank to be honest. Though I do remember someone from the next table getting up around 10 p.m., right after the Japan team had made those three shots on goal."

This "someone from the next table" must have been H, of course.

Female customer D: "I didn't see anyone either. Everyone was watching the match. Pretty sure we'd have noticed if someone got up."

The customers seated at the counter chime in:

"Nobody went to the toilet between 9.30 p.m. and 10 p.m."

"Yeah, it's true, we were all too caught up in the game. Everyone was glued to their seats."

"I mean, it was a 3–3 tie at that point. Not the kind of game you can tear your eyes away from."

Everyone at Table ② says pretty much the same thing. In other words, if you don't count F – me – who discovered the body just after ten, the last person to use the Gents toilet was H, just before. But here's where it gets sticky . . .'

———

A look of pain flashed across Shiki's face, as if for a moment he had forgotten his role of actor.

'*H refuses to give a statement, saying, "I'm exercising my right to remain silent." Consequently, he's taken into custody.*
Cut!'

No way! Shiki's friend was arrested . . . ?

Silence fell once more, but Kaede broke it.

'Does anyone know who the victim was? He doesn't sound like one of the regulars at Haruno.'

'I don't think so. The owner said she'd never seen him before, and I remember one of the cops saying that he didn't have any ID on him.'

'And I wonder who that "knife-like object" belonged to,' Kaede continued.

'That was determined pretty quickly,' Shiki replied. 'I overheard the forensics team talking. The victim had a leather holster for a butterfly knife attached to his belt.'

Iwata ruffled his already-messy hair.

'So that means the killer must have grabbed the victim's own butterfly knife and stabbed him with it.'

'Looks that way.'

'Then the solution is indisputable. I'm sorry to say it, Shiki, but I think your friend H stabbed the victim on impulse. Three minutes is plenty of time. The fact that he's refusing to talk is extremely suspicious. A decent, honest person wouldn't act that way.'

'But, Senpai, that's the thing. H is one of the most decent and honest people I know. Almost fatally so for an actor.'

'Fatally?'

'Right.'

Shiki looked his baseball senpai straight in the eyes.

'In the theatre world, being too nice can be a problem. H has none of that cut-throat ambition to trample on others just to get a role. But I can at least vouch for his good character. He's not the type to kill anyone. He's serious, kind and has a strong sense of justice – in that sense he's like you, Senpai.'

'Cut it out,' said Iwata, but his face crinkled with obvious pleasure. 'Am I such a great guy?'

'No, that's not what I said. I meant the bit where I said *at least* I could vouch for his good character.'

'Hey!'

'Sorry.'

'I guess I'll have to let this one slide as well,' said Iwata with a roll of his eyes.

'Anyway, don't you think that if H was the culprit, he'd have stopped me when I tried to go to the toilet right after he came back?' said Shiki.

'That's a good point. So why is H refusing to talk? Well, no, what's more important . . .'

Iwata ran his hand through his curly locks again.

'. . . is the case itself: who murdered the tattooed man? And where and how was he killed?'

'Nothing about it makes sense,' Shiki admitted. 'Let's go over the timeline again, outlining the key points and what likely occurred. First of all, nobody went to the toilet after 9.30 p.m. At exactly 10 p.m. H headed to the men's room. He returned three minutes later, and when I asked him if the toilet was free, he clearly stated, "It's free." I went directly to the Gents toilet, but found the door locked from the inside. I knocked and called out, but there was no response. I climbed onto the sink and looked over the door, I saw a body that had been stabbed in the back.'

'There was no window in the toilet, was there?' Iwata asked. 'Nothing that someone could sneak through?'

'No. It's exactly as shown in the diagram.'

'Then how about this theory? Perhaps the guy was stabbed outside and, as he was dying, he somehow staggered into the izakaya?'

'Impossible. Look, when I saw the body, the blood was still gushing out of the wound. It means he must have died instantly. And if a dying man came staggering into a bar, despite all the excitement about the football game, somebody would have noticed.'

'Then the key question remains—'

'Yes, it's just as you said, Senpai. The case is: who

murdered the tattooed man, where and how? And, if I may add one more element . . . where did the killer disappear to?'

The longer silence that followed was broken by the hoot of the owl in the wall clock.

Kaede had been listening without comment, but finally she spoke up.

'This case is an extremely complex puzzle, which is why you needed to consult with us, right?'

Shiki shrugged.

Aha! Caught you! You're in the habit of shrugging your shoulders too . . .

'Do you mind waiting until tomorrow? I think I might have something useful to share with you then.'

The next day was a national holiday. She could pay a visit to her grandfather.

Kaede quietly pressed stop on her voice memo recorder.

3

The rainclouds cleared right as Kaede arrived at her grandfather's house.

There was no logical basis to think it, but she had a feeling that her grandfather would be in better health today. As she made her way through the garden where fallen leaves glistened with rainwater, through the open study window she could hear a voice.

'Ah–eh–ee–oo, eh–oh–ah–oh'

'Ah–eh–ee–oo, eh–oh–ah–oh'

Vocal exercises must have been part of today's rehabilitation. Modern rehabilitation practices meant that care was offered by a team of specialists according to specific needs. It was rare for only one therapist to be assigned to a patient. Speech therapists were a relatively new addition to a rehabilitation team; they assisted with aspects of speaking, listening and swallowing.

Kaede knocked at the study door and announced herself.

'Come in!' came a pleasant, welcoming voice. 'Ah! Your granddaughter's here, Himonya-san. It's great that you're in such good form today.'

Just as *rakugo* storytellers of old had been named after their neighbourhood – with nicknames that translated as something like 'Master of X-town' – Kaede's *rakugo* enthusiast grandfather had always been fond of his 'Himonya' nickname.

Kaede bowed and entered the study to see a middle-aged man with a slight build and a balding head, his remaining hair closely cropped. The man was just putting on medical gloves to begin a throat massage. He was about the same height as Kaede – five foot three – or perhaps a little shorter.

'You know how some elderly people have sagging flesh on their necks? A bit like a camel?' he explained to Kaede.

The Izakaya Locked-Room Murder Mystery

'It's because their throat muscles have got weaker. Their ability to swallow also deteriorates. Regular massage makes a big difference.'

'That sounds very beneficial. Thank you,' Kaede replied.

'But you have a magnificent head of hair still, Himonya-san. I'm quite envious.'

The man turned and tipped his gleaming smooth head towards Kaede and her grandfather, and got smiles in return.

'But even your impressive head of hair is nothing on my daughter's,' the man went on. 'The length, and the smoothness, and above all the shine.'

'Naturally,' replied Grandfather laughing. 'You can't compare your daughter to an old man like me. You know if you go on this way I'm going to have to give you a nickname too – how about "Doting Father"?'

Grandfather enjoyed giving nicknames to people he got along with. He and Doting Father must have been close. Their rhythmic banter gave the room a kind of barber's shop atmosphere, and Kaede took pleasure in listening. It reminded her of the famous essay by Edogawa Ranpo, 'Ka-no mondo: Reflections on John Dickson Carr'.

'I hope my grandfather isn't bothering you with all his tales,' Kaede said, but Doting Father immediately waved the question away, looking genuinely offended by the suggestion.

'Not at all,' he protested. 'I'm always impressed by Himonya-san's vast knowledge.'

His rather puffy nose with its wide nostrils gave him the look of a slightly cheeky monkey.

'To use a sporting analogy, he's like a decathlon champion. He's so well informed in every field that just listening to him is an education. I ought to be paying him for the lessons.'

It wasn't flattery. The twinkle in his eyes with their many laughter lines suggested a vibrant sense of curiosity.

'A decathlon champion? Now that's an interesting comparison.'

Grandfather raised one corner of his mouth in a devilish grin.

'Now let's see if Doting Father can name all of the decathlon events.'

'Oh no! There he goes again!' replied Doting Father, clearly perplexed. He turned to Kaede and rubbed his smooth head.

'You see, Kaede-sensei? He always manages to get the better of me.'

'Well then, perhaps I'd better answer for you,' Grandfather cut in. 'There's the one hundred metres sprint, then the long jump and the high jump—'

'All right, all right! And victory goes to Himonya-san yet again!'

The Izakaya Locked-Room Murder Mystery

Kaede couldn't help laughing at the perfectly timed interjection.

As if sounding the end of today's physical therapy session, a bell cricket chirped out in the garden. Those days, it was rare to find crickets living in the garden of a private home in the city, and this was one of Grandfather's points of pride.

'Right then, I'd better be going,' said Doting Father.

Grandfather raised a hand in thanks, but then brought up a new topic, perhaps trying to get his friend to stay longer.

'Did you manage to record that group of crickets the other day?'

'Perfectly. My daughter was thrilled when she heard it.'

'That's wonderful. It's so rare to come across three crickets on the same leaf all chirping together.'

'That expensive recorder was worth it. Now I know the real meaning of soothing.'

'For sure. Sei Shonagon wrote, "Of all insects, the bell cricket." She put them at the top of the list of insect calls.'

'Oh sorry, that's not what I meant,' said Doting Father, with a playful tilt of his head. 'I was soothed by the smile on my daughter's face as she listened to the recording.'

'Ha ha, you got me. There's no besting you is there?'

'Goodbye, Kaede-sensei.'

Doting Father bowed to Kaede several times as he left, the two of them right at eye level.

Grandpa's lucky . . .

Having someone like this who not only cared for his health but also made him laugh – Kaede was truly grateful.

While she was drawing up Grandfather's schedule, the care manager had told Kaede, 'The most important aspects of caregiving are teamwork and smiles, including from family members.'

These words still resonated with Kaede. She pressed her hands together in a gesture of gratitude.

Then she turned to her grandfather. It was time to outline the case of the Izakaya Locked-Room Murder.

Grandfather was proud of the fact that his hearing hadn't deteriorated at all. After listening to Kaede's summary of the case and the voice memo, he began to murmur half to himself, his gaze distant.

'Ah, Haruno. I haven't been there in a while, ever since my legs stopped cooperating. You know the proprietress makes the best offal stew. The perfect balance of sauce and dashi broth – remarkable how she could achieve a flavour that exquisite, running that place single-handedly as she does.'

He took a slow sip from his favourite olive-green coffee cup. Kaede realized that she too had been drinking coffee non-stop since last night. She knew that coffee was

The Izakaya Locked-Room Murder Mystery

supposed to be beneficial to Lewy Body Dementia patients, but was also aware that her grandfather consumed too much of it.

'Whenever I came in, the proprietress would ask me, "Himonya-san, how long can you stay today?" When I told her what time I needed to leave, she'd lean in close and say, "Well then, we'll keep it to two problems this time. How about a flask of sake?" I'd barely have sat down before she'd start negotiating. Then, once the number of customers began to thin out, she'd spread out her maths and English textbooks on the counter. Circumstances had forced her to drop out of school when she was young, so she was studying to take the high school equivalency exams. The grin of delight on her face when she got the answer to a problem . . . well, it doesn't matter if you're a primary school kid or a grown adult, it's always the same. And of course that made me feel content too. I'd end up helping her with five or six problems, and be there until she closed up – every single time.'

'And did she pass her exams?'

'Of course. Who do you think was her tutor?'

Grandfather raised his eyebrows in an attempt at playfulness, but there was a trace of melancholy in his voice.

'It was such a comfortable place . . . I also knew that young man with the square jawline, the one you're calling H. He was a regular there too. A gentle soul; I recall how he always used to say, "I'll just have anything. Don't worry about me," whenever the place got too busy. I know he saw traces of his late mother in the proprietress. And although he probably wasn't aware of it, in his own awkward way he had begun to be conscious of her as a woman, not just a mother figure.'

'Really?'

'Now then . . .'

Grandfather shifted gears, ready to get down to business.

'First of all, shall we proceed under the assumption that this Shiki fellow had no part in the crime?'

'I think so. Otherwise, we wouldn't have a tale to weave, would we?'

'But before we get to the crime itself, there's one more puzzle that we mustn't overlook. Let's call it "The Mystery of the Menu".'

'The Mystery of the Menu?' Kaede repeated, with a quizzical tilt of her head. 'I don't recall that bit.'

'After Shiki discovered the body in the toilet, he went into the kitchen to report it to the proprietress. He found her *resting her chin in her hand and writing a note for the menu board to let the customers know she'd run out of something*. But the moment she saw Shiki, she *dropped her marker pen and tore up the paper*. Why do you think that was?'

The Izakaya Locked-Room Murder Mystery

'Shiki said it himself, didn't he? She just got distracted and made a mistake. Is that such a big deal?'

'It's a huge deal.'

Grandfather placed his cup on the side table.

'Even if she did make a mistake, why tear up the paper? Surely her priority should have been listening to what Shiki had to say? I know the proprietress, and such a rough and impulsive act is completely out of character. Why did she deliberately tear it up? Or, rather, why did she *have to*? This is The Mystery of the Menu. Only when we can solve that puzzle logically, can we begin to understand the true nature of this crime.'

Now that Kaede thought about it, she realized that her grandfather had a point. Although she had only met her a few times, she thought the owner didn't seem the type to tear up a piece of paper over a small error, especially not in front of a customer.

But then what does that mean . . . ?

Grandfather held his hands out in front as if measuring something, then pulled them back and gave a dismissive wave, as if suggesting they should put The Mystery of the Menu aside for now.

'Now, normally I'd ask you to start weaving your tales right about now, but I feel it's only fair that as a long-time regular at Haruno I go first. I do have something significant to share.'

A shadow passed across Grandfather's face.

'I have an idea of the identity of the tattooed man.'

'What?'

Kaede's eyes grew wide.

'It's a man who has been casting a dark shadow over the life of Haruno's proprietress ever since her high school days. I believe he always used violence to get his way. She's mentioned to me more than once that there was some kind of bad man in her past. I've even seen a tattooed man standing near the entrance to the izakaya.'

'You have?'

'Then, about a year ago, there was a freezing cold night with one of those relentlessly bone-chilling winds that makes everyone feel a bit down. I was at the izakaya, tutoring the proprietress for her exams as usual, but that day she'd been drinking.

'"Himonya-san," she said, resting her chin in her hand, "that's enough studying for tonight. I'll treat you to some sake, if you wouldn't mind listening to my story. I want to tell you about that man who showed up at the door the other night."'

Resting her chin in her hand . . .

In Shiki's account too, she'd been resting her chin in her hand as she wrote the notice. It was a cute habit that suited her cheerful personality, Kaede thought.

'I already knew most of what had happened between

them,' Grandfather continued, 'so I said, "He's out, isn't he?" She laid her head on the counter and began to cry.'

'Out? Out from where?' Kaede ventured.

'Prison,' replied Grandfather, matter-of-factly. 'Twenty-odd years ago there was a major case that caused quite a stir. A couple – a tattooed man and a young high school girl – committed a string of home invasion robberies across the country. One of their victims tried to resist and ended up dead. Of course, this man was the mastermind; he was at least a decade older than the girl. His accomplice, the girl, well she just followed along, doing whatever he told her to. She was small and rather athletic, so her role was mostly to climb up and slip in through high windows, or to secure their escape route. However, the public saw it differently. The pair became notorious, nicknamed "the Japanese Bonnie and Clyde".'

Bonnie and Clyde . . .

She'd heard those names before. Bonnie Parker and Clyde Barrow, the infamous couple whose bank-robbing spree across the American Midwest in the 1930s had inspired one of the iconic films of the New Hollywood era.

'You're saying the female half of that couple was the izakaya owner back when she was in high school?'

'Exactly.'

Deep furrows appeared in Grandfather's forehead.

'The pair was finally arrested in the far north of the

country. The man was sent to prison, and the girl was placed in a juvenile detention centre. That much I knew from news reports at the time.'

'I see.'

'Years had passed, but the moment I saw that tattooed guy in the shop doorway I recognized him as "Japan's Clyde". After all, he had been on the nation's most wanted list. And by extension, the proprietress must have been "Japan's Bonnie". After those long years in prison, Clyde had the nerve to show his face again to Bonnie.'

'How awful.'

'Whether it was the alcohol talking, or some need to unburden herself, the proprietress began to tell me the story of what happened after their arrest. She'd grown up in poverty, and it was in the detention centre that she learned for the first time that people regularly eat three meals a day. She told me that the stewed dishes she ate there were so delicious that she couldn't stop thinking about them. That's how she made up her mind that someday she would have her own restaurant.'

Kaede found the story deeply moving. While her own 'adventure' had been to become a primary school teacher, this woman's had been to open a restaurant where she had total freedom to serve her own homemade cooking.

'For her, getting arrested was like divine intervention,' Grandfather continued. 'Her chance to sever ties with that man and start over. But then out of nowhere Clyde tracks her down and appears at her door. His leverage? Very simple: "How do you feel about people knowing your past? The survival of this place depends on me now." The proprietress had no choice but to comply, giving him money. I told her not to give in to his demands again and asked her to contact me immediately if he ever came around again, but . . .'

He broke off, glancing at his walking stick, propped up against the side table.

Even if the owner of Haruno had managed somehow to contact him, there was no way in his current condition that he could have made it to the izakaya. Not even with that stick to help him . . .

Kaede pretended not to notice, quickly steering the conversation back to the main subject.

'And then that day finally came,' she prompted.

'Indeed. Totally shameless, he turns up to extort more money from her. He must have been grinning to himself to see how well the place was doing, thinking about how much more money he was going to get out of her. He would never have guessed that this was going to be his last day on Earth. Well, the police will discover his identity soon enough. That's probably the reason they haven't made the murder public yet – they need time to confirm that the victim is really that infamous ex-criminal.'

Grandfather clasped his hands together and looked straight into Kaede's eyes.

'Right now, I believe we have all the elements of the case laid out before us. Let me ask you again, Kaede, what do you think happened that night? What tales are you going to weave?'

This was it. The moment had arrived.

Kaede swallowed hard before beginning to weave her first tale.

'Tale Number One: H was the killer. There was some kind of confrontation between H and the tattooed man, and he killed him in the Gents. After locking the door from the inside, he used the toilet paper holder and the bolt as footholds to climb over the top of the door. Then he returned to his seat as if nothing had happened and lit a cigarette. His refusal to answer the police's questions would appear to support this story.'

Grandfather stroked the stubble along his strong jawline a moment or two before shaking his head.

'There's a flaw in that narrative,' he declared. 'If H were the culprit, then why when Shiki asked him if the toilet was free, would he have replied, "Ah, yes, go ahead. It's free"? Having just locked the door from the inside, surely he would have wanted to delay the discovery of the body as long as possible? Considering he was the last person to have used the toilet, it's only natural that he'd be a

The Izakaya Locked-Room Murder Mystery

suspect. No, this isn't convincing from a psychological standpoint.'

It was true. If H were the killer, his words and actions were flaunting his crime. Besides, having heard that he was a serious and kind soul, it pained Kaede to accuse him.

She felt greatly relieved, but also somewhat perplexed, as she moved on to her next tale.

'Tale Number Two: H is not the killer. Someone else murdered the man, locked the door from the inside and climbed out over the door.'

But no sooner were the words out of her mouth, than Kaede dismissed her own theory: 'But that's impossible. There are even more contradictions in that narrative there than there were in the first one.'

Grandfather's smile was enigmatic.

'Nobody used the toilets after 9.30 p.m., and if we believe H's assertion that the toilet was empty after he returned from using it at 10 p.m. . . .'

It took some courage for Kaede to say the next words.

'In a matter of just a few minutes, the victim had to suddenly appear in the toilet and the killer to vanish. That would make this case essentially a locked-room murder mystery.'

'That's exactly what it is.'

Grandfather's gaze was fixed on a corner of the study where the bookshelves cast a shadow.

'Yes, I can see the picture now,' he murmured. 'The proprietress was the culprit. I can see her now right there, getting ready.'

Kaede let out a small gasp. Getting ready? To do what? To escape?

'Your second tale is undoubtedly the correct version. This is, without doubt, a locked-room murder mystery,' Grandfather declared with complete certainty. 'Let's go over again exactly what occurred that night.'

The deep furrows in his forehead were back.

'Up until 9.30 p.m. customers had been using the toilets regularly, but as the football game heated up, all eyes were fixed on that TV screen. Then around 9.50 p.m. when Japan's repeated attacks on goal had everyone on their feet and the din must have been deafening, Clyde came around again, looking to extort more money. Only the proprietress from her spot behind the counter noticed him there in the doorway. Whether he beckoned her over, or she signalled to him to meet her by the toilets, we can't know for sure. However, as she must have feared making a scene, the latter seems more likely. Besides, meeting him in the kitchen would have been too dangerous with all those sashimi and filleting knives around. The man was the very definition of a violent criminal, so it was much more prudent to choose the toilets.

'With all the customers' attention on the game, the

The Izakaya Locked-Room Murder Mystery

proprietress slipped away from the counter, and Clyde moved stealthily along the wall to the toilet area, opened that door and snuck inside, unnoticed by anyone. They began their conversation in the Gents, but things escalated very quickly. The proprietress must have summoned up the courage to refuse his demands – probably for the first time ever. Enraged, Clyde turned violent. I'm certain he tried to strangle her.'

'Strangle her – you think it was self-defence?'

'Yes. It's a clear case of self-defence,' said Grandfather. He screwed up his face as if he had just licked a palmful of coarse salt. 'I'll explain later how I reached that conclusion.

'Next, Clyde tried to stab the proprietress with his butterfly knife, but in the struggle, she accidentally stabbed him.'

Kaede's head was instantly assaulted by a vivid tableau of contrasts. Bright red blood. Pure white slowly becoming seeped in crimson. An image that summoned unwelcome echoes of a long-ago incident . . .

'"What should I do? I didn't mean to stab him!" The proprietress no doubt tried to perform first aid on Clyde, but he was already gone. She desperately tried to figure out what to do. She was a kind and conscientious person – the idea of turning herself in must have been the first to cross her mind. But then she thought about the future of her restaurant. Even if the incident was ruled self-defence, the damage to her reputation would be unavoidable. After her years of hard work, taking on debt to get her place up and running, if people now learned that the proprietress of Haruno was none other than Japan's Bonnie, the business would collapse. Besides, who would want to eat at a place where a violent murder had been committed?

'In her panicked state she thought that if she could just keep Clyde's body hidden for one night – or at least until the football match ended and she could get the customers out – that would buy her some time. But then, right at 10 p.m., as she opened the door and peeked out, one of her regulars, H, came to use the toilet. In a split-second decision she locked herself back inside and called out to H, "So sorry, the Ladies was occupied so I'm using this one. I'll be right out."

'Then when H had gone, she removed Clyde's wallet and other personal belongings, putting them in the pocket of her apron; leaving the door locked, she used the paper dispenser and the bolt as footholds to climb out over the top of the stall.'

'Eh?'

Kaede looked sceptical.

'You say she climbed through the gap at the top of the toilet door. Could she really pull off something like that?'

Grandfather put a finger to his temple with a knowing smile.

'Don't forget that in her former life of crime her speciality was crawling in through high windows. She's small and remarkably athletic; and she always wears jeans. Escaping from that toilet would have been a breeze. When people think of the proprietress of a traditional izakaya they picture someone in a kimono with a long *kappogi* apron over it, but there's no rule that says she's obliged to dress the traditional Japanese way.'

That was true. It was precisely because of the owner's casual style that Kaede had felt comfortable inviting Iwata to the izakaya that time. The same must have gone for Shiki and the other young theatre troupe members. The casual atmosphere was what attracted them to the place.

'Now, once she had climbed out, an idea struck her. If she put an Out of Order sign on the door, then no one would find the body.'

'Makes sense.'

'However, H turned around and went back to his seat. Although the Ladies toilet door was closed, it wasn't locked, but H didn't bother to check. The proprietress said she'd be right out, and it didn't cross his mind to use the Ladies.'

'But, Grandpa—'

'I know the problem you have with this, Kaede.'

Grandfather nodded, as if to acknowledge that she had a point.

'You find it unconvincing that the proprietress would use the Gents toilet, but it's common practice in the service industry. It's rather bad manners for a man to complain when a woman needs to use the facilities. Especially in an izakaya, it's not uncommon to see a sign saying, *Please understand that the staff may need to use these facilities.*'

Kaede had to agree, especially as there was no toilet in the kitchen area. The owner would naturally have to use the same facilities as the customers.

Grandfather continued his tale.

'When H got back to his seat, he likely thought, "I'll have a cigarette before I go back again." That's a very common habit among us smokers. And it was this very habit that created the conditions that led to this being a seemingly "impossible crime".'

Grandfather focused his gaze once more on the corner of the study.

'If H hadn't been a smoker he might have lingered outside the door, in the bit of corridor that led back to the main restaurant area, waiting for the proprietress to come out. And if he had waited there, even with all the noise, somebody at Table ① would surely have spotted him.'

'For sure,' Kaede agreed. 'And during the police's questioning, somebody would have mentioned that they thought they'd seen someone waiting for the toilet.'

'Precisely. But because H was a smoker, he chose to return to his seat. Now think back to when F – Shiki that is – asked him, "Is the toilet free?" Remember H's odd

The Izakaya Locked-Room Murder Mystery

response: "Ah, yes, go ahead. It's free." Don't you find that a bit odd? The first part just seems redundant. The second half – "It's free" – should have been sufficient. Why would H say, "Ah, yes, go ahead" to his fellow theatre troupe member after he had apparently just come back from using the toilet? Odd phrasing, don't you think? And it wasn't because he was deferring to his older senpai either.'

Yes, Shiki had mentioned that everyone was around the same age.

'In that moment, over Shiki's shoulder H must have caught sight of the proprietress leaving the toilet. That's why the odd phrase "Ah, yes, go ahead" slipped out. In this context he actually meant, "Ah, I was about to go myself, but I've just lit a cigarette and the proprietress just came out, so please, go ahead."'

'Then why did all the customers testify that nobody had gone to the toilets after 9.30 p.m.?' Kaede asked. 'They said nobody used them.'

Grandfather had a definitive reply.

'That's because the person who came out of the toilet area wasn't a customer. It was the proprietress. And she was carrying supplies.'

Kaede experienced a moment of recognition.

Could it be . . . ? Was this a case of the 'invisible man'?

'For example, if she emerged from there carrying a wastepaper basket filled with paper towels, would anyone think she had just used the toilet? No, they'd assume she just went in there to tidy up and restock.'

As I thought!

'At that moment the proprietress had become what G. K. Chesterton would have termed an "invisible person". Oh and of course it goes without saying that inside that wastepaper basket was her blood-stained apron along with Clyde's belongings.'

The call of a bell cricket drifted in from the garden.

Kaede felt as if most of the events of that evening had been explained. Still, she ventured one more question.

'This may be too much of a stretch of the imagination, but is it possible that the owner and H were in on it together?'

'No, it's not. If they were, why would H have let Shiki go to the toilet? If they were in cahoots, then they would surely have found an excuse to close up the restaurant right away.'

'Then how about the possibility that the owner planned the crime, but alone?'

'That's even less likely. It makes no sense to risk committing murder in a crowded restaurant.'

'Of course not. You're absolutely right, Grandpa, but . . .'

But . . . Was it OK to say it?

'You're talking as if you saw the whole thing with your own eyes.'

The Izakaya Locked-Room Murder Mystery

'That's right,' he said simply.

He narrowed his eyes as he continued to stare into the corner of the room.

'Right now, the proprietress is having a heated argument with Clyde. Or maybe she's talking to H through the toilet door. And now, reluctantly, she's stabbing him. I can see it all happening. Could you ask for any more conclusive evidence than this? Though, to be precise, it's not something I witnessed happen, more something I'm watching happen right now.'

Kaede covered her mouth in astonishment.

This was an unprecedented method of deduction. Taking into account the owner's warm personality and Clyde's past villainy, he was able to analyse all the information instantly and thoroughly. Then the irrefutable truth was revealed to him as a vision.

The lone cricket chirped once more.

'Now then, let's finally delve into this Mystery of the Menu,' Grandfather announced.

'Are you saying you've solved it? The mystery of why the izakaya owner tore up the menu?'

'Of course. As I said before, the solution to this puzzle is the key to revealing the whole truth.'

'Is there any rational reason why she'd tear it up?'

'There certainly is. And that mysterious action reveals not only her involvement in the killing, but that her actions were in self-defence. Let me ask you a question, Kaede. Imagine you're the proprietress, rushing back to the kitchen. Say you want to make sure that nobody uses the Gents toilet, what would you do?'

'Let me think . . .'

Kaede took a moment before replying.

'I'd quickly make an Out of Order sign to stick on the door.'

Grandfather made a gunshot gesture.

'Exactly.'

'But . . . that's not what the owner did. She was making a sign for the menu board to say she was out of offal stew.'

Kaede stopped and put a hand to her mouth.

Not out of *offal*. Out of *order*!

'You've got it, haven't you?'

Grandfather raised a long slim index finger.

'She'd locked the door to the Gents, so she'd never expected the body to be discovered so quickly. And as you said, she'd run back to the kitchen to write an Out of Order sign. But what with the pain she felt in her neck from Clyde's attempt to strangle her, along with her state of panic, maybe she wasn't as quick as she would have liked to be. And that brings us to a vital point. She wasn't idly propping her chin on her hand. She was rubbing her neck in pain. That unconscious gesture is what tells us her action was in self-defence.'

The Izakaya Locked-Room Murder Mystery

'I see. And that's when Shiki arrived.'

'Right. That was a terrible miscalculation on her part. Shiki saw the blood seeping out from under the toilet door, discovered the body inside, and burst into the kitchen.'

'And he saw her writing "Out of o . . ." on a piece of paper.'

'Everything happened so quickly that it's not surprising he misinterpreted the sign. When he saw the words she was writing, he naturally assumed she had run out of something, probably her famous offal stew, and was making a sign for the menu board. But naturally the proprietress couldn't let anyone see that she was writing an Out of Order sign for the toilet door, as it would reveal her involvement. That's why she reflexively tore up the paper. Well, think about it logically – would she really have time to stick papers on the board in the middle of a busy evening in the restaurant? And to sit there calmly resting her chin in her hand? It would have been easier just to tell a customer she'd run out of something.'

'Out of' – a phrase commonly used with both menu items and something that was broken. Neither out of place in an izakaya setting.

'It's no wonder that when Shiki told her he'd discovered a body she was in shock. And her voice trembled when she called the police. The body had been found before she'd had a chance to put up her sign.'

'But, Grandpa, there's still something I don't understand.'

'What's that?'

'What happened to the bloody apron and the man's belongings? I mean the police must have searched for them.'

Grandfather's smile had a hint of mischief.

'Oh, Kaede, I wish you'd picked up on that. There's only one place that would be a challenge for the police to search. Where else could she have hidden them but in that massive pot of her famous stewed offal as it marinated in her signature sauce?'

'Ah!'

'I imagine she must have struggled with that decision. She was trying to cover up the incident to protect her restaurant, but hiding an apron and wallet in her stew would ruin her prized broth, an action that would also be detrimental to her business.'

Kaede let her imagination roam. What would she have done in that situation? She couldn't decide.

'Let me ask you one more question,' she said. 'Why do you think that H stayed silent, even when the police took him away?'

Grandfather squinted as if peering into space to capture the fragments of a vision.

'The most convincing theory is that he's protecting the proprietress. In other words, by the time the police arrived, he'd realized there was no other possible culprit. Maybe H really is a kind and just man. Or maybe she had confided in him previously about Clyde's threats.'

'That seems like the saddest possible ending for both of them.'

'Why do you think that?'

'You implied before that the owner might be getting ready to leave. Is she planning to escape while H keeps his silence?'

'No, that's not it after all,' said Grandfather, his eyes narrowing even further. 'She's not getting ready to run away. I see her, right there in front of me. She's calling the police. She's decided to turn herself in to save H.'

This vision sounds a bit like wishful thinking . . .

However, given how sure of himself her grandfather sounded, she couldn't help but believe it was true.

At that moment, there was a chorus of chirping from the bell crickets in the garden. Simultaneously, Grandfather's eyes flew open.

'Oh, I see! How could I have missed that!'

He turned towards the window, a wry smile on his lips.

'I was on the verge of overlooking a crucial fact. In the world of the bell cricket, it's only the males who chirp. I should probably thank Doting Father for drawing my attention to those crickets. It seems I've made a serious error.'

What? Crickets? What mistake?

Bewildered, Kaede watched her grandfather stroke his stubbly beard.

'And yet, once you're bothered by stubble, it continues to bother you.'

All Kaede heard were meaningless ramblings.

'I should have got the home helper or Sanae to shave it for me. When I leave it to you, it always ends up feeling rough. So instead of asking you to give me a shave, I'd like to ask you a favour.'

She knew it. The familiar phrase was coming.

And just as she'd predicted . . .

'Kaede, pass me a cigarette, would you?'

Grandfather exhaled a cloud of Gauloise smoke, then settled deep into his chair.

Was he closing his eyes completely or just squinting?

Eventually, he peered deep into the purplish haze and began to speak again.

'Kaede, I'm sorry. The tale I've woven was not the optimal solution. There's a significant flaw in the narrative.'

'Huh?'

'I promise I'm not teasing you. When I'm examining possibilities, the picture keeps on shifting. Frustratingly, it's

The Izakaya Locked-Room Murder Mystery

the pictures I see in the smoke that seem to have the fewest inconsistencies.'

Peering deeper into the smoke he began to mutter, as if to himself.

'The proprietress wasn't the killer after all. It was H all along.'

There was a chilling silence. Somehow all the crickets in the garden had stopped chirping.

'No matter how many crickets there may be, only the males make a sound,' Grandfather went on. 'Consequently, in order to calculate the exact ratio of males to females we'd have to count them visually. However, the male to female ratio that day at the izakaya is already known.'

Male to female ratio?

'Is that relevant to the case?' Kaede asked.

'Let's think about it. Remember the seating plan for that evening. Including the two tables and the counter, that evening there were thirteen customers in total, labelled A through M. Of those, only two were women, sitting at Table ①. In other words, eleven of the customers were men. Once the football match ended, it's likely that they'd rush to the men's toilet at once.'

'Right.'

'And there is the major flaw in the tale I wove,' announced Grandfather, his eyes glinting from beneath a fallen lock of hair. 'With that risk of a sudden flood of male customers at any moment, why would the proprietress choose the Gents toilet for her conversation with Clyde?'

'Oh, I see!'

Kaede finally caught on.

'From her perspective, the kitchen would be out because of all the sharp knives in there,' she said. 'If she wanted to have a quick conversation then get rid of Clyde quickly, she could have talked to him in the bit of hallway in front of the toilets, or as a last resort, the Ladies toilet. The Gents would be the least likely place for her to choose.'

'Exactly. Then, let's revisit those vital missing three minutes. First, around 9.50 p.m. Clyde appears at the entrance to the izakaya. The proprietress signals to him to meet her over by the toilets – this much fits in with our earlier theory. But then their discussion takes place in the hallway outside where the washbasin is, not inside the Gents toilet. They get into a violent argument, and Clyde grabs her by the throat. Then he pulls out his knife and tries to stab her. At that moment H arrives to use the toilet. He tries to save the proprietress by wresting the knife out of Clyde's hand, but in the struggle ends up accidentally stabbing him in the back.'

'Yes, that makes sense. I doubt the owner would have stood a chance by herself against an enraged Clyde.'

Grandfather raised a finger.

'And this is key – if the proprietress were the killer, Clyde would have been stabbed in the abdomen during the struggle. The fact that the wound was in his back points to the involvement of a third person – namely H.'

Well, now that you mention it . . .

'At that moment, Clyde was still alive. Though the wound was probably fatal – when a knife is deeply embedded in either the stomach or the back, survival is unlikely – at that moment neither the proprietress nor H thought he would die. She pulled the groaning, cursing Clyde into the Ladies toilet where there was a lower risk of him being seen. "H, I'm sorry. I'll handle this. I'll call an ambulance if necessary," she said, ushering H back into the restaurant. She'd have been talking gently to Clyde, asking him if he was OK, if he needed an ambulance, but then in his growing rage he attacked her again. At this point, the embedded knife was acting as a kind of plug, keeping most of the bleeding internal. The proprietress fled into the hallway again, and when Clyde charged after her like a crazed killer, she pushed him backwards and he fell into the Gents toilet. The door had probably been left open. He fell against the toilet tank and the force of his fall pushed the knife further into his back, severing an artery.'

'I see. And then she locked the door from inside and climbed out over the top. She tossed Clyde's belongings and her apron into the wastepaper basket and left the hallway.'

'I believe those actions were less about the restaurant's future and more about preventing H from being implicated.

Meanwhile, back at his seat, H had completely forgotten about needing the toilet, and lit a cigarette to calm his agitation. And then, when Shiki asked him if the toilet was free, he caught sight of the proprietress leaving. As far as he knew, the men's toilet should have been unoccupied, so he reluctantly replied, "Ah, yes, go ahead. It's free." However, due to unexpected circumstances, a bloody corpse was now in the men's toilet. H probably assumed that the proprietress had stabbed him again, and consequently kept silent to protect her. He has no idea that he himself is the real killer.'

The expression on Grandfather's face was complex as he gazed deep into the swirling tendrils of smoke. Was he searching for H's familiar gentle expression?

'I can see H sitting there in the interrogation room, his fists clenched beneath the table, determined not to speak unless the proprietress comes. He's resolved to make his testimony match whatever she has to say. If she gives the true version of events, he'll confess without hesitation that he stabbed the victim. And then . . . Ah, yes, I can see it.'

Grandfather frowned as if trying to pierce the fog with his stare. Without a doubt, he was seeing a scene from the future, the very near future. Apparently, sometimes that smoke screen could project images of days yet to come . . .

'The proprietress has broken down in tears. Undoubtedly,

she's saying, "Yes, H did stab him, but he never meant to. He was trying to help me." And when he hears what she said, H will murmur his usual line, "Don't worry about me." And in that moment H will finally understand his true feelings for her. What he had thought of as admiration of her maternal nature was in fact something else. He loved her as a woman. He was in love.'

Inexperienced as she was in matters of the heart, Kaede felt she could understand H's feelings. Maybe the time he had spent alone in silence would be a chance for him to do some soul-searching, to understand his true feelings for Haruno's owner.

Kaede pondered some more. How would the police judge H's actions? Would they see they were an instinctive response to an emergency situation? And how would they view the actions of Haruno's owner?

Kaede wanted to believe that the kindness of these two people would be key to lighting a new path forward for them.

After a while, the Gauloise in the ashtray burned out.

Grandfather stared into his coffee cup, and mumbled in a drowsy voice, 'Kaede, could you pass me some chopsticks? The offal stew here is truly excellent.'

Grandpa, I'm sorry that I can't take you out with me much any more . . .

But she'd made up her mind that if the izakaya ever reopened, she would take him there.

Chapter 3:
The Vanishing Person at the Pool

1

Perhaps it was due to all the ongoing redevelopment, but the Shimokitazawa station area was spotlessly clean and litter-free. Kaede wasn't getting any sense of what her grandfather always called 'the perfectly seedy charm' of the neighbourhood.

But then she came across two street performers frozen in the pose of a pair of Kongo Rikishi guardian statues, surrounded by a crowd of young people watching with earnest expressions, and not a hint of derision. *There's the real 'Shimokita' vibe after all*, she thought.

The little theatre building was tucked in beside a fitness club that had once been a famous old movie house. Outside was a board propped up on an easel, bizarre lettering scrawled on it in bold marker pen.

The Blue Corner theatre troupe presents their quarterly performance of The Author is You: Part 3

What kind of show was *The Author is You*? But the addition of *Part 3* suggested a regular event with a loyal following.

Kaede descended the stairs, enveloped in the wafting aroma of fried chicken from the next-door karaage restaurant.

She was greeted by a woman with short, flaming red hair and a welcoming, dimpled smile. Her lipstick was a bold red that matched her hair colour perfectly. She may have been working front-of-house, but this woman clearly belonged to the theatre world, Kaede thought.

'Here you go,' said the staff member, handing her a piece of paper and a pencil.

Probably a feedback form. Looking forward to writing all my thoughts down.

But then the woman added some unexpected directions.

'This is your "suggestion sheet". We'll be collecting them fifteen minutes before the curtain goes up, so please complete it by then.'

Kaede looked down at the paper.

'Please describe a character you would like to see performed on stage. A glimpse into the life of . . .'

Oh, I get it. It's an improv play . . .

Opening the theatre door, Kaede found a tiny space with seating for no more than thirty audience members. It was almost full already. As she squinted in the low lighting,

The Vanishing Person at the Pool

looking for an empty seat, she heard Iwata's voice calling out, 'I saved you a spot!'

She thanked him and sat down, noting that he was already busy scribbling.

'This format's a first for me too,' he said proudly, twirling his pencil. 'I don't suppose you're any good at these things, Sensei?'

'You mean writing scripts and stuff?'

'Right. You have to suggest a person and an odd situation to put them in. You know, I'm really into comedy.'

'That's the first I've heard of it.'

'Oh, is it? Anyway, this kind of thing must be challenging to someone as serious as you, Kaede-sensei.'

He might be right about that, she thought, her pencil frozen in mid-air.

The audience members' suggestion sheets were collected, Kaede's included. About five minutes later, the voice of an announcer rang out, sounding like a boxing match emcee.

'Ladies and gentlemen, thank you for your patience! From the theatre troupe Blue Corner, please give a warm welcome to our director!'

Shiki, dressed in a slim-fitting suit, stepped out on stage accompanied by lively dance music.

'Huh, he got promoted to director,' Iwata muttered.

The audience, particularly the younger women, burst into energetic applause.

It was hard to tell whether Shiki was aware of his own popularity, but he waited for the applause to die down before launching into the usual greetings. Then he raised his voice a notch.

'Thank you to everyone for your wonderful script suggestions,' he said with a deep bow.

Kaede felt her heart skip a beat. That voice – low but carrying to every corner of the room. A familiar texture, reminding her of something from the distant past.

'Right then . . . as usual I've taken the liberty of selecting five of your suggestions. Our theatre troupe will now perform these scenes to the best of our ability. No rehearsals, no staging, everything impromptu. *The Author is You: Part 3* is about to begin. Ready?'

In unison the audience shouted out in English, 'The show must go on!' All except Kaede, that is.

She realized it must be a Blue Corner ritual. Kaede had the sense of being an outsider as the stage lights faded to black. Shared nerves and a sense of anticipation filled the small theatre as the audience prepared to be both onlooker and author. As a buzzer sounded, the stage lit up.

The following ninety minutes were filled with joy and energy as audience and performers brought the stage to life.

There was *A scene from the life of a veteran umpire who*

The Vanishing Person at the Pool

returns the ball to the pitcher at 150 km/hour, followed by *A scene from the life of soldiers in Japan's self-defence force who, after a time-travel mishap, find themselves in the Heian period where nobles compose* waka *poems and play courtly games of* kemari.

The next, *A scene from the life of a champion shogi player, clenching his fist in the waiting room moments before a title match, declaring, 'I'll win this for you!'*, turned into one of the most intense, thrilling love stories that Kaede had ever seen.

Then, *A scene from the life of woman in her twenties who, after losing her life savings at the racetrack, sets sail on a tuna fishing boat.*

Kaede silently rejoiced.

Yes! They picked mine . . .

Each new improv script was first introduced by a narrator, sparking laughter before the scene had even begun. However, the essence of each performance was profoundly serious. Kaede didn't know a lot about improv theatre, but she realized there was something very fresh and unique about this.

For the grand finale, performed by the entire company, and lasting over thirty minutes, there was an epic tale starring an elderly circus couple: *A scene from the life of a trapeze artist couple who, the night before their show, get into a violent, almost deadly argument.*

2

The play after-party was to be held at a *mizutaki* hot pot restaurant, about a seven-minute walk from the theatre. As they walked along a street lined with an oyster restaurant, an assortment of second-hand clothing shops and a darts bar, Iwata grumbled to Kaede.

'I can't believe he rejected my scene.'

'Oh really? What was yours about?'

'A primary school teacher who used to be on the school baseball team.'

You just wrote about yourself!
And you really thought that would get picked?
Your over-confidence is stunning.

A variety of possible responses flashed through Kaede's mind, but finally she settled on, 'That's a shame.'

They arrived at the *mizutaki* restaurant and settled into the tatami floor seating. With the pot bubbling in the centre of the table, the drinking began.

The place was famous for its generous all-you-can-eat and all-you-can-drink specials.

Kaede recalled her grandfather telling her that theatre performers weren't in it for the plays, but for the after-parties. Sitting in the midst of the current racket, she finally understood what he meant. Although Blue Corner was a small troupe of barely ten members, including the crew, their explosive energy surpassed that of all thirty-two kids in Kaede's primary school class combined.

She'd already heard that the owner of the izakaya Haruno had turned herself in to the police, and although it had been confirmed that it was H who had stabbed the victim, it was likely that they would rule there was no criminal intent. Perhaps that was why his companions were able to celebrate so freely tonight.

In the end, Grandfather's deductions had proved perfectly accurate. However, Kaede was aware that it would be tasteless to make the izakaya murder case the topic of conversation tonight.

Around the large rectangular table, the troupe was well into their toasts – each one preceded by a shout of 'The show must go on!' Although Shiki had invited her to join, Kaede had a hard time matching their high spirits, and felt a little out of place. Iwata, on the other hand, despite only having seen them perform a handful of times, had blended right in, discussing scenes as if he were a seasoned actor. Kaede reflected how this warm approachability was one of the reasons the children in his class adored him.

About an hour must have passed when Shiki, wearing a T-shirt and with his long hair tied back, squeezed in between Kaede and Iwata. He was carrying three mugs of beer.

'Sorry I couldn't hang with you earlier,' he said. 'You

know what's good about the all-you-can-drink here? They don't make you get a new glass each time, so you can really drink all you like.'

'Nah, I'm good on the beer.' Iwata grimaced and patted his stomach. 'Don't want to end up with a beer belly. I envy you, though. How do you maintain that body when you say you hate sports so much?'

Kaede was wondering the same thing. When she first met Shiki, he'd seemed delicate, almost girlish, but now she could see he was muscular, his six-pack visible through his T-shirt.

'Bodybuilding and sports are different,' Shiki replied, pushing a mug of beer towards Kaede. 'How can I put it? I think my dislike of sports might be connected to why I just can't get along with classic translated mystery novels.'

Ah he's setting me up again, I can feel it . . .

'How do you mean?' she asked anyway.

'You know that satirical haiku that goes,

> *Famous detective*
> *calls all suspects together*
> *'Now then,' he begins*

'As I mentioned before, these old-school foreign mysteries are too locked into a certain pattern. For example, after identifying the culprit, the detective always proudly "twirls

The Vanishing Person at the Pool

his moustache" in self-satisfaction. Why the need to twist your moustache if there isn't even a mirror nearby? Surely that would throw off its balance completely? There's no persuasive power in a deduction delivered with a lopsided moustache. If I were the culprit I'd be in stitches.'

I'll give you the benefit of the doubt, no – a thousand benefits. You have just come off stage after a big performance . . .

'I kind of see what you're saying, but what does that have to do with hating sports?'

'It's the same thing – those sports commentaries, the post-game interviews, they all follow the same rigid patterns. There's so much I hate about them. They're so predictable I just can't stand it.'

Meanwhile, Iwata was somehow sprawled face-down on the table again. The all-you-can-drink system was clearly not for him.

'Take the Most Valuable Player interview in pro baseball,' Shiki went on, ignoring Iwata. *Broadcasting booth, broadcasting booth, we're live with the MVP interview* – and cut! This might have made sense back in the day when the signal was unreliable, but why the need to repeat the phrase "broadcasting booth" twice? Isn't once enough? And anyway, the term is totally outdated. But there's the reporter continuing without an ounce of self-reflection. *And today's MVP is Whatshisname who hit the game-winning home run. The moment he struck the ball, you could tell it was going out of the park!* And cut! There's no way of telling the moment the ball makes contact with the bat that it's going to be a home run. You realize it a split-second later, by judging both the sound the hit makes and the angle and speed of the ball. But everyone's so bound by these clichés that they end up telling what is actually a shameful lie. And then of course, there's the worst—'

Shiki broke off mid-rant to take a gulp of beer, possibly to keep his throat from getting dry.

Hey, Iwata-sensei!

'Do you know the number one baseball cliché that I never want to hear again?'

Hey, Iwata, wake up! Save me, please!

'*Two out, bases loaded, full count – three balls, two strikes. We're at a crucial moment where one hit could win the game.*'

It was no use. Iwata was out cold. There was no stopping Shiki now.

'*And the runners are poised to set off on the next pitch. Here it comes, the sixth pitch. He hits it! It's a high fly to the shortstop . . . This is interesting.* OK, cut, cut, major cut! *This is interesting*? No, it isn't. It isn't *interesting* at all. Fans from both teams are watching mesmerized, barely daring to breathe. How condescending is it to call this *interesting*? The only ones permitted to use a line like that are the gods of baseball or maybe one of the true baseball greats. So, in conclusion, er . . . what I'm trying to say is . . . we shouldn't misunderstand a situation, based on our own arbitrary assumptions.'

Huh?

What's up with him? So weird. This is not just being verbose. Is he totally drunk?

Kaede reckoned it was high time to change the subject, and that she'd better do it while Shiki was still at least somewhat coherent.

'Hey, Shiki, I haven't given you my thoughts about today's performance yet,' she said, surreptitiously moving his beer out of his reach.

'Oh, please. I'd love to hear it.'

Kaede sat up slightly before starting.

'It was amazing.'

She meant it. Her grandfather had also told her, 'When actors ask for feedback after a performance, there's only one answer: *It was amazing!* They're on a high, and they just want to be praised.' But in this case, it was a genuine response from the heart.

Shiki's expression softened into an unfamiliar smile, the most unguarded expression Kaede had ever seen from him.

'Thank you,' he said.

'Not only was the improv excellently done,' Kaede went on, 'but I was impressed with how everyone moved so seamlessly between different roles. For instance, there were so many female characters.'

'Right.'

'You played a few of the female roles yourself, too. And you really pulled it off. In fact, I was wondering whether that was why you'd been growing your hair long.'

'No, nothing like that. I'm just too lazy to get it cut.'

Shiki tried to run his fingers through his hair, and spectacularly missed. He was drunk enough to forget he'd tied it back.

'You have only one woman in your theatre troupe,' Kaede continued, glancing at the red-haired front-of-house staff member across the table from them. 'And yet you managed to create these ensemble pieces with all those male and female characters. It's really impressive.'

Several people burst out laughing at this.

'Kaede-sensei,' said Shiki, his words slightly slurred, 'I hate to break it to you, but we don't have any women in this troupe.'

The red-haired woman reached up and with a flourish, pulled off her wig.

'Right now, we're recruiting women members. How about it, Kaede-san?'

Exhaustion from playing multiple roles, coupled with the pressure of leading the theatre troupe seemed to catch up with Shiki. He leaned back into his floor chair and promptly fell asleep. At which point Iwata's head popped up from the table.

The Vanishing Person at the Pool

'Looks like his batteries finally ran out.'

'What?' said Kaede. 'I thought you were passed out drunk?'

Iwata chuckled.

'Didn't you notice? I switched to oolong tea ages ago. I knew this guy was going to crash eventually,' he added, as he gently draped his coat over the sleeping Shiki. 'Besides, he was going off on one of his sports rants, and I couldn't be bothered to engage. Tonight was one of the shorter ones. Usually once he's done with baseball, he'll start complaining about football commentary, and then move on to marathon coverage too.'

Ha! So that was no improv performance. It had been a well-rehearsed routine.

Iwata looked down with surprising tenderness at Shiki who was sprawled out with his mouth slightly open.

'Actually, there's a reason he came to hate sports.'

'Oh yes?'

'Back in high school, I was the baseball team captain and the catcher. And although he was only a freshman, Shiki was made our ace pitcher because of his fast ball. Well, when I say *was made* – in reality the teacher who was our club adviser didn't know much about baseball, so I was the one who picked him.'

'Really?'

What they call a baseball battery: a pitcher and catcher

duo . . . Kaede didn't fully understand, but she had already sensed that their bond went deeper than the typical senior–junior relationship.

'For us third years, it was our last summer of high school baseball. It was the bottom of the ninth inning, the opposing team at bat. The score was tied, bases loaded, two outs and a full count – three balls, two strikes.'

Exactly the same scenario Shiki was just complaining about . . .

'I signalled to Shiki to throw a fast ball straight down the middle, but his hand must have been sweaty and the ball slipped. It was a wild pitch. The ball struck the batter right in the face, and of course we lost the game on a walk. But it didn't matter about the game. Rather than the end-of-game whistle, it's the wail of the ambulance siren that has stuck with me. That ball hit the batter so hard that the boy lost the sight in his left eye.'

Kaede had no words.

'Shiki quit baseball for ever that day. And he's grown to hate any kind of sport where there's any risk at all of injuring an opponent.'

Kaede understood. But . . .

What if he's just pretending to hate it? Maybe he still loves them deeply – baseball, other sports . . .

She had a feeling she might be right.

The Vanishing Person at the Pool

'Kaede-sensei, shall I tell you how I knew he was going to crash tonight?'

'Please.'

'Right before today's performance, when Shiki and I were talking backstage, a familiar face dropped by to say hello. It was Shiki who recognized him first.'

'Don't tell me . . .'

'Yes. Somehow word must have reached him, because the batter from that day came to the performance for the first time. Shiki broke down in tears.'

Iwata's voice trembled as he spoke.

'You can see why he'd want to drink himself into oblivion after that. Kaede-sensei, this guy – he's got a sharp tongue, but a soft heart. He's the type you want to protect because he's so vulnerable. But . . .'

Iwata forced a smile.

'Like I told you the first time you met him, he's a prize weirdo. Whatever you do, don't fall for him.'

3

Well, here I am, hangover and all . . .

Kaede was kind of surprised at her own daring. It had been about three years since she'd last shown up at one of these reunion lunches for her university class. Lately she'd sensed a shift in herself towards being more sociable. It might have something to do with meeting Shiki – so different from herself with his bizarre need for attention.

She walked into the western-style restaurant near Shinjuku-sanchome station, famous for its handmade hamburger steaks and inexpensive lunch sets. It wasn't exactly a high-end establishment, and that suited Kaede just fine. The last time she'd attended one of these reunions it had been at a fancy bistro in Omotesando, but with more friends bringing babies along these days, the choice had shifted to something simpler.

Still, the neat interior featured elaborate decorations. Halloween was a couple of weeks away, and each table was topped with a small jack o'-lantern. A variety of Halloween costumes and accessories were on display on the wooden latticed walls. A silver masquerade ball mask with vivid red feathers caught Kaede's eye. It reminded her of the theatre troupe member's red wig from the previous day.

Lunch was over, and the woman Kaede had been chatting with decided to leave early because her baby was fussing. Kaede walked her to the door, helped her to calm the child, then returned to find another old friend had arrived and taken the empty seat across from her.

'Kaede! It's been ages. Your skin is still so beautiful.'

'Please! I'm pale and washed out from a hangover.'

Kaede was happy to find how easy it was to chat even though they hadn't met for three years. Misaki was one of

The Vanishing Person at the Pool

the few friends she'd regularly had lunch with during their student days.

But maybe we were just casual friends really . . .

She wondered when it was that she'd started to fear getting close to people.

Well, it must have been back then – after learning what had happened to her mother. Since then, it hadn't only been romantic relationships she'd avoided, but even just meeting people, forming close friendships. That old unhealable wound . . .

'Anyway, I've got something to tell you,' Misaki said with excitement. 'Right now, I'm teaching at the primary school where your grandfather used to be principal.'

'Really?'

'Yes. There aren't many teachers as cool as your grandfather was. How is he these days?'

'Um . . . well, fine . . .' she answered vaguely.

It wasn't that Kaede was ashamed of her grandfather's dementia, but it didn't feel like the right moment for that particular conversation. Still, she was surprised to hear that Misaki was teaching at the same school. Most of her classmates in the Education Faculty had gone on to become teachers, and many of them at primary schools, but this felt like quite the coincidence.

'You know how your grandfather was nicknamed "Principal Window Wiper"? Well, even now, fifteen years since he retired, he's still a legend in the Parent Teacher Association. People tell stories about him.'

Wow . . .

Kaede felt genuinely proud.

'Anyway, here's the best part,' said Misaki, glancing towards the restaurant window, which was adorned with paper cut-outs of ghosts, witches and black cats. 'The current principal is pretty cool too. After hearing the stories about your grandfather, the new headteacher started cleaning the school windows with the same amount of dedication, earning the nickname, "Second-Generation Principal Window Wiper".'

Her grandfather's window-cleaning habit hadn't just been for show. He'd begun not only because he wanted the windows to be shiny, or to chat with children as they walked around the school; there had been another hidden purpose – to put the 'Broken Windows Theory' into practice.

Kaede recalled his explanation.

When the windows of abandoned houses or vehicles are left broken, or graffiti in the underground isn't removed, people start thinking 'This is normal' or 'Nobody cares anyway'. And so more windows get broken and more graffiti appears. The moral standards of the local residents gradually decline, and these minor crimes eventually lead to more serious, violent crime. Or so the theory goes.

The Vanishing Person at the Pool

So how to prevent crime before it happens? By cleaning windows.

In the early 1990s, facing a surge in violent crime, the mayor of New York City invested large sums of money into scrubbing off all the graffiti in the subway network, in accordance with the Broken Windows Theory. As a result, the crime rate plummeted, and there was a dramatic improvement in safety – or so the story went.

'Not that I think the kids around here are going to turn to crime,' Grandfather had laughed. 'But if the windows are clean, then they're going to want the hallways and floors to be clean too. The dust in the classrooms will even start to bother them. Windows are like the heart. When you look through a clean window, your heart becomes cleaner too. I truly believe that.'

Kaede was ruminating over her grandfather's words when she was interrupted by Misaki's voice.

'Hey, Kaede, are you listening?'

'Sorry, sorry. What were you saying?'

'I was telling you that Second-Generation Principal Window Wiper also likes watering the flowers in the schoolyard, just like the original. They've even given up that spacious office on the second floor to move into a much smaller room right in front of the flower beds. I'll never understand being that much into flowers.'

Misaki grinned, showing her charming snaggleteeth.

Misaki was proud of her protruding canines, so much so that she'd stubbornly refused her parents' offer to get braces.

They suit you, Misaki . . .

Kaede admired her friend's unshakeable self-confidence, which was all part of her adorable charm.

Far more confidence than I'll ever have . . .

'By the way, this is a bit random,' said Misaki, 'but are you still into mystery novels?'

A bit random? Total change of subject.

'Yeah, mysteries are pretty much my only hobby,' Kaede admitted.

'Then listen to this. Something puzzling happened at our school. Well, I'd say it was a proper mystery.'

'No way! Tell me everything.'

Misaki leaned in.

'You know how there are different types of mystery story, they're divided into all those sub-genres, right? Like Locked-Room Mystery or Unbreakable Alibi or whatever?'

'Uh-huh.'

'What would you call a case where someone just disappears in front of everyone's eyes?'

That'd be a vanishing person mystery.

Kaede didn't want to seem too much of a mystery nerd so she kept it to herself. If she'd answered immediately, the excitement would doubtless have turned her voice too shrill.

The Vanishing Person at the Pool

Ellery Queen and John Dickson Carr, those giants of classic detective fiction, had often sat '*far into the night*' discussing the genre, as Carr wrote in a dedication to Ellery Queen in his novel *The Curse of the Bronze Lamp*. They had concluded that the '*miracle problem*' of a person vanishing was '*perhaps the most fascinating gambit in detective-fiction*'.

'I'm not so familiar with all the genres,' said Kaede casually. 'But would you mind if I recorded you telling the story?'

She quickly hunted for her phone's voice memo icon.

'I get nervous when I'm being recorded,' said Misaki with an embarrassed smile. 'But anyway, where to begin . . . ?'

She paused a moment to think.

'OK, well in spring of last year we got a new teacher at the school. She was young, fresh out of college. Strong, chiselled features, a great figure – totally beautiful. How can I put it? Like a classic Showa-era beauty.'

Showa-era beauty! Kaede chuckled to herself. Just the word 'beautiful' would have been enough, but Misaki typically never just gave a simple compliment.

'I can't use her real name, so for the purposes of this story I'm going to refer to her as "Idol-sensei". No, hold on, she has that Showa-type face, I think I'll go with "Madonna".'

'You've taken that straight out of Natsume Soseki's *Botchan*. And besides, that book was written in the Meiji era.'

'Whatever. Anyway, she had that kind of vibe.'

Kaede felt a slight chill from the use of the past tense.

'Well, you know how it goes in every workplace – there's a hot new colleague and the place gets all stirred up. Our school was no exception. The single male teachers, even some of the pupils' dads, started acting all strange around her. There was an unsettling feeling that something was going to happen.'

'I see.'

'Come to think of it, you're a beauty too, Kaede. Only in a different way. Do you get strange vibes at your place too?'

'No, no,' Kaede protested, waving her hand in denial, but for a brief second Iwata's smiling face flashed through her mind. 'Nothing like that! Go on.'

'Right. It was around spring this year when Madonna-sensei suddenly stopped smiling. She'd always been totally cheerful before, and a rumour went around that she was dealing with some kind of trouble in her personal life. Nobody knew what exactly. But then in June, around the start of the rainy season, she started taking more days off. Something was definitely going on.'

'Yeah.'

Kaede nodded in agreement. Thinking back, she couldn't imagine taking multiple absences in her second year as a teacher.

The Vanishing Person at the Pool

'Then came the day in question. It was the last day of classes before the summer break.'

Misaki lowered her voice, as if worried someone might overhear.

'They'd just announced the official end of the rainy season, and it was one of those scorching hot days with a brilliant blue sky. Madonna-sensei had thirty fourth-grade kids, and fourth period class was swimming. I can still remember it clearly – the sound of their excited voices from the classroom next door.'

Kaede could picture it clearly. Her own face would always break into a smile when she saw the kids' excited reaction to the instruction, 'Everyone get changed and meet by the pool!' It was one of those moments that made her grateful she chose this profession.

'So, Madonna-sensei's swimming class began. But . . . you know what? It'd be easier to explain the next bit if I drew you a diagram. Hold on a sec . . .'

She reached into the oversized tote bag she always carried that somehow suited her petite frame perfectly. She pulled out a pen and a personal planner, and using a shop loyalty card as a makeshift ruler, she skilfully sketched a map of the pool area. Watching her, Kaede was reminded for some reason of Shiki, who performed improv scenes so effortlessly. This kind of talent had to be innate.

'This is about right,' said Misaki, deftly tearing out the

page from her planner and securing it on the table with her phone as a paperweight. 'I'll explain what happened next, as I heard it from the children.'

She opened her planner again. The type to handle everything with brisk efficiency, Misaki also seemed to be a dedicated note-taker.

'The lesson began at 11.15 a.m. Madonna-sensei had been on the swim team herself, and she was very thorough teaching the children proper breathing techniques. Fourth-graders can be very cheeky as you know. Some of the boys were saying things like, "Sensei is cute even in a swim cap and goggles," and there were girls whispering that they wanted a figure like hers.'

Yeah, that's classic fourth-grade behaviour, Kaede thought.

'Perhaps Madonna-sensei got that great body from being on the swim team,' Misaki mused. 'Anyway, at 11.40 a.m. precisely she blew her whistle and announced, "All right everyone, the last twenty minutes of class is going to be free time!"'

Kaede was sure the pupils must have been ecstatic. There were two things that kids always loved – curry for lunch and free time in the pool. And especially on this perfect summer day, their last swimming lesson before the summer holidays.

'All thirty children were in lanes 1 to 3 – the right-hand side of the pool in this diagram. Some of them played

The Vanishing Person at the Pool

underwater rock paper scissors, others were racing each other at crawl or butterfly. There was quite a racket apparently.'

Misaki paused to take a sip of her carbonated water. Staring at the tiny bubbles reminded Kaede of the clarity of a swimming pool in summer.

'At exactly twelve noon, the school bell rang. Naturally the kids kept on splashing around, but then Madonna-sensei, who was standing at Point Ⓐ, blew her whistle and raised both arms, signalling them to get out. The kids reluctantly climbed out of the pool at Point Ⓑ. All they had to do was take a quick shower and get back to their class. But right then they heard the splash of someone diving into the pool. They turned back to look, thinking Madonna-sensei was going to have a quick swim.'

'She used to be on the swim team, right?' commented Kaede. 'Nothing wrong with swimming a couple of solo laps.'

'Sure. And checking the pool for lost swim caps or goggles is routine for teachers anyway. But of course, kids being kids, they started complaining that Sensei was having all the fun.'

Misaki smiled, showing off her cute snaggleteeth.

An image of that summer day floated into Kaede's mind. A body, beautifully toned from years of swimming, tracing an elegant arc through the air. The brilliant sunlight casting

Swimming Pool Diagram

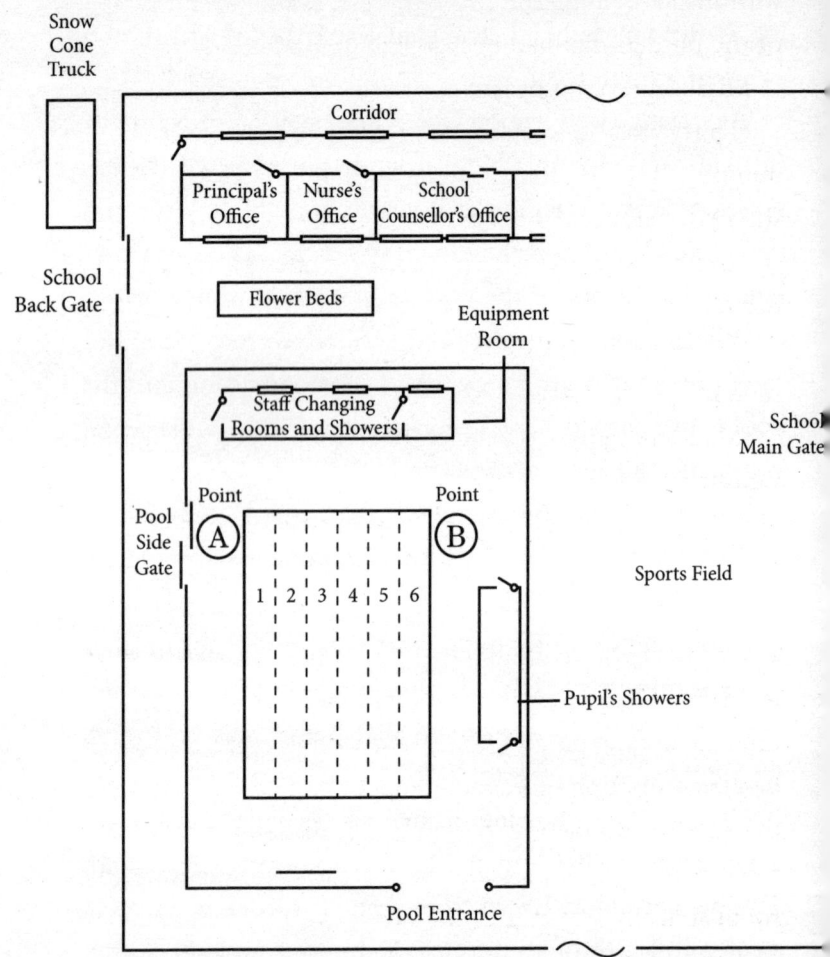

The Vanishing Person at the Pool

a silhouette on the shimmering surface of the water. This young woman was struggling with something in her personal life. Behind those swim goggles were her eyes filled with shades of anguish? Or brightness, as she was finally free of the burden that had been weighing on her?

Misaki's next words had Kaede snap back to the present.

'Thirty seconds passed, then fifty seconds, then a full minute. But Madonna-sensei didn't surface. Someone shouted, "Hey . . . did she . . . drown?" Four or five of the strongest swimmers jumped back into the pool to search for her. But . . .'

Misaki broke off for a moment, and her expression turned serious.

'Madonna-sensei wasn't in the pool. She had simply vanished.'

Their conversation ought to have gone unheard by their university classmates at the other tables. And yet, at the utterance of the phrase 'simply vanished' the restaurant that had been buzzing moments earlier fell eerily silent. Perhaps the cardboard cut-outs of witches in the window had cast some sort of dark spell that made the commotion in the room similarly vanish into thin air.

Don't be silly . . .

Kaede broke the silence by asking, 'What do you mean by vanished? I mean nobody actually saw Madonna-sensei dive into the pool, did they? All they heard was the splash of somebody entering the water. So, isn't it possible that—'

'I know where you're going with this,' Misaki interrupted, holding up a hand to stop her friend from continuing her thought. 'Look, I enjoy a good mystery as much as anyone. You're thinking that Madonna-sensei wanted to perform some sort of disappearing act, so she threw a block of ice or maybe dry ice into the pool instead. While the kids were wondering why she hadn't surfaced and were fussing about looking for her she changed into her street clothes in the locker room, laid low for a while, then slipped out through the pool's side gate and escaped through the back gate of the school. That's the trick, right?'

Kaede nodded. With mystery novels, mirrors or ice were always the first suspects. That was basic stuff.

'But look,' Misaki continued, pointing to the plan. 'The children were adamant that the sound they heard was a person diving into the water. And you know what? It's not difficult to believe them. I mean, think about it. How can you mistake the sound of a block of ice for a human body entering the water? Of course, it's not impossible, but highly unlikely.'

'Yeah,' Kaede agreed, silently cursing the rather simplistic

The Vanishing Person at the Pool

tricks in old mystery novels, 'it is practically impossible to mistake one for the other.'

'Right. But now let's say, for argument's sake, that the children did mistake a different sound for a person diving in. It still doesn't all add up.'

'How do you mean?' Kaede asked.

'Take another look at this diagram,' said Misaki, pushing the paper closer to Kaede. 'Let's go over the events of that day along with their timeline. The moment the bell chimed at noon, Madonna-sensei was here at Point Ⓐ, blowing her whistle and gesturing for the children to get out of the pool. They reluctantly got out here at Point Ⓑ and started walking towards the showers. At that moment they heard what they were sure was the sound of someone diving into the pool behind them. They waited about a minute, but nobody surfaced. Several panicked pupils jumped into the pool but no one could find Madonna-sensei. Are you with me so far?'

'Yep.'

This is already a classic vanishing person mystery . . .

'The kids got changed as quickly as they could, then they ran up to the staffroom on the upper level, announcing to all the teachers in there that "Madonna-sensei dived into the pool and disappeared!"'

Kaede could only imagine the heightened emotions of the students at that point.

'And as it happens, guess who was one of the teachers in

the staffroom when it happened?' announced Misaki with a touch of the dramatic. 'I ran straight down to the ground floor to inform the principal. You see . . .'

She paused to point to the diagram again.

'The principal's office is right here on the ground floor, and the bushes in the flower bed in front aren't particularly tall. That means there's a clear view of the pool from the office window. The protective barrier around the pool is no more than a chain-link fence. It's practically like looking through glass. So, I asked if there'd been anything out of the ordinary, like someone leaving through the side gate of the pool or the back entrance of the school.'

'And what did the principal say?'

'"I happened to be cleaning my office window so I would have noticed if anyone went in or out of the gates. I didn't see a soul."'

Kaede voiced what had probably been on everyone's mind since that day.

'I hate to say it, but how do you know that the principal wasn't lying?'

Their old classmates had gradually begun to leave the restaurant, but right now Kaede didn't feel like stopping to say proper goodbyes.

'Plus, even if the principal was cleaning the window the whole time this went down, there is a chance something could have been missed,' she added.

The Vanishing Person at the Pool

'You're right, Kaede, but the principal wasn't the only person to testify that they didn't see anything.'

Misaki indicated the diagram again.

'See this back alley here? As you know, it's kind of a tradition at our school – every summer at the stroke of noon when the bell rings, a *kakigori* snow-cone vendor sets up right here outside the back gate. And this vendor swears that from noon when he set up shop until 6 p.m. when he closed, not a single person came through that gate.'

'Then what if . . .' Kaede began, knowing it was unlikely, but wanting to eliminate all possibilities, 'she didn't leave through the back gate, but just walked out of the school's main gate? If she timed it right, she could have avoided the principal's gaze. That looks as if it could have been a blind spot.'

'I think that would have been quite a challenge – practically impossible really. On the west side of the pool is this sports field, and there were football and softball lessons going on at the time. To sneak past dozens of pupils and leave by the front gate . . . she'd need to become as transparent as this sparkling water.'

There was a brief moment of silence.

'Well, then . . .'

Kaede pointed to another part of the diagram, although she knew she was quickly running out of countertheories.

'Setting aside the issue of the splash for now, couldn't

Madonna-sensei have been hiding in the staff changing room here? Or this equipment storage room next to it?'

'Ah well, that's the thing,' said Misaki. 'After the children were dismissed for the day, one of the teachers suddenly said, "What if she's collapsed in the changing room or the equipment room?" and we all went over to check it out. We were really nervous. The doors weren't locked so we could get in, but then . . .'

Misaki seemed to get caught up in the resurfaced memory. Unable to hide the fear in her expression, she clutched at the collar of her tunic.

'There were just the small lockers, kickboards, ropes and cleaning supplies. No sign of anyone. Just as the children had claimed, Madonna-sensei had dived into the pool and vanished.'

'Hold on a minute, Misaki,' said Kaede, her tone a little stern. 'This is a case of a missing person, or a disappearance – something that warrants a proper investigation. Should you be dramatizing it with a word like "vanished"?'

'That's why I came to ask your advice,' retorted Misaki, her voice louder than Kaede's. 'Sure, she stood out because she was so beautiful, but she was also a sincere person, who did what the senior teachers asked of her, and she had a great deal of respect for the principal. I really liked her. I think it was the first summer when she was a brand-new teacher, we went on a school trip to the beach, and it was

The Vanishing Person at the Pool

while she was playing the watermelon smashing game with the kids, she suddenly burst into tears. I discreetly pulled her aside to talk, and that's when she told me she was from a remote island. The smell of the ocean reminded her of home, which made her cry. Then I realized that a group of four or five boys were hiding behind some nearby rocks eavesdropping on our conversation. When I got angry with them, they ran off down the beach. I thought they were going to spread gossip about the new teacher who started crying when reminiscing about her hometown, but that's not what happened. Those boys brought back the biggest chunk of watermelon for Madonna-sensei, saying, "Here you are, Sensei; please don't cry."'

Misaki briefly flashed a tearful smile, and dabbed the corner of her eye with a handkerchief.

'I was hoping to get the chance to work with her so much more. So, I wondered if you might be able to figure out what happened to her that day, instead of the police.'

So sorry, Misaki. I was the one being insensitive, more interested in the mystery than in the fact that a human being had gone missing.

'The police aren't investigating?'

'That's right. Her only living family member – her father – didn't file a missing person report for some reason. So that was the end of the matter. Even if a family member does file a report, their disappearance isn't necessarily considered a police matter. Apparently, someone only begins to be officially considered a missing person after a report is filed, but Madonna-sensei hasn't even been afforded that status.'

Misaki's really done her research.

Kaede had heard from her grandfather's caregiver that dementia patients who were in the habit of wandering off frequently ended up as missing person cases, although thankfully, her grandfather had never exhibited such tendencies.

Until recently, people reported as missing were categorized into two types: 'general runaway cases' for those presumed to have left of their own volition, and 'special runaway cases' where foul play was suspected. These days, though, out of consideration for the feelings of family members who preferred that their loved ones were not labelled 'runaways', the terminology had changed, and they were now referred to as 'general missing persons' and 'special missing persons'. In other words, Misaki had used the correct terminology when she referred to Madonna-sensei failing to be treated as a missing person.

'But, Misaki, this is all hypothetical,' Kaede pointed out. 'What if Madonna-sensei chose to disappear of her own free will, and somehow slipped away from the school unnoticed?'

'Then what?'

'Then she would have caught a train from the nearest station . . .'

Kaede recalled that there was a station barely five minutes on foot from that primary school.

'Or perhaps she'd parked a car nearby so she could escape that way. Or isn't there a possibility she used a bus?'

'I don't think so,' said Misaki firmly. 'The shopping area in front of the station has a lot of security cameras. And just between you and me . . .'

Misaki pressed her index finger to her lips in a hush gesture.

'One of the teachers who was a big fan of hers is friendly with the chairman of that shopping district association. He pulled some strings to get all the camera footage in the area checked. But there was no sign of her that day or the next. She'd have to pass by the station to get to the bus stop, so she couldn't have taken the bus. As for a car, well, she didn't own one. In fact, she didn't even have a driving licence.'

What else? What else? Kaede thought, rifling through the filing cabinet of her mind. But no more conceivable options emerged.

'So, you see,' said Misaki, staring absently into her glass of now-flat soda water, 'she simply dived into the pool and vanished.'

Kaede realized that the remaining eight classmates in the restaurant had dwindled down to just Misaki and herself.

Misaki looked down as she stirred her water with a muddler.

'You know what, Kaede?'

Perhaps it was the moment of shared melancholy over the disappearance of Madonna-sensei, but Kaede found it pleasant to be called by her name.

'Unless something is treated as a criminal case, they say the gossip fades away in seventy-five days.'

'Right.'

'They quickly found a temporary teacher to take over for her,' Misaki continued. 'When classes resumed after the summer holidays it felt as if the adults at the school had slipped back into their normal routine. In the staffroom now there's this unspoken rule that you just don't mention her any more . . . That kind of thing, it hits you pretty hard, you know?'

Kaede understood. It wasn't uncommon for young teachers to disappear from school due to mental health issues, or family circumstances. Among Kaede and Misaki's own university classmates there were at least three people who'd been so devastated by the loss of family members that they'd been unable to continue teaching. The 'school refusal' phenomenon didn't only refer to pupils. Teachers were human too, and sometimes they simply stopped attending school. Even at today's lunch gathering there were two former classmates who'd stopped coming with no explanation. They must have had their reasons.

'Oh, that reminds me . . .' said Misaki, her face brightening, and her snaggleteeth putting in another appearance. Kaede reflected that her friend was one of the strongest in their group – or at least the best at putting on a strong front.

'Next time you visit your grandfather, you should definitely show him this.'

Misaki picked up her phone and sent Kaede a photo.

'That was taken on last year's staff trip. Isn't she lovely?'

The photo was of a beautiful young woman in a yellow dress, standing in front of some temple or shrine. Even though it was a solo shot, you could tell at once that she was tall and elegant, her small face accentuating her graceful proportions.

Was it the bright sunlight in her eyes, or perhaps she'd been caught off guard by the photographer. Her hastily constructed, shy smile was totally charming. There was no hint of the troubles that would later plague her.

What burden could she have been carrying?
And why had she suddenly vanished?

As she pondered these questions, Kaede gently touched the screen to zoom in on the young teacher's face.

4

Kaede visited her grandfather's home after checking in with the morning care worker about his condition. Patients with Lewy Body Dementia, especially those with Parkinson's-type symptoms, often struggled when the temperatures dropped, causing their circulation to worsen. Fortunately for her grandfather, the balance of medications seemed to be working well and there was no significant deterioration in his health.

As she stepped into the entryway, she could hear Grandfather conversing with a young man in the study down the hall. The recently installed sliding door didn't fit properly, allowing sounds to leak through freely.

'Did you manage to record the bell crickets clearly?' Grandfather was asking. 'I was worried a mobile phone might not do them justice.'

'It turned out perfectly. I'm already using it as my ringtone.'

Grandpa, you're so cute . . .

He really was proud of those crickets in his garden.

After a little while, Grandfather's physiotherapist, a man that Kaede had met a couple of times before, emerged from the study.

'He's doing very well today,' the physiotherapist said with

The Vanishing Person at the Pool

a broad smile. 'Although as soon as rehab was over, he went right back to his book.'

Physiotherapists help restore motor functions compromised by various conditions, providing massage and electrotherapy treatments and more. When people think of rehabilitation, this is probably the profession they picture.

Her grandfather's therapist appeared to be in his early thirties, with close-cropped hair and a sturdy build. His hamstrings – a name Kaede remembered only because Iwata had called them 'the muscle group that sounds more like something you'd tie meat up with' – bulged through the fabric of his tracksuit trousers. His sharp features and stoic demeanour reminded her of a certain famous baseball player who'd been setting hitting records overseas.

As he excused himself to leave, a sweet fragrance tickled Kaede's nose.

'Is that vanilla essence?' she asked. 'It smells lovely.'

'No, actually it's vanilla beans,' replied the physio, raising a thick, well-defined eyebrow with a smile. 'Our shop is committed to using real beans for our soft-serve ice cream. My father says it would tarnish our reputation if we took shortcuts by using essence.'

'Oh, I see. My apologies.'

'No problem at all. I'd love to bring you some, Kaede-sensei, but it would violate workplace regulations. Please come by our shop sometime.'

'I'd love to.'

'Well then, I'd better be going.'

Kaede had already heard from her grandfather that his physiotherapist's family owned an ice-cream shop. It was no surprise to Kaede that Grandfather had given him the nickname 'Soft-Serve Guy'.

The building that housed the ice-cream shop was right in front of a major railway station, and his parents owned the entire building. The family must have been rather wealthy. If he'd wanted, Soft-Serve Guy could have lived a life of relative leisure by taking over the family business, but instead, inspired by the experience of caring for his late grandmother, he had chosen to become a physiotherapist.

When time permitted, he sometimes helped out at the shop, which must have been why the faint scent of vanilla lingered on him today.

Kaede only met him occasionally in passing, but it had taken a whole month to learn these details about him. He was naturally reticent in nature, but would respond cheerfully when spoken to, as he did today.

He's different from any of the guys at our school, Kaede thought.

Being quite reserved and shy herself, Kaede felt a certain kinship with Soft-Serve Guy. Among her grandfather's caregiving team, he seemed particularly good-hearted and earnest.

The Vanishing Person at the Pool

'Oh, hello there. I'm afraid you've just missed Sanae again,' said Grandfather from his chair in the study.

He smiled as he closed his book and set it down on the side table. It wasn't a novel, but a book of shogi problems. In the past, Grandfather used to enjoy solving crossword puzzles, but lately he was frustrated by the trembling of his hands, and preferred shogi puzzles. But he only engaged with these kinds of problems on his good days, which meant that his mind must be working at full capacity today.

I don't understand the rules at all, but I love shogi anyway, thought Kaede, rather absurdly.

She started out with some small talk, telling Grandfather all about the performance by Shiki's theatre company a couple of days earlier, including the events of the after-party. To her surprise, he seemed extremely impressed.

'Sounds like an excellent play. Its brilliance is that it doesn't solely rely on the audience members' prompts. After all, what matters most is how captivating the story becomes afterwards. If the story itself isn't engaging, nothing else matters. Gimmicks are just that – gimmicks and nothing more. What counts is whether you found the way they performed the stories to be compelling or not.'

A tiny tremor ran through Grandfather's fingers as he made the gesture of placing a shogi piece in check.

'A hundred points for that performance.'

A hundred?

A perfect score to a play performed by a theatre troupe he'd never even seen? In all the years he'd given Kaede prompts, and she had woven tales for him, Grandfather had never once awarded her a hundred points. Yet for some reason she felt joy to hear this. She didn't even understand it herself.

Oh well, that's not important right now . . .

Kaede related the episode of the Second-Generation Principal Window Wiper that she'd heard from Misaki at the alumni reunion. Then she asked Grandfather to listen to the recording she'd made on her phone.

Grandfather listened, arms folded, to the tale of Madonna-sensei. Occasionally his face would contort in a peculiar way, or he'd bring both hands up to cover his mouth. Kaede wasn't sure if his expressions were from laughter, or if he was gripped by fear. She guessed that he was concerned about Madonna-sensei's whereabouts – or even for her life. Anxious to hear her grandfather's tale as soon as possible, she was barely able to keep quiet during the playback.

She knew she was being impatient, but the moment the recording ended, she asked him what he thought. Of course, he didn't give her a direct reply.

'Let's set that aside for now,' he said. 'First, could you show me that photo of her in front of the temple? And then I want to hear your tale.'

The Vanishing Person at the Pool

As Kaede watched him examine the photo with keen interest, she couldn't help imagining what Shiki would say at this moment: *Why do detectives, both past and present, feel they have to delay their conclusions for dramatic effect?*

Eventually Grandfather put down the photo and turned to Kaede.

'Right then, let me start by asking you something. Assuming everything Misaki told you was true, what kind of tale would you weave, Kaede?'

Kaede took a deep breath before starting.

'Tale Number One: Madonna-sensei didn't get out of the pool. To be precise, she couldn't get out.'

It was a little painful to continue.

'The teacher drowned due to some unforeseen circumstances. But then, why wasn't her body discovered? Well, it was because of the drain. Every year in Japan there are tragic accidents where people get a body part sucked into a pool drain. It's no wonder Madonna-sensei's body didn't resurface. Her body is still caught up somewhere in the drainage system.'

Kaede waited nervously for her grandfather's reaction, and was secretly relieved when he pointed out the inconsistencies in her tale.

'It's true that accidents like that happen, but they typically occur in those lazy river-type flowing-water pools, and the victims are tragically almost always small children. It's very unlikely that a mature adult woman such as Madonna-sensei would get caught in a drain. Besides, I don't think there's ever been a case of a body remaining undiscovered in a pool drain accident.'

'Tale Number Two: Madonna-sensei never dived into the pool at all. She made secret plans to escape from her life. The fact that she had taken so many days off school, apparently burdened by some personal issues, supports this theory. But then why did all the pupils claim that she dived in and never resurfaced?'

Kaede paused and looked her grandfather in the eyes. She was more confident of this version of events.

'The entire class was lying,' she continued, answering her own question. 'They collaborated to help out the teacher they loved so deeply with her plan to escape.'

Grandfather pinched the bridge of his nose – a habit of his when he was deep in thought.

Kaede felt a flutter of anticipation. Was this tale close to her grandfather's own?

But then, 'Seventy points. No, let's make it sixty.'

What?

He'd been scoring her?

'It's better than Tale Number One, but there are still some major plot holes. How could all thirty children possibly keep their story straight? You just can't keep people from blabbing, especially not primary school children.'

The Vanishing Person at the Pool

His tone reminded Kaede of the line from the Harry Kemelman detective novel they discussed last time: 'A nine-mile walk is no joke, especially in the rain.'

'And where did Madonna-sensei disappear to?' Grandfather continued. 'The principal and the snow cone vendor both confirm that nobody left through the back gate. The other teachers verified that she wasn't hiding in the changing room or the equipment shed. How do you explain her absence from the surveillance camera footage around the station? You can't possibly believe that they're all colluding, can you? Until these discrepancies are cleared up, Tale Number Two just fundamentally falls apart. In other words . . .'

Perhaps because that day he was focused on solving Japanese shogi puzzles, it was a cup of green tea that the coffee-loving detective paused to sip from.

'There exists another tale: Tale X.'

Such elegance of form!

Kaede couldn't wait for his next words. Then, whether he was aware of it or not, he spoke the very phrase she had been anticipating.

'Kaede, pass me a cigarette, would you?'

Have you ever smoked a Gauloise?

According to her grandfather, there had once been a popular song with that odd title.

The study filled up with the purplish smoke of Grandfather's Gauloise. Although it was supposedly twelve tatami mats in size, the rows of bookshelves seemed to compress the room down to about six. And yet, looking at those multi-layered rows of books, the room felt endlessly vast, like catching a glimpse of oneself in an infinity mirror.

Grandfather blew a smoke ring in the direction of the cracked-open window.

'I've seen the picture now – but without harnessing the power of hallucination.'

Without harnessing the power of hallucination . . . ? What exactly did that mean?

Is this mystery child's play to Grandpa?

'Let's start by considering what kind of personal problems Madonna-sensei might have been struggling with. Generally, people's problems can be divided into three basic categories: illness, money or relationships. So, which was hers?'

Grandfather's gaze turned briefly to the smoke drifting out of the window. Was he wishing that Madonna-sensei's problems could vanish just as easily?

'Given her youth and background as a swim team member, I think we can rule out illness. She was a stunning beauty who attracted the attention of the young male teachers, so let's hypothesize that her troubles were of the relationship variety. More specifically, some kind of complicated romantic entanglement. What if she was involved with one of the male teachers? That scenario could answer most of our questions.'

Kaede's eyes went immediately to the photo still open on her phone.

Sure. A woman that beautiful must have had something going on . . .

'Let's reconstruct the timeline of that day. First, 11.15 a.m. – fourth period swimming class begins. It's perfect pool weather, and given it was the last swimming class of the semester, the children must have been very excited. At 11.40, right on schedule, Madonna-sensei blows her whistle and calls out, "All right everyone, the last twenty minutes of class is going to be free time!" Up to this point, there was nothing suspicious.'

Kaede nodded in agreement.

'But from here the situation escalates to murder.'

'Whaa—?'

'The children were splashing around in the pool, paying no attention to their teacher. That was the moment that from the shadows of the changing room someone beckoned her over. Someone she didn't dare to refuse, and who if they happened to be spotted wouldn't seem out of place, say someone who frequently occupied themselves with watering the flowers, or cleaning the school. Moreover, someone who was involved in an affair with

Madonna-sensei. Or to put it more plainly, someone who was part of a love triangle.'

A chill ran down Kaede's spine.

'No way!'

'Yes, Second-Generation Principal Window Wiper was the culprit,' Grandfather declared. 'The crime must have been committed between 11.45 and 11.55 a.m. The principal killed Madonna-sensei in the pool changing room. Given the lack of blood, strangulation with a rope from the storage room seems the most likely. They then temporarily hid the body in the storage room, and removed their own clothes, hiding them in locker. Then, already having a swimsuit concealed under their clothes, they added a swim cap and goggles before exiting the changing room.'

Hey, hold on, just a minute . . .

Kaede had an immediate concern, which she voiced without delay.

'Wait a minute, Grandpa. Are you saying that the principal disguised himself as Madonna-sensei? Isn't your theory a bit far-fetched?'

Grandfather let a tiny smile cross his lips.

'Haven't you worked it out yet? The principal is a woman.'

'No! That's impossible,' said Kaede, her voice coming out louder than she intended. 'I mean, this is the headteacher we're talking about.'

The Vanishing Person at the Pool

'Women principals aren't all that unusual,' Grandfather replied. 'And lately it's quite common for talented young teachers to be made principal. It was a few years back now that there was that big news story about a thirty-two-year-old becoming the youngest in Japan's history.'

Kaede recalled seeing it on the TV news.

'These days, no one would be surprised at a woman around forty being a primary school principal. In fact, if you heard about a teacher who's always cleaning windows and tending to flower beds, wouldn't you picture a woman right away? You were too influenced by the image of me doing the same things, and automatically assumed it was a man.'

'But if that's the case, why didn't Misaki tell me? If the Second-Generation Principal Window Wiper was a woman, wouldn't that be the first thing she'd mention?'

'Exactly,' Grandfather acknowledged. 'After telling you the current principal's nickname, she undoubtedly added something like, "And she's a young woman." But maybe you were momentarily distracted – perhaps thinking about me – and missed what she said?'

Kaede froze.

It was true.

She thought back to that moment. She'd been lost in thought, overlaying the image of her grandfather onto Second-Generation Principal Window Wiper, and contemplating the Broken Windows Theory.

She couldn't believe it – due to her wandering mind she'd missed probably the most crucial detail of the story.

'Looks like I was on the mark,' commented Grandfather. 'But then again . . .'

He narrowed his eyes.

'. . . I'd have thought you'd work out for yourself that the principal was a woman.'

'Why do you say that?'

'That play you went to see the night before – wasn't it full of hints not to make assumptions about gender? They were scattered throughout.'

Ohhh! That's right.

'First of all, there was that flame-haired troupe member that you assumed was a woman but turned out to be a man. But more importantly, how about the script idea you gave to the actors to perform? Wasn't it about a woman in her twenties who blows all her money on horse racing and ends up working on a tuna fishing boat? Not that I fully understand the modern sense of humour . . .'

He drew slowly on his cigarette.

'But I'm guessing the comedy you were aiming for was the twist that a character whose behaviour is so stereotypical of a man turns out to be a young woman, wasn't it?'

Kaede had no response. It was embarrassing to have the comedy behind her own idea explained so meticulously.

'And there was yet another hint. At the after-party, didn't

The Vanishing Person at the Pool

Shiki say something like, "We shouldn't misunderstand a situation, based on our own arbitrary assumptions"? Pure coincidence, but it was almost as if he was alluding to this misunderstanding over the principal.'

It wasn't so much Grandfather's observations that astonished Kaede as another separate realization. How was it that he could remember an exact line from a reported conversation, one that hadn't even been in her voice recording? But for now, she had one lingering question . . .

'Grandpa, how can you state so definitively that the principal is a young woman? I mean, sure, it's possible but isn't it still fairly rare?'

'That's simple. By understanding Misaki's intentions, that's the natural conclusion.'

'I don't follow.'

'Yesterday, right before you parted, Misaki-sensei said this to you: "That reminds me . . . next time you visit your grandfather, you should definitely show him this." Right?'

'That's right.'

'Think about it. The photo she wanted to show me, First-Generation Principal Window Wiper? Naturally, from both a psychological perspective and simply out of courtesy, wouldn't that be a photo of the Second-Generation Principal Window Wiper? It's difficult to believe that she would so casually send out a photo of a missing woman. In this age of privacy concerns, isn't that the very reason Misaki avoided using her real name, and gave her that Madonna-sensei nickname?'

Kaede looked down again at the photo on her phone.

'So, the woman in the yellow dress is—'

'Yes. She's the murderer. Second-Generation Principal Window Wiper.'

The fragrance of *kinmokusei* – the osmanthus tree – wafted in through the open window.

If Kaede remembered correctly, the meaning attached to this flower was 'truth'.

'Let's return again to the events of that day,' Grandfather said. 'At exactly twelve noon, the school bell rang for the end of classes. The children were still splashing around in the pool when from the dark of the staff changing room the principal emerged, dressed as Madonna-sensei in a swimsuit. Standing at Point Ⓐ, she blew her whistle and made that grand gesture with both arms that means "get out of the pool". Wearing a swim cap and goggles and having a similar figure to Madonna-sensei, who would have noticed the switch? On one hand, a youthful-looking principal in her late thirties or early forties; on the other, a Showa-era beauty, with a Showa-era nickname, mature for her age. Put

The Vanishing Person at the Pool

them both in swimsuits, and even adults wouldn't have been able to tell them apart.'

'I see what you mean.'

'And so, the children, suspecting nothing, climbed out of the pool at Point Ⓑ and headed for the showers. Checking that nobody was watching, the principal went back into the changing room.'

'I follow so far,' said Kaede, 'but what about the biggest mystery of all – the big splash? All the children said that they heard their teacher dive in.'

'Not quite everyone,' said Grandfather, raising a playful index finger. 'As a primary school teacher you've probably experienced the same thing . . . after the whistle is blown one kid, likely one of the boisterous, attention-seeking boys, jumps back into the pool just to get a laugh.'

Yes, it was possible . . .

Or rather – yes, it happens in my own lessons . . .

Ending pool time with just a whistle was nearly impossible. Usually there were one or two kids who would pretend not to hear it and jump back in.

To tell the truth, I find those antics kind of endearing . . .

'Got it. So, this boy dived under the water, held his breath, and stayed hidden?'

'Exactly.'

'But is it possible for a fourth-grade boy to hold his breath for over a minute?'

'Let me ask you, how long do you think the world record is for holding your breath underwater?'

'Um . . .'

She thought of the film *The Big Blue* starring Jean Reno as a deep-sea diver; unfortunately, the only image that came to mind was his big round glasses.

'Maybe about five minutes?'

'Nonsense!' Grandfather laughed out loud. 'From what I remember, the record used to be about twenty-four minutes. It could be even longer now. Even a fourth-grader can manage a minute.'

Now that he said it, she realized it was true. There were no flaws in her grandfather's logic. She recalled countless videos of children as young as first grade of primary school holding their breath underwater for over a minute.

'After about a minute, around four or five children, worried about Madonna-sensei, jumped into the pool. Meanwhile, the mischievous boy who was already underwater ran out of breath and resurfaced, but startled by all the commotion, he quickly ducked back under.'

'I see. And after that he got scared . . . the atmosphere just wasn't conducive to admitting that it was he who dived in and not Madonna-sensei.'

'Precisely. He could never have imagined that his little prank would have led to such a major mystery.'

I'll have to let Misaki know . . .

The Vanishing Person at the Pool

'Next, having changed back into her regular clothes over her swimsuit, the principal laid low in the changing room, waiting for the commotion to die down, and the pupils to leave the pool area. Then she slipped out through the side gate of the pool and returned to the principal's office through the side door at the end of the corridor. What's important to note here . . .'

Grandfather paused.

'. . . is that the principal's office door opens outwards into the corridor. She left it open in advance, so that after committing the murder she could re-enter the building by that west side door without being seen, even if someone happened to be in the hallway.'

Kaede looked at the diagram she had printed out.

I see . . .

After the twelve o'clock bell, it was unlikely that anyone would be in that ground-floor hallway, especially in the vicinity of the nurse's office or the school counsellor's room. But the principal couldn't have been certain.

If she crossed the edge of the flower beds, entered by the side door, and went those few metres along the hallway there was a blind spot due to the open office door. Then she could slip back into her office unseen.

'Soon after that, the pupils reported the event to the teachers in the staffroom, and in turn those teachers came downstairs to notify the principal. By that time . . .'

Grandfather glanced at his teacup on the side table.

'. . . She was probably taking a breather and sipping tea.'

'But where did the body hidden in the equipment room disappear to? When Misaki and the other teachers went to search it, there was nothing there.'

'She'd dealt with it before they got there. As she often tended to the flower beds, nobody would be surprised to see her there. She must have brought a wheelbarrow or hand-cart in through the back gate of the school, loaded the body of Madonna-sensei into it and covered it with a blue tarp. Then she could have left it parked in full sight by the flower beds.'

A horrific image passed through Kaede's mind.

'You're saying that Madonna-sensei—'

She stopped as a shiver ran down her spine.

'In the middle of the night, by moonlight, the principal buried her body in the flower bed?'

'That appears to be the only explanation,' Grandfather confirmed. 'And even now, the principal continues to wash the windows of her office every day, all the while keeping watch over the flower bed where Madonna-sensei is buried and pondering when and where to relocate her body.'

'It's absolutely chilling, but it suddenly makes sense now – the real reason the principal moved her office from the first floor to the ground.'

The Vanishing Person at the Pool

'Indeed. And I can't help thinking that the moving of the office is also connected to the motive for the murder.'

'Eh?'

'How about this tale? A beautiful and talented forty-year-old female principal is in a romantic relationship with a young male teacher. However, this male teacher falls instead for the newly arrived young Madonna-sensei. Now, within the school, where would be the ideal location for their secret trysts?'

Inspiration hit Kaede at once.

'The staff changing room by the pool!'

'Exactly,' Grandfather nodded. 'One day, the principal catches sight of her lover and Madonna-sensei sneaking into the changing room together. At first, she may have tried to convince herself she was mistaken, but after witnessing the same thing several times over, she decides she can tolerate it no longer. She moves her office down to a room on the ground floor with a clear view of the changing room through the pool's chain-link fence. Now, I know well from my time as principal and the connections I made with members of the Board of Education, that it wouldn't have been difficult at all to convince them to let her make the room change, especially with the use of a few choice phrases such as "the need to nurture a love of nature among the student body". Had her pressure tactics worked on her lover and she'd managed to lure him back to her side, then she might have forgiven the affair. However, the young couple kept up their clandestine meetings, until finally—'

Kaede finished the thought: 'It led to murder.'

A slightly chill breeze carried in the scent of osmanthus once more. Kaede recalled that the other meanings of the osmanthus flower were 'temptation' and 'intoxication'.

Kaede decided that she should go home and get Misaki's opinion before going to the police.

Unusually, however, Grandfather asked for a second cigarette. He exhaled the purple smoke in the direction of the osmanthus, embodying perfectly the image of intoxication.

She couldn't leave before ensuring his cigarette was completely extinguished, so Kaede brewed some more tea. As she was pouring it, Grandfather spoke.

'You know, sometimes with shogi problems, there are multiple correct moves.'

What was he talking about?

'From the puzzle writer's point of view, it's preferable to have one single correct solution. It makes for a tighter, more elegant problem.'

He picked up the shogi puzzle book from the side table.

'But rarely, there turns out to be another correct solution that even the creator didn't spot, and sometimes it's even more elegant. I've found two such solutions in this book alone.'

What's he saying? Surely not just bragging . . .

'I think it's time to consider this case again. I want to describe to you another elegant picture.'

Eh?

'Grandpa, are you saying there's another tale?'

'There is. And I think this one will be more to your liking.'

What the . . . ?

Kaede felt the sweat forming on her forehead.

'Weave it for me, Grandpa,' she said, reopening her folding chair, and settling down to listen.

'Let's start by reconsidering Madonna-sensei's troubles. As I already said, people generally have three kinds of problems: illness, financial troubles and relationships. If we remove illness and relationships from the previous tale, we're left with one possibility.'

'Money troubles?'

'Right. Madonna-sensei lost her mother early on, and Misaki mentioned that her father was her only living parent. So then, why didn't her father file a missing person report when his beloved daughter disappeared? Doesn't that strike you as odd?'

'Now that you mention it, yes.'

'Let's suppose her father was in debt and forced to

declare personal bankruptcy. Despite that, those unsavoury debt collectors with ties to criminal organizations are not going to just give up. They'd probably go after Madonna-sensei, demanding she repay not only the principal amount, but exorbitant interest rates. As you know, public employees like her make ideal co-guarantors on loans.'

It wasn't entirely impossible. But wasn't it a bit of a leap of imagination?

'Then who would Madonna-sensei confide in? Naturally the principal, a woman she deeply respected. How's that so far?'

'Well, I feel as if we're stacking hypothesis upon hypothesis,' said Kaede candidly. 'But go on.'

In that moment she heard her grandfather laugh out loud.

'After listening to Madonna-sensei's plea for help, and giving the situation careful consideration, the principal proposed that she do a moonlight flit.'

'Moon . . . moonlight flit?'

It took a while for Kaede to grasp the meaning of the unexpected phrase.

'The principal and Madonna-sensei came up with the plan that I just described to you earlier, orchestrating a "vanishing person mystery" at the pool. The difference is that it wasn't a murder, but simply an identity switch of two women dressed in swimwear.'

Gradually the truth was taking shape in Kaede's mind.

The Vanishing Person at the Pool

But still . . .

'At 11.40 a.m., after announcing free playtime at the pool, Madonna-sensei entered the changing room. The principal was probably waiting for her in there. Madonna-sensei put a dress over her swimsuit, concealed her damp hair under a straw hat or something, grabbed the travel bag she'd prepared, and exited through the side gate of the pool to the school's back entrance. This wouldn't have taken more than a few minutes, especially with the principal's help getting changed.'

I guess not.

Anyway, this tale's much more appealing than the previous one . . .

'Around ten minutes before the snow-cone vendor shows up at noon, Madonna-sensei emerges on the back street behind the school and jumps into a taxi that she's arranged in advance. They drive past the nearest train station and on to a smaller one without any security cameras. She blends into the crowd at the station and finally boards a *Shinkansen* bullet train for a distant location.'

'That means Madonna-sensei is still alive? And her father is in on it?'

'That's how a moonlight flit has always worked.'

But Kaede had some doubts.

'Even if the young principal was so kind and proactive,

would she really have come up with such an elaborate escape plan?'

'Well then, how about this?' Grandfather continued. 'Perhaps when approached by Madonna-sensei for advice, the principal turned to a certain other person with whom she kept in touch. Maybe this person was someone who loved the school dearly, having once worked there. He also cared about the woman now nicknamed the Second-Generation Principal Window Wiper, and even in his weakened condition, where writing a few words on a piece of stationery had become a challenge, he managed to keep up a correspondence with her. What if this person had the connections to discreetly secure a teaching job at a private school in some regional city for someone who had done a runner?'

Grandfather glanced across at a low bookshelf with a letter holder on top.

'Among those letters, there might be a note from Madonna-sensei addressed to Misaki-sensei, to be handed over after all the brouhaha has died down. Of course, as it's personal correspondence, this "certain person" hasn't opened it, but it's clear to them that it will be filled with warm feelings towards her dear mentor, Misaki-sensei. No, in fact they are sure of it.'

No way!
Seriously?

The Vanishing Person at the Pool

Grandfather exhaled a cloud of smoke towards the window. Through the haze he assumed the pose of a triumphant shogi player, bringing his right hand down with dramatic flair.

'Checkmate.'

This time his hand didn't tremble in the slightest.

'Kaede, I knew the ending of today's tale from the start so I couldn't help but laugh. For a bit of fun, I considered other possible "correct solutions", although the bit about transporting the body in a wheelbarrow might have been a bit of a stretch. The other thing I'd like you to understand is that people who love flowers can never be evil. Second-Generation Principal Window Wiper loves them even more than the first did, and that's the real reason she moved her office from the first floor.'

Unbelievable. The mastermind of the whole plan had been right here before her eyes the whole time!

But there was still one thing she didn't understand.

'Hey, Grandpa, I have to ask you something.'

'What is it?'

'Why did this "certain person" go to all the trouble of orchestrating this vanishing act at the pool? It doesn't make sense. If the goal was to do a moonlight flit, then couldn't Madonna-sensei simply have ordered a taxi to pick her up in the middle of the night and take her to a remote train station?'

Grandfather began to chuckle.

'Wouldn't that make for a dull story?'

'What?'

'I said the same thing about Shiki's play. If the story itself isn't engaging, nothing else matters.'

Kaede was speechless.

Could that be it? The motive behind the whole incident . . . Just to make things more interesting?

It was absurd.

'The final swimming lesson right before summer break. The sky cloudless after the rainy season's end. In the scorching heat, their beloved Madonna-sensei vanishes like a mirage. The children had a tale they could tell for the rest of their lives. To a child there has never been anything more captivating than a mysterious summer ghost story.'

At that moment, with a soft hiss, the Gauloise's ember extinguished.

'Oh, there's water coming in,' Grandfather groaned.

A hallucination . . .

A common phenomenon with patients with Lewy Body Dementia was to hallucinate that the floor was flooding.

'Over there on the pier stands Madonna-sensei, her face full of hope. She watches the waves crashing and wishes that summer would hurry up and come. She's thinking how she wants to swim freely along the shoreline of this island, leaving all her cares behind.'

The Vanishing Person at the Pool

He mentioned an island. Good thing none of those loan sharks were listening...

He must have arranged for Madonna-sensei to teach at a primary school on a remote island, deliberately choosing somewhere that would remind her of her own hometown.

Kaede gently placed a blanket over her grandfather, who was already drifting off to sleep.

Chapter 4:
They Were Thirty-Three!

1

'Your grandfather's been claiming there are otters nesting under his bed,' his home helper told Kaede over the phone. 'No matter how much I try to stop him, he keeps trying to move the bed.'

Kaede's heart sank a little as she set off for Himonya.

Her grandfather was generally aware that the visions he saw were a product of his DLB, but on rare occasions he became convinced that they were real. Whenever that happened, it was a sign that his health was in decline, often triggered by some kind of stress.

Kaede knew what was causing his stress.

He can't hear the children's voices any more . . .

As a child, Kaede had called this neighbourhood (well at least the three hundred square metres of it that made up her world) 'Red Candy Town'. Typical of old Tokyo neighbourhoods, it was a maze of tiny criss-crossing roads, dotted with red triangular stop signs. To the young Kaede these looked just like a popular brand of candies sold at the local sweet shop.

The street that passed her grandfather's house was also narrow, with one of those red candies just by his gate. But a few days earlier the sign had been taken down to make way for a sewage reconstruction project that was scheduled to last for the next year.

Because of the construction, the children from the nearby preschool were forced to take a detour on their way to and from school. Kaede's grandfather could no longer hear their sweet, cheerful voices.

Kaede opened the front door and the home helper – a woman in her late forties – immediately took her hand and steered Kaede into the hallway.

The woman wore her hair in a severe bob, trimmed precisely at her jawline, giving the impression of someone devoted more to her work than fashion. She was the one to suggest that, as they were going to be working together for a while, they should keep things informal, and so Grandfather and Kaede called her by the affectionate nickname 'Okappa-san' after the popular wooden dolls with the same haircut.

'I've thought it over, and I think the only thing to do is make him look under the bed,' Okappa-san told Kaede.

'I understand. I'm sorry my grandfather is causing so much trouble,' Kaede replied.

'No, no, it's fine. But to think such a brilliant man would end up like this . . . It's such a mysterious illness, isn't it?'

Her bluntness somehow made her more trustworthy to Kaede.

'Shall we get on with it then?'

Okappa-san nudged Kaede towards the living room.

The hydraulic bed was rather heavy, and not something one person could easily move alone.

'You'll see when you move it, there are two, maybe three otters under there.'

Ignoring Grandfather's rather sullen expression, Okappa-san and Kaede shifted the bed aside to reveal nothing but a bare floor.

'See, Grandpa? There's no need to worry any more. It looks like the otters have moved out.'

'Ah . . . yes. So it seems.'

Grandfather was trying to sound as if he agreed with Kaede, but it was clear that he couldn't quite believe it.

'Maybe it's because it's got so cold lately,' he added, his shoulders visibly slumping. He must have felt foolish now that he realized the otters had been a hallucination.

It was hard to tell whether he had been trying to get rid of the otters or he had enjoyed having the creatures nesting under his bed. Kaede suspected it was the latter.

Okappa-san left, and the two of them returned to their usual seats in the study. Grandfather was quick to change the subject.

'How are things at school?' His voice was a little drowsy.

It was as she'd thought. He was lonely without the sound of the children's voices. That was probably why he brought up the topic of Kaede's school.

'Well . . . this isn't something that happened recently – more than six months ago.'

Kaede had prepared a story in advance.

'It's part ghost story, part fantasy, but in the end turned out to be more of a mystery.'

'Ohh!' Grandfather's face lit up, a stark contrast to a moment earlier. It wasn't only mysteries that he loved. As long as the story was interesting, he enjoyed most genres, including horror, fantasy, or even science fiction.

Kaede paused for a moment, then lowered her voice.

'That day there were thirty-two people in the classroom. But then suddenly there were thirty-three . . .

'Well, Grandpa, I was teaching a sixth-grade class for the first time. In that class there was a rather unusual trio – two boys and a girl. How can I describe them? Imagine the little trio of wizards from J. K. Rowling's Harry Potter series, and you'll get the idea.

'The first one was a justice-loving but rather mischievous boy who wore glasses. We'll call him Harry. The other boy was timid, kind-hearted with very cute freckles. Let's make him Ron. And then the final one was a strong-willed girl who was incredibly popular with all the boys in the class because she was such a badass. Of course, she's our Hermione.

'On the surface, these three seemed to have nothing in common, but somehow they were totally inseparable and always at the centre of class activities. Later I discovered that they'd connected over a shared love of mystery and fantasy novels.

'On that particular day, the three were their usual boisterous selves. Last period was an English conversation class. Nowadays it's common for public primary schools to teach English from around fifth grade. This class had thirty-two pupils, sixteen boys and sixteen girls. That might sound small compared to your teaching days, Grandpa, but it's the norm these days. I brought along a seating chart I made to show you. Now where are your glasses? I'll get them for you . . .

'When the bell rang for the start of the class, I clapped my hands to get their attention and said, "Please get into pairs as usual, and practise speaking. Use English only. You can use the phrases in the textbook if you need to. But absolutely no Japanese allowed! Anyone who uses Japanese won't be allowed to graduate."

'There were pretend shrieks of horror and a lot of giggling. Although it was part of the curriculum, this kind of lesson had a game-like quality to it, and I think everyone was ready to have some fun with it.

'But then Harry got to his feet, pushing his glasses up with his middle finger, and raising his other hand.

'"Isn't that kind of boring?" he said. "As class representative I'd like to make a suggestion. Can we have a scary story contest instead?"

'I quickly told him that it wouldn't count as a lesson, but the whole class got immediately excited. They were all shouting, "Let's do it!" "We want to hear ghost stories!" Even Hermione, usually the serious one, joined in. "Come on, Sensei!" Of course, all the boys followed her lead, especially Ron, who was totally smitten with her. He wasn't going to raise any objections.

'And so, we struck a deal – we'd hold the scary story contest, but on condition it was only for fifteen minutes.

'After a few of the children shared familiar stories – the kind that the other kids had heard before and they couldn't help smiling at – Harry stood up.

'"I'll go next," he said. "Have you heard the ghost story of the girl about our age who might turn up in our classroom?"

'Behind his glasses, there was a flicker of fear, but his expression was, as always, unreadable. The classroom which had been so lively a moment earlier suddenly fell silent. Harry ignored this reaction and continued.

They Were Thirty-Three!

' "Last night my great-grandpa told me something. He said that during the war there was an air-raid shelter near our school, and you could hear children crying inside it. He said nothing was scarier than the sound of crying in the darkness. He said that until the day he dies he'll never forget the sound of the air-raid sirens and the sad voice of one little girl—"

' "Just a minute!" I'd been preoccupied with that girl, and now found myself cutting Harry off. "I think that story is really valuable testimony, but just because this air-raid shelter was near the school doesn't mean that ghosts are likely to turn up in this classroom."

' "Well, Sensei, that's what I'm trying to tell you. Yesterday I went to the library and looked it up, and I discovered something interesting. The air-raid shelter wasn't just near the school."

'He pointed to the back of the classroom.

' "It was right there, where we're all sitting right now."

'The whole class turned to look at the back of the classroom.

'After that, it didn't matter who told a ghost story, the atmosphere stayed eerily quiet. To be honest, I thought it had all gone way beyond a fun little activity, so I clapped my hands again and announced, "All right, the scary story contest is over!"

'The children seemed relieved. And we finally got on with the proper English conversation lesson.

Classroom Plan 1

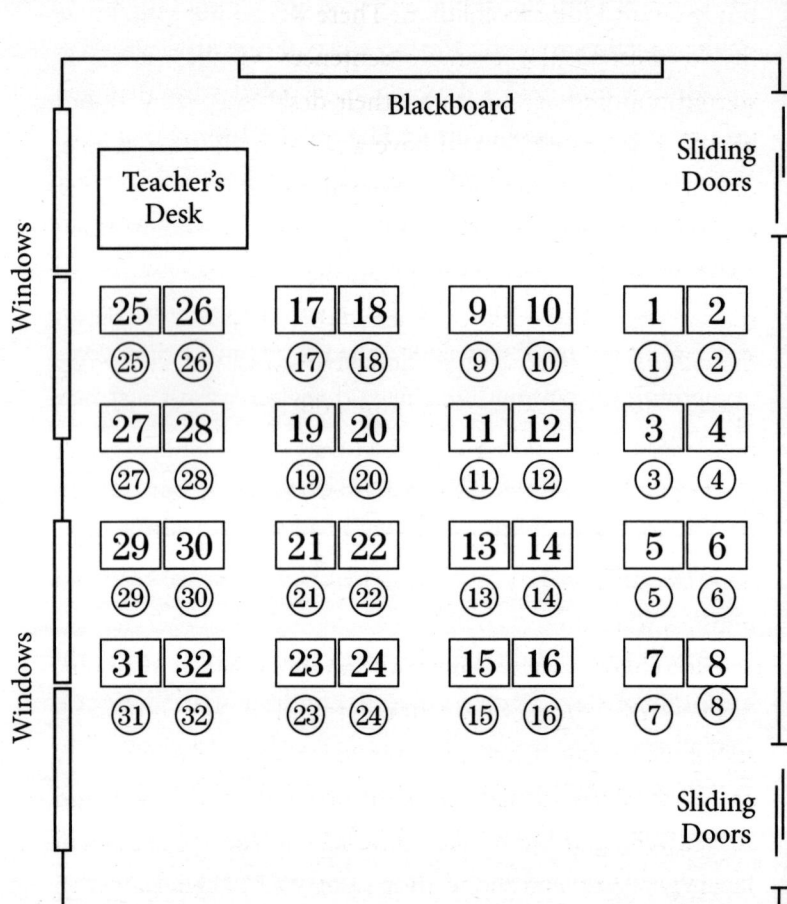

They Were Thirty-Three!

'"OK, you have two minutes. Ready? Go!"

'Everyone divided into boy–girl pairs, or groups of three. They huddled up shoulder to shoulder as they began to speak in English together. Two minutes may seem short, but it can feel long to children. There were a few who, once they'd finished the example sentences in the textbook, started pointing at objects on their desk and asking things like "Is this a book?" or "I have a . . . pencil!" Just simple, obvious stuff, but even that seemed to get the class quite excited, and there was a lot of laughter.

'I was walking around between the desks, listening, and making my way towards the back of the classroom. Through the window I could see the cherry blossoms, not quite fully open – maybe halfway – but from a distance they looked to be in full bloom. When I reached the pair in the middle at the back – it was Ron and Hermione – I turned back to face the blackboard and took a moment to observe all the children. I checked the classroom clock and saw that the two minutes were up.

'Now, here is where things got strange. When I called out, "Time's up!" the pair right beside me, Ron and Hermione, suddenly sprang apart and started arguing. Ron, usually so quiet and mild-mannered, turned red in the face and started yelling at Hermione, "I heard you! You just spoke in Japanese!" But Hermione shot right back, "What are you talking about? You were the one speaking Japanese!"

'As I tried to calm them down and listen to both their versions of events, they continued to insist that they'd clearly heard someone speaking Japanese. And that the voice had been "lonely and tearful". They both claimed that the voice had come from somewhere behind them.

'I'd been standing right by them, and I certainly hadn't spoken. And I can state with absolute confidence that there was no one behind me at the back of the classroom. Soon the whole classroom was in uproar, speculating that a thirty-third pupil had appeared in their class, and that it was the ghost of the girl who'd been crying in the air-raid shelter.

'Just then, a ray of sunlight shone in through the window onto the back of the classroom, which today had been feeling darker and more cramped than usual, almost like an air-raid shelter . . . At the same moment, a breeze from the hallway stirred up some dust motes which swirled and sparkled in the sunlight. Several children pressed their hands to their mouths as if trying to stifle a scream.

'It was an unseasonably chilly day so all the classroom windows were locked from the inside. The front and back doors were slightly ajar, but no one had come in. Our classroom was right at the end of the building, so there was no possibility of hearing sounds from a neighbouring class either. Harry, Ron and Hermione were not the type to lie, nor were they trying to play a trick on anyone.

'So that's the story – how a thirty-third suddenly turned up in a class of thirty-two. Grandpa, what tale would you weave from this?'

Kaede had intentionally told the story without a single pause, hoping to keep her grandfather from nodding off. But she needn't have worried; his voice was clear and alert.

'Kaede, pass me a cigarette, would you?'

2

The noise of the sewer construction had stopped some time ago; probably lunch break for the workers. In its place, the soft cooing of a bird carried on the crisp winter air.

'That's a turtle dove,' Grandfather said. 'Sounds just like an owl.'

His expression brightened.

'Rather fitting for your story, isn't it?'

Kaede was delighted. The young wizard, Harry Potter, kept a snowy owl . . . The fact that he was making this immediate connection meant that Grandfather's intellect was firing back up.

'This is not one of those "Challenge to the Reader" puzzles, but a "Challenge to the Elderly Living Alone",' Grandfather added, slowly rotating his neck to loosen up his shoulders, a smile on his face. 'Cleverly concealed in your story are all the clues we need to solve the mystery. And if we were to give it a title, it would have to be, "They Were Thirty-Three!"'

Kaede understood. He was referencing the classic manga series *They Were Eleven!* by Moto Hagio, which her grandfather had once recommended to her. It was a tale set aboard a spaceship – the ultimate locked-room setting – where an eleventh person inexplicably appears among a crew that should only have numbered ten.

Grandfather stopped rotating his neck and fixed his gaze on his granddaughter's face. 'Right, then. There's one major discrepancy in this story, and once you spot it, the mystery of the thirty-third person can be solved instantly.'

Kaede's heart quickened. 'So, what's the discrepancy?'

Grandfather narrowed his eyes slightly as if trying to peer into her thoughts.

'It's also clearly visible in the floor plan. The clue is in the fact that although it was an unseasonably chilly day, both the front and back classroom doors were cracked open.'

She'd known it – mystery was the best medicine for her grandfather.

'The windows were locked shut from the inside, so why not close the doors as well? Why were they left open far enough that there was a draught? The answer is simple: for ventilation. Around six months ago we were still in the Covid pandemic, weren't we? Perhaps you were testing my memory there, Kaede?'

They Were Thirty-Three!

He rolled his eyes mischievously.

'And then there was your description of Harry. You said, "Behind his glasses, there was a flicker of fear, but his expression was, as always, unreadable." No, you weren't lying, Kaede. A very careful choice of words.'

Grandfather slowly placed a finger on his own lips.

'It was only natural that his expression was unreadable, because, like all the other students, Harry was wearing a mask.'

'Brilliant as ever, Grandpa.'

'Which brings up another discrepancy in the story. Namely that despite the risk of infection, the boys and girls huddled up shoulder to shoulder to practise their English conversation. Now would the curriculum really be so reckless about the risk of spreading droplets? For such a lesson plan to exist, there's only one way it could be done. The children weren't paired up side by side. They were paired up with the pupil sitting in front or behind them.'

Kaede swallowed hard.

'Let me explain using the floor plan,' Grandfather went on. 'The pupils in the first and third rows would have stayed where they were. But the children in the second and fourth rows had to make some adjustments. They'd all have pushed their desks back and brought their chairs around to the other side, placing them back-to-back with the chair in front. They then started their conversation sitting back-to-back. This arrangement would allow them to properly observe social distancing. Your description of them being "shoulder to shoulder" wasn't technically untrue, but they were in fact doing it back-to-back while remaining seated. I remember seeing news reports about schools across the country having to conduct classes this way. And when you say that the back of the classroom seemed more cramped than usual – well that makes perfect sense, because it actually would have been. The children facing backwards wouldn't have been able to fit their knees under the desks, so the space between the rows would have been wider than usual, inevitably making the space at the back of the classroom narrower.

'How am I doing? Does my explanation make sense? If it's hard to follow, you'd better get out that second diagram that I suspect you prepared in advance.'

Wow. He saw right through me . . .

Accepting defeat, Kaede unfolded the second piece of paper and showed it to the master sleuth.

Somewhere in the distance the turtle dove made the same owl-like sound. Kaede recalled a certain Italian restaurant she'd visited where an owl lived in its wall clock.

Owls were the messengers of wizards. And her grandfather was a wizard of mystery.

'Now we can easily identify the thirty-third person,' he said softly. 'Kaede, it was you.'

They Were Thirty-Three!

Kaede nodded her confirmation.

'That was your first year as a sixth-grade homeroom teacher. It was mid-March, spring just beginning, and graduation just around the corner. That English conversation class was one of the few chances you had left to interact with your pupils – possibly even the last chance. When you look at it like that it makes sense that Harry suggested the scary story contest. It was to create some class memories. And it's easy to see why you'd let them do it too. It was your first ever homeroom class of graduating pupils, and when the day came it wouldn't be the children who were crying. I know from experience; it's always the teacher who ends up in tears.'

Grandfather briefly closed his eyes as if savouring his own memories.

'Those children, who just a year ago had seemed so young, were now confidently practising their English together. How reassuring that must have felt. As you walked slowly towards the back of classroom, the half-open cherry blossoms beyond the window seemed in full bloom already to your eyes. Standing just by Ron and Hermione, you turned to take in the view of the whole class one last time. And that's when, without even realizing it, you murmured something aloud, your voice tearful. Perhaps something like, "No, I don't want to say goodbye."'

It was true. She couldn't remember clearly exactly what

Classroom Plan 2

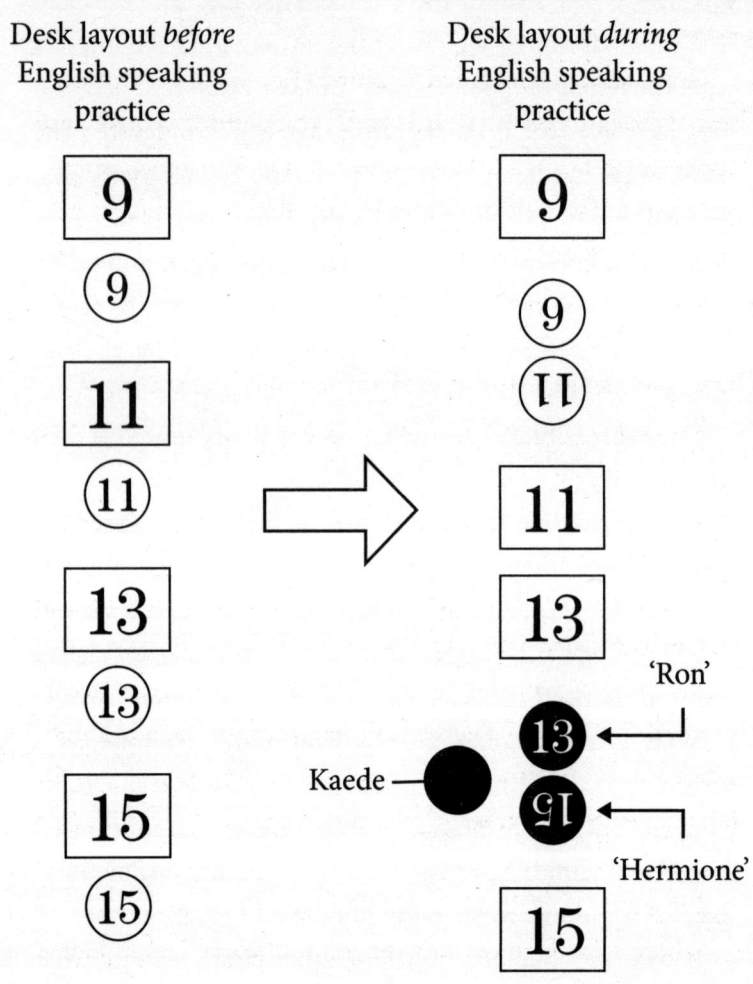

They Were Thirty-Three!

had happened, but later she'd realized that she was the one who had let some words slip out. But it had happened as Grandfather had described. Only after all the commotion had died down had she understood that she herself was the thirty-third person.

Grandfather continued. 'Now, Ron and Hermione, seated back-to-back, heard your voice from somewhere above their heads. Ron assumed it was Hermione speaking, and Hermione thought it was Ron. The murmured voice of a young woman can seem both ageless and genderless. But after the two minutes were up, and they realized that it wasn't their conversation partner who had spoken in Japanese, the incident quickly turned into a ghost story.'

Kaede lowered her head as if defeated, but secretly she was sticking out her tongue in defiance.

Then, just as she was about to ask, 'Is that all, Grandpa?' she was pre-empted.

'But of course,' he continued, with a smile, 'that's not the end of the story, is it? This wasn't just a challenge to the reader. The "Challenge for the Elderly Living Alone" consists of two parts. That story was merely the prologue. There's a second story that completes the tale. There was, in fact, another, separate thirty-third person,' Grandfather declared.

I don't believe it! How could he have figured that out . . . ?

'There's a clue in the first diagram. Look at Seat ⑧ in the

back corner of the classroom; its chair is the only one tucked underneath the desk. In other words, there was nobody sitting there. Desk ⑧ belonged to a girl who hadn't been coming to school in a long time. It's common for a desk in the back of the room near the door to be assigned to pupils who haven't been attending, to make it easier for them to return to class when they're ready. And in this case, that would be Seat ⑧.'

'B-but how do you know that seat belonged to a girl?'

'I'll explain that later. First, I want to discuss Harry's behaviour during that class. You described him as someone who was justice-loving but mischievous. Do you really think he would have wanted to spend one of his last ever classes at primary school – one of his precious last moments with you, Kaede – telling ghost stories just to scare everyone? I think we can assume he had an entirely different motive.'

As ever, not a single flaw in Grandpa's logic . . .

'I imagine he had visited the absent girl's home many times before this final class, trying to persuade her to come back to school. He might have said, "Everyone wants to see you," or "Let's all say goodbye to Kaede-sensei together." His persistence paid off, and unbeknownst to you and the other pupils, she made up her mind to come to school for the first time in ages. But mischievous Harry wanted to make this reunion with her classmates a surprise.

'Most likely he planned it this way: first he'd tell the ghost

They Were Thirty-Three!

story about the girl in the air-raid shelter. Then when the English conversation class was over, he'd shout, "Hey, everyone, look at the back of the room!" That was the moment the girl would step in through the rear classroom door. Her classmates, who had all been worried about her, would burst into applause. Or at least that was the plan. If you look at the first diagram you drew, the door at the back of the classroom is slightly further open than the front one. It wasn't just for ventilation; it was to make it easier for her to slip in without feeling too self-conscious.'

'Um, Grandpa, I have two questions,' Kaede cut in.

'Ask away.'

'First of all, how did you even know there was a student absent that day?'

'Because when you were talking about the English conversation lesson, you said, "Everyone divided into boy–girl pairs, or groups of three." If there had been thirty-two pupils in the classroom they should have divided evenly into pairs. Why would there be any need for a group of three? Clearly, somebody was missing. And besides, when you began the story you said, "That day there were thirty-two people in the classroom." You were simply stating a fact. Yes, there were thirty-two people in the classroom that day – thirty-one pupils and you, making thirty-two in total.'

'Then let me ask the same question from earlier. How did you know the absent pupil was a girl?'

'That was because you clearly indicated that it was.'

Ah he spotted that too . . .

'Right after Harry told the story of the girl in the air-raid shelter, you said, "I'd been preoccupied with that girl, and now found myself cutting Harry off." Think about it – the way you put that was rather odd. If you were referring to the girl in Harry's story you would probably have said something like "I started thinking about her", or "the girl in the story" but you said "I'd *been preoccupied* with *that* girl" which suggests you were thinking of a *different* girl. Harry's story made your mind wander to the absent pupil from your class. It reminds me a little of that scene in *Death on Gokumon Island* where the great detective Kosuke Kindaichi is troubled by the matter of an apparently strange use of a preposition, although in this case it's a matter of a demonstrative pronoun and a slightly odd use of the past participle. Anyway, unlike that grim tale, I'm sure that this story had a much happier ending. Yes, I can picture it now . . .'

Grandfather peered through the purple smoke from his Gauloise.

'"Hey, everyone, look at the back of the room!" At Harry's signal, the girl shyly steps through the rear door of the classroom, her eyes on the floor. You and the rest of the class are momentarily startled, but then you all break into heartfelt applause. Having succeeded in his mission, Harry

They Were Thirty-Three!

removes his glasses to wipe away tears of joy. "See, not a ghost after all! OK, everybody? Let's welcome her back. One . . . two . . . three . . . Welcome back!" The girl's mother, who brought her here and is waiting outside the classroom, also dabs at her eyes. Now, with Kaede, and this girl in the classroom, all thirty-three class members are finally present. And that is the happy conclusion to the tale of "There Were Thirty-Three!"'

As if to signal the end, with a creaking sound Grandfather slowly leaned back in his recliner.

At that moment, multiple voices called out from the entryway to the house.

'*O-jama shimasu!* Sorry to intrude!'

For Kaede, the timing couldn't have been better, but she felt a twinge of embarrassment at her failure to teach proper etiquette.

'I told them they should ring the doorbell first,' she lamented.

'And who might *they* be?' Grandfather enquired.

'Harry, Ron and Hermione.'

'I'm sorry, what did you say?'

'I happened to run into the three of them on the train the other day. They're all at the same junior high school now, and at Hermione's suggestion they formed a Mystery, Sci-Fi, Horror and Fantasy study group. But they've already pretty much got through the school library's stock of those genres, so I asked them if they'd like to come over to my grandfather's house.'

'May we come in?' came a voice that Kaede fondly remembered as Harry's.

Wow, his voice is starting to break . . .

'We should clear out this smoke,' Grandfather said, unable to conceal his delight as he hurried to open the window and waft the purplish haze outside.

'Come on in!' Kaede called out.

The trio came piling in, a varied mix of heights and personalities. Of course, they didn't really resemble the characters from *Harry Potter*, but Kaede couldn't help seeing the similarities.

First to speak were Ron and Hermione, exuberant in their excitement.

'What's this room? Whoa, awesome! It's all books!'

'That's rude. You should greet people first.'

'I heard there are lots of bell crickets in your garden. I brought the latest encyclopaedia of insects.'

'That's not what I meant by greetings.'

Hurried self-introductions were made.

'Principal Window Wiper, aren't you?' Harry began, pushing his glasses up with his middle finger as he gazed at the expansive bookshelves, and cutting straight to the point. 'We heard that there are a lot of scary books here that we

They Were Thirty-Three!

haven't read yet. Would it be OK if we came by to borrow them sometimes?'

'That's not polite!' Hermione corrected him. 'May we humbly request you bestow on us the favour of borrowing your books?'

'That doesn't sound right either,' said Ron.

Grandfather burst out laughing.

'Feel free to come over and borrow them anytime,' he said. 'When it comes to horror novels, I think I have all the notable titles. For example, let's see . . . you all wished that girl, the school refuser, would come back to class, didn't you? How about a tale where any wish can come true?'

'That just sounds like a typical fairy tale. Not scary at all,' said Ron.

'Is that what you think?' asked Grandfather, a look of mischief on his face. Then, pointing to the corner of the nearest bookshelf, in his most theatrical voice he spoke the name of a tale that could chill any reader to the bone, a tale of unimaginable terror.

'Kaede, would you pass me the short story collection that contains "The Monkey's Paw" by W. W. Jacobs?'

Chapter 5:
The Phantom Lady

1

The first time your picture was taken,
You didn't notice, did you?
A 'two-shot' of you and me.
You didn't notice, did you?

I didn't know Saturday mornings could be this lively, Kaede thought.

A slow-moving river wound its heavy way through this traditional old neighbourhood on the outskirts of Tokyo. Sitting on the bank hugging her knees in the soft winter sunlight, Kaede watched the way only the water nearest to her seemed to flow. Far across, by the opposite bank, a dredging boat doing work on the embankment moved at such a leisurely pace it almost appeared stationary.

In stark contrast to this languid scene, the walking path behind Kaede bustled with an endless stream of people enjoying their walks and jogs. From the floodplain came constant cheers from people absorbed in baseball, tennis or croquet. But to Kaede's ears, these enthusiastic voices reminded her of the sleep-inducing rhythmic vibrations of the heated train she'd taken here.

It's no good. I'm still sleepy . . .

As she stifled a yawn, she was jolted by a voice barking at her from somewhere above her head.

'How long is this break going to last?'

Iwata stood behind her, arms crossed and expression stern, like a temple guardian statue. He was fitted out from head to toe in running gear.

'The longer you rest, the stiffer your muscles get and the heavier your legs become. And wearing regular trainers like that? It shows you're not taking this training seriously.'

'Regular trainers?' She'd made sure to pick shoes in the same boring colour as Iwata's own. 'I bought proper running shoes like you told me!'

'All the more reason to push harder. Come on – hydrate, and then get up.'

He's a monster!

She had no choice but to take a swig of her mineral water, climb back up to the walking path, and jog after Iwata again.

In three weeks, the primary school where Kaede and Iwata worked would hold its annual cross country event. Usually, someone as athletically challenged as Kaede would have zero involvement, but this year was different. Somehow, she had been assigned to run at the very back, watching over the slowest children. Most likely, this was all part of some conspiracy of Iwata's, who volunteered to lead the front every year.

Kaede glared resentfully at Iwata's back as he set the pace, his shoulders moving rhythmically. She failed to see the point of travelling all this way, taking multiple trains, and having to stash her belongings in a station locker, just to run on this particular path. Still, as she jogged along aimlessly, she was beginning to see why Iwata liked this place and this time of day.

The paved promenade was about five metres wide – plenty of space for people to comfortably pass each other. An elderly couple, well dressed, and walking a large dog, greeted Iwata with a cheerful 'Good morning!' as they passed. Their Irish setter wagged its tail vigorously, the dog apparently also acquainted with Iwata.

Next a young man dressed in serious running gear – a track jacket and leggings – nodded and called out a greeting as he passed by. He adjusted his neck warmer to reveal a bright smile.

I see – this is actually rather pleasant . . .

Coming to this promenade on a Saturday morning, you could enjoy stimulating interactions with other regular users.

The next person to catch Kaede's eye was a woman in about her mid-thirties in a hoodie, her elbows pumping rhythmically at precise right angles as she strode towards them. Spotting Iwata, she paused briefly to say, 'Good morning, Iwata-sensei. Dedicated as always!' She took a sip from her water bottle, which was wrapped in a garish, character-themed hand towel, while giving Kaede a quick once-over.

'Ooh,' she went on, tucking her drink bottle under her arm and covering her mouth with both hands in an exaggerated gesture. 'Isn't she lovely? Your girlfriend, by any chance?'

Really, lady? There's no point in pretending to cover your mouth. I can hear every word.

'No, no . . . at least not yet.'

What do you mean, 'not yet'?

The woman in the hoodie gave Kaede a knowing smile.

'Sorry for interrupting your run. Take care, you two!' she said before power-walking off.

Great, now she's totally got the wrong message . . .

Kaede slapped her thighs, which were beginning to feel a lactic acid build-up.

Still, Iwata-sensei did introduce me to this lovely spot, so maybe I'll forgive him this time . . .

Without saying anything, she began to jog along behind

The Phantom Lady

Iwata again. However, being totally unused to exercise, she soon found herself out of breath.

Hey, hold on, Iwata-sensei. I think you've picked up the pace!

It's no good. I can't keep up . . .

Iwata turned to talk to her. His voice showed not the slightest hint of exertion.

'Shiki didn't turn up after all. I guess he really does shut down on Saturday mornings.'

'Huh? Wha . . . ?'

'Oh no.'

Realizing that Kaede was gasping for breath, Iwata stopped and crinkled his whole face into a huge grin.

'Looks like you've shut down too, Kaede-sensei. Let's make that next bridge the finish line.'

Under the guise of doing a cooldown, Kaede wobbled along behind Iwata towards the road bridge just up ahead. At which point they heard the echo of a familiar baritone.

'Nice work, you two.'

The voice belonged to Shiki. He emerged from the bridge's shadows, pushing back his long hair.

'This is what you need after working up a sweat,' he announced, producing cans of beer from a convenience store bag.

The bridge cast a long shadow over the riverbank. The three of them sat down in a row on a sunny spot on the dice-patterned concrete embankment, and opened their beers. The cold liquid, chilled by the winter air, seeped into their warmed bodies.

'So good,' said Kaede without thinking. She'd always found beer too bitter, but now she finally got its appeal.

'Oh man, there go all the calories we just burned off,' grumbled Iwata, gulping down his beer in one. 'I'll accept your kind donation anyway,' he added, glaring at Shiki. 'How come you didn't show up on time?'

'Give me a break,' replied Shiki, a relaxed grin crossing his face.

In that moment, Kaede realized what the two men had in common. Although they each had completely different smiles, she found both charming.

'You never seriously expected me to go for a run on a Saturday morning, did you? It's insane.'

'We're talking ten o'clock. It's not like it's even early.'

'It is for me. Besides, I know you secretly enjoyed it being just the two of you.'

'Shut up and pass me another beer.'

'Yes, sir,' Shiki replied, tossing a can to Iwata with perfect control. Then he turned to Kaede and changed the subject.

'So, what boring mysteries have you been reading lately?'

Here we go . . .

Today he's diving right in with that 'boring' premise.

The Phantom Lady

'Won't listening to me talk about all those boring mysteries be way too boring for you?' she retorted.

'That's exactly what makes it fun – the chance to pick apart all their flaws. It's a unique pleasure reserved only for that literary form known as the mystery genre.'

'Hold on, hold on!'

To Kaede's surprise, it was Iwata who cut in.

'You two are always having your cosy little chats about mysteries. Let me have a turn for once.'

'Eh?' said Shiki. 'Do you even know anything about mystery novels?'

'Don't underestimate me,' replied Iwata, taking a large swig of beer in preparation. 'I've come up with an unprecedented new theory. Prepare to have your minds blown. It's called "The Pro-Wrestling and Mystery Equivalence Theory".'

'Let's hear it,' said Shiki. He seemed genuinely intrigued.

Encouraged by the interest, Iwata took a deep breath. His nostrils flared slightly.

'You know, Kaede-sensei, that I'm a fan of pro-wrestling?'

'That's the first I've heard of it.'

'Oh, is it?'

Iwata scratched his nose a little sheepishly before turning back to Shiki.

'Anyway, pro-wrestling and mysteries have a lot in

common. For example, there's a certain word that always features in a mystery. But that same word is also quite common in the world of pro-wrestling.'

He raised his voice a little.

'I know! Let's make this a quiz. Here's the question: what two-syllable word is frequently featured both in mystery novels and pro-wrestling? Quickest answer wins.'

Kaede and Shiki responded in unison.

'Bloodshed.'

'Um . . . correct . . .' said Iwata with a groan of frustration. 'How come you both knew that?'

'Iwata-senpai, that's just superficial.'

'Too obvious.'

'No need for you both to chime in,' said Iwata huffily.

Shiki adopted a concerned expression.

'Please don't tell me that's all you've got?'

'Don't be ridiculous. There's tons of evidence to support my pro-wrestling equals mystery theory.'

Iwata produced a notebook from his waist pouch, licked his finger and began flipping through the pages.

'I've done my research. There used to be this famous wrestler called Karl Kox, and his nickname was amazing: "Killer Karl Kox".'

'Superficial.'

'Obvious again.'

'Stop saying things in unison! There's more. Let me

The Phantom Lady

see . . . Wrestlers with mystery-related nicknames . . . For a start, there's "Dr Death" Steve Williams. Just the idea of a murderous doctor has to be terrifying, right? Then how about "Machine Gun" Karl Anderson? That weapon's a public safety nightmare – what are the police even doing? I've got more . . . Yes, the ultimate must be "The Convict". Get this, his whole schtick is that he's a death row inmate in prison uniform who gets special release just for matches.'

Iwata snapped his notebook shut with a theatrical flourish. He looked rather pleased with himself.

'What? That's it?' Shiki asked.

'That's it. That should be more than enough evidence.'

'Ugh, this is exhausting,' said Shiki, running his fingers through his hair. 'If you're going to propose a pro-wrestling and mystery equivalence theory, I wish you'd focus more on the fundamentals. I agree there are many parallels between the two. But wrestlers' macabre personas and the image of murderers in mystery novels are just superficial commonalities. Why not take a broader perspective and look at the entire structure of a pro-wrestling show?'

'This is starting to sound complicated,' Iwata complained.

'It's quite simple. In any well-staged wrestling event, there's always some kind of "incident" in the opening match that shocks the audience. Maybe it's some new wrestler, rumoured to be something of a powerhouse making his debut and absolutely crushing the reigning champion. Or perhaps there's some kind of interference, or even a betrayal, that completely reshuffles the alliances between the wrestlers. These opening match happenings are the equivalent of what we refer to as the "inciting incident" in a murder mystery.'

Once Shiki got going there was no stopping him.

'Once they start their national tour, the unexpected incident of the opening match evolves into numerous storylines with a variety of themes. Grudges, friendships, justice, revenge – occasionally even the topic of ageing. These parallel the mid-story twists and developments in a murder mystery plot.'

Shiki pressed on, unfazed by his audience's stunned silence.

'All these storylines converge perfectly at the final match in the grand arena. Everything is resolved, and there are no loose ends left hanging. The flawless champion is akin to the brilliant, all-knowing detective, defeating his most powerful nemesis with an unexpected move. The catharsis experienced by the audience as they leave the venue is much like the satisfaction a reader feels after finishing a well-crafted mystery. This affinity exists precisely because both genres are essentially masterfully constructed works of fiction. What's more—'

'Enough already!' Iwata interrupted, unable to contain

himself any longer. 'Don't just hijack my theory and try to make it sound all deep.'

'Senpai, you are simply too shallow.'

'Shut up. Anyway, you hate sports. Why are you suddenly so passionate about pro-wrestling?'

'Because pro-wrestling isn't sport. It's romance.'

'Ro-romance?'

'That six-metre-square ring is a canvas where the wrestlers paint the stories of their lives. And the—'

'Give it a rest, will you? Are you drunk or something? Do you even understand the words coming out of your own mouth?'

As the banter continued – ironically reminiscent of a pro-wrestling match, Kaede thought – she opened a second can of beer, and breathed in the gradually warming winter air. And in that moment, she realized that just like the beer, the atmosphere was perfectly enjoyable with the three of them together.

But then she sensed from somewhere above them an odd kind of gaze. Cautiously she raised her head, and made out a figure leaning on the handrail of the bridge's walkway, staring intently down at them. No, it would be more accurate to say they *appeared* to be staring down, because due to the backlight, all Kaede could see was a dark silhouette.

Yet to Kaede, it felt as if this 'shadow' had deliberately

calculated the effect of the backlighting, and was intentionally keeping their face turned in the threesome's direction.

'Hey, sorry to interrupt your fun,' she said, turning to her two companions, and lowering her voice. 'You see that person on the bridge?'

'Yeah,' said Iwata.

'I see them,' said Shiki.

'I've had this feeling for the past month that someone's been following me. I mean, I know I sound paranoid, but . . .'

Her voice faltered a little, and she continued uncertainly.

'But right around a month ago I started getting these silent phone calls every day . . . Ha ha, no, I'm sorry. It's probably just me overthinking it.'

Before she could say another word, Iwata jumped up and dashed off towards the stairs leading up to the bridge.

'Hey, Iwata-sensei!' Kaede called after him.

'No, let him check it out.'

Shiki placed five slender fingers on his chiselled jaw.

'Kaede-sensei, these calls were from unknown numbers, I assume?'

'Yes. But more often they were from public phones.'

'Is there a phone box near your apartment?'

'Yes, there's one right in front of my building. Even though it's kind of rare to see phone boxes these days.'

The Phantom Lady

Shiki stared at the sparkling surface of the river. Unable to stand the silence, Kaede forced herself to smile.

'I'm sure they're just prank calls. I'm sorry for bothering you with my personal stuff.'

'No,' Shiki responded with a seriousness that Kaede had never seen in him before. 'This isn't something that should be ignored.'

At that point Iwata returned, out of breath.

'The guy got away. He must be quite a runner.' And then, echoing Shiki's words, 'This isn't something we should ignore.'

2

I wonder if you noticed
How many times I talked to you today?
From a place much,
much closer than you might think.

Saturday morning, one week later, Iwata was running alone on the same riverside promenade.

It felt colder than last week, even though the weather forecast had predicted temperatures three degrees higher.

Could it feel colder because . . .

An embarrassing thought flitted through Iwata's mind, one he was very reluctant to acknowledge.

. . . because Kaede isn't with me?

No, stop it. You're being pathetic, Iwata . . .

This had been his Saturday-morning routine for ever – making the hour-long trek to get here all by himself – and yet he had never felt so lost and lonely. He had been the one who insisted she not come here again, telling her if she really had a stalker, it was best to avoid the riverbank.

Come to think of it, he had been just as pathetic last week too. He should have invited her, and her alone, to come.

But I was afraid she'd reject me, so I invited Shiki too . . .

And at first, when Shiki hadn't turned up . . .

I was so happy about it . . .

Shaking his head to clear his thoughts, Iwata picked up his pace. Fortunately, the windbreaker he'd worn in anticipation of the forecasted rain acted like a sauna suit, quickly warming up his body. Nodding to the silver-haired couple with the Irish setter and exchanging greetings with the young man in the track jacket and leggings, the chill in his heart began to dissipate.

All right, this feels good. This place really is the best. I wish I'd had the chance to bring my mum and dad here too . . .

He reached the foot of the bridge where they'd drunk their beers the previous week.

I'll take a short break . . .

About fifty metres ahead of him on the walking path he spotted the woman in the hoodie from last week. Iwata

The Phantom Lady

raised a hand in greeting as he stepped off the promenade onto the riverbank. Distant thunder echoed from somewhere beyond the clouds. It might rain today after all. Perhaps that was why there were no people on the riverbank.

No, there is someone . . .

Iwata had spotted two men grappling in the shadow under the bridge. The words 'Oi, you!' carried across to him on the icy wind. It looked serious.

'Is everything all right there?' he called out as he ran down the concrete embankment towards them.

It wasn't clear whether his voice hadn't reached them or they were simply ignoring him, but the men continued to scuffle, gripping each other's arms even more fiercely.

One of them, a middle-aged man in a suit, looked to be around fifty. The other was a young man, probably in his twenties, and wearing an orange T-shirt. The younger man yelled something in a high-pitched voice. In response, the older man appeared to decide the fight was over, and shoved the young man away with force.

'Don't mess with me!' he shouted, his hand swinging like a pendulum.

'Are you kidding?' the younger man muttered, clearly surprised.

Without even glancing in Iwata's direction, the middle-aged man set off running. The younger man's knees buckled under him, and he began slowly to collapse. Iwata caught him right before he hit the ground, somehow preventing him from banging his head.

'Are you OK?' Iwata asked, but the young man didn't reply. His eyes were closed and his face was rapidly losing its colour. Iwata was taken aback by how young he looked.

Reminds me of the kids in my class. He's barely a teenager . . .

His hand brushed against something hard that protruded from the boy's body. A distinct, solid sensation that made his stomach turn.

Please don't let it be . . .

But there it was, exactly what he had feared: a knife, still embedded in the young man's stomach. The man's neck, cradled in Iwata's arm, was drenched in sweat, but sweat was not the only fluid soaking his body. A darker colour was spreading across his orange T-shirt, staining it a brilliant crimson.

Bloodshed. Murderous. Weapon.

Words from last week's mystery discussion flashed through Iwata's mind.

What am I doing? This isn't the time . . .

'Stay with me! I'm calling an ambulance right now.'

Still supporting the young man's body with his left arm, Iwata reached for the phone in his waist pouch. But the zipper wouldn't budge.

The Phantom Lady

Why won't it open? Damn it!
Oh, I see.

Iwata finally realized why the zipper wouldn't move. His hands were too slippery from their sticky coating of blood.

Don't panic. Stay calm. Every second counts . . .

Right then without warning fat raindrops began to fall. Iwata looked up, and saw the woman in the hoodie standing at the top of the embankment, her hand over her mouth.

Thank god!

'Did you see what happened?' he called to her.

The woman nodded several times.

'Did you see the man who ran away?'

She nodded more forcefully.

'Please could you call an ambulance?'

Even if he managed to get his phone out, he wasn't confident he could press the buttons with his blood-slicked fingers.

But the woman did something completely unexpected. As if she hadn't even heard his pleas, she turned and strode away with determined steps.

'Hey, wait! Wait!'

For a moment, Iwata thought he was going to cry.

'What are you doing? Hey! Heeyyy!'

Why? Weren't they friends, always exchanging greetings? Why would she run away?

He stayed there, mouth hanging open, staring at the point on the walking path where the woman had disappeared. The rain intensified, pelting his cheeks, and snapping him back into the moment.

That's right. I still need to call an ambulance!

It was at that moment he heard a gentle yet firm voice from behind him.

'Stay calm, son.'

He turned his head to see an older uniformed police officer, a baton in his hand.

'Stay still. Just like that. Don't move.'

'Officer, please! We need an ambulance!'

'One's been called. Now, very slowly let go of it.'

Of it? Of what?

Looking down, he realized he was gripping the handle of the knife with his right hand.

What am I doing?

Iwata hurriedly released his grip on the knife still embedded in the young man's stomach. He must have subconsciously debated whether removing it would be beneficial, and his hand had found its way to the hilt.

'Could you slowly raise your right hand?'

Obediently, Iwata lifted his hand as if hailing a taxi. Out of the corner of his eye he caught a glimpse of his own bloodstained palm.

There was a gurgling sound. Bloody bubbles emerged

The Phantom Lady

from the mouth of the young man, still supported by Iwata's knee and left hand.

Please don't die.

'Turn your face away, sir. Yes, like that. Stay that way . . . Please don't look back.'

The police officer's voice was too calm. Iwata felt a sense of unease. His overly polite manner was somehow irritating, given that the crucial ambulance hadn't even turned up yet.

'Emergency alert. Emergency alert. Notifying headquarters and all PCs in the vicinity . . .'

The officer appeared to be on his radio. 'PC' likely stood for 'patrol car'.

'. . . incident involving bodily harm near the railway bridge. Suspect is currently in visual range. What . . . Lost connection? Do you copy? Repeating, suspect currently in visual range. Believe I can secure him, but cannot rule out resistance. Requesting immediate back-up from nearby PCs. I repeat – urgent assistance required.'

'Hold on, officer. It wasn't me! It was the man who ran away.'

'Don't say anything.'

As the officer slowly approached, Iwata could hear the jingle of metal.

Handcuffs?

The rain had become a downpour.

3

Immersed in her morning reading, Kaede hadn't noticed the rain.

She rushed onto the balcony to bring in her laundry, and then settled back on the sofa bed, picking up her book. It was by Hillary Waugh, a mystery writer who was back in fashion in recent years. The title – *That Night it Rained*. Kaede reflected once again how elegantly understated the title was.

As she carefully removed one of her treasured laminated obituaries of the critic Takeshi Setogawa, which she used as a makeshift bookmark, she noticed something unusual: the voicemail icon on her mobile phone was showing the number 15.

Lately she'd been getting more of those anonymous phone calls, so she'd been keeping her phone on Do Not Disturb most of the time. That explained how she'd missed the calls, but fifteen of them?

Were they from an unknown number? Or a public phone?

With trepidation, Kaede checked her call log.

Iwata-sensei

Iwata-sensei

Iwata-sensei

What? Was this for real?

The Phantom Lady

Rather ominously, the same name filled the screen, line after line. All fifteen calls were from Iwata, and they'd all come within a five-minute window, around half an hour earlier.

She shuddered.

Something's wrong . . .

Trying to calm her racing heartbeat, she returned to the home screen, where she also found three one-word text messages from Iwata.

Woman

Disappeared

Find

The texts had been sent right after the fifteen missed calls.

What's going on? What could have happened?

No, this was no time for puzzle-solving. Immediately she called Iwata back.

However, no matter how many times she called, all she got was a robotic female voice telling her, 'The number you are trying to reach is either out of range or has been turned off.'

I'm sorry, Iwata-sensei. I'm so sorry I didn't pick up.

But he might try again. Kaede turned off the Do Not Disturb setting and opened her contacts. She searched for Shiki's name, intending to ask his advice, but before she'd found it, she was startled when the phone began to ring loudly.

'Aagh!' she yelped, and immediately dropped it. She scrambled to retrieve it, and saw an unfamiliar phone number on the screen.

Iwata-sensei's home number?

She hurried to answer.

'Hello, I'm terribly sorry to call you on a weekend,' a rather raspy male voice said. 'Am I speaking with ___san?' he asked, using Kaede's family name.

'Yes, that's me.'

'This is Officer___ from the A— police station.'

The caller stated his name and title in a formal manner, then continued in a mechanical tone.

'I'm calling to inform you that your colleague, Iwata-san, has just been arrested on suspicion of assault resulting in serious bodily injury. We are currently processing the paperwork for his detainment.'

'Sorry, what?!'

Assault?

Arrested?

Detainment?

It took her several seconds to process this string of unexpected words.

'Hello? Can you hear me?'

'Ah, y-yes I can hear you.'

'When we asked Iwata-san for an emergency contact, he told us he had no parents or siblings. He indicated he had no other relatives either. He said that if he had to name someone, then it would be you. Now, is everything clear so far? Hello?'

Kaede was speechless once more. Pressing her hand to her chest, she struggled to get her breathing under control.

'Yes, I understand.'

'Under normal circumstances we don't immediately contact colleagues. However, given the situation, and since we want to prevent any unfortunate incidents while in our custody – well, our chief has instructed me to reach out.'

'Wait a minute. By "unfortunate incidents" are you referring to . . .'

She forced herself to articulate the difficult words.

'. . . Are you talking about suicide?'

'I'm afraid, under the chief's directive, I'm unable to comment on that. Now I'd like to go over visitation procedures. Please have something ready to take notes.'

Stay calm, Kaede . . .

And who is this 'chief' anyway?

'Before that, could you please tell me more details of this assault incident?' Kaede asked.

'I'm unable to provide any details, as this is an ongoing investigation. Additionally, we must ask you to refrain from discussing the incident during your visitation. If you do, we may have to terminate the visit.'

'And that's—' Kaede barely stopped herself from asking if that was also the chief's directive.

'So, as I previously mentioned, could you prepare to take notes?'

Her hand trembled as she reached for a pen and a paper.

She was of course shaken by the news of Iwata's arrest, but there was something that had come as a greater shock. That was the information that someone as cheerful as Iwata had no parents or siblings. There was a burning behind her eyes as she wrote down the instructions.

'Hello? Shiki? Are you awake?'

'No . . . I mean, yes,' he replied, groggily.

He sounded practically dead.

Kaede had resolved never to call him on a Saturday morning, but this was an emergency.

'Sorry, but you really need to wake up.'

She briefed him on everything that had happened.

'This is serious,' he said, fully awake now. 'I'm guessing Iwata-senpai made those phone calls right before or right after his arrest. And the texts – they were probably sent in desperation, frantically typed in the back of the police car or something.'

'Yes, I think so too.'

The Phantom Lady

A fresh wave of regret washed over her. Why hadn't she noticed? If only she'd glanced at her screen she could have answered in time.

'I guess they'll have confiscated his phone by now,' she added.

'Most likely,' Shiki agreed. 'We need to go and visit him as soon as possible and get the full story from him directly. But I do remember that back when my theatre troupe was researching a courtroom drama, I learned that discussing a case during visiting hours is strictly forbidden.'

'That's what the police said too.'

'And typically, during the first three days – what they call "those crucial first seventy-two hours" – the focus is on interrogation so visitation is likely to be denied. But I'll still apply for it,' he added.

'I will too,' said Kaede.

'In any case,' said Shiki, doubtless running a hand through his hair on the other end of the line, 'let's strategize before the visit.'

His voice was reassuringly steady.

'I'll come up with a plan.'

4

Despite multiple attempts, they weren't granted permission to visit Iwata until Wednesday, four days after his arrest.

As it was a weekday, Kaede was forced to call in sick to school, but there was nothing else for it. As for Iwata, Shiki called up pretending to be his younger brother, and claimed there was an urgent family matter that required a week of leave.

But to Kaede, the situation looked dire. The fact that Iwata hadn't been released after those initial seventy-two hours suggested that the police had requested an extension of the detention period from the prosecutors. In other words, they were becoming more convinced of his guilt.

As she and Shiki completed the visitor entry procedures at the detention centre, Kaede did her best to recall what little information they'd gathered so far.

News of the incident had first appeared on the day it occurred, but only a few lines in an evening tabloid paper. There was barely anything to be gleaned from that article:

Around 11.00 a.m. on Saturday, a stabbing occurred on the bank of the A— river. The nineteen-year-old victim remains unconscious and in critical condition.

It was also reported that a twenty-seven-year-old suspect (clearly Iwata, although he wasn't named in the article) was arrested at the scene on suspicion of inflicting bodily injury, although he continued to deny any involvement.

And that was all the media reported.

The Phantom Lady

The only other clues they had were the three words that Iwata had texted to Kaede: *woman*, *disappeared* and *find*.

I hate to think about it . . .

A grim scenario flashed through Kaede's mind.

If the youth were to die, the charges would immediately change from assault resulting in bodily injury to assault resulting in death, or to perhaps even murder. And Iwata's name would be widely reported along with that ominous label: 'suspect'.

How much of the truth could they hope to uncover during today's visit? When the detention period was up and the case handed over to the prosecutors, an indictment would almost certainly follow. And once indicted, the reality of the Japanese judicial system meant that there was a 99 per cent chance that he would be found guilty.

Knowing Iwata's stubborn nature, it was unlikely that he would already have got himself a lawyer. In order to prove his innocence, Shiki and Kaede were somehow going to have to extract information from Iwata himself. The problem was that, while casual conversation was permitted, discussion of the case was strictly forbidden. Electronic devices like mobile phones or voice recorders were off limits. Moreover, visiting time was strictly limited to fifteen minutes . . .

It's going to be a race against the clock . . .

A young uniformed officer opened the door. Kaede and

Shiki exchanged a silent glance before entering the visitors' room.

Just as Shiki had described, the first thing Kaede noticed was the transparent partition that bisected the room. It was just like the ones she saw in TV dramas. In the centre of the partition was a circular pattern of holes within a frame. Kaede had learned through her preparations for the visit that these were known as speaking holes, and that the far side of the partition was known as the detainee side and the near side the visitors' side.

No one had appeared yet, but the moment Kaede and Shiki took their seats on the folding chairs provided, they readied the items they'd brought in their bags, and got out their notepads, placing them on their laps. They couldn't afford to waste a single second.

Soon they heard footsteps approaching from the detainee side and an impeccably dressed older woman with perfect posture appeared. Adjusting her spectacles, she introduced herself as an officer from the detention supervision department.

'Not good,' whispered Shiki, just loud enough for Kaede to hear.

Indeed, to Kaede too, this woman looked like someone who would be rigidly 'by the book', a stickler for the rules. A rather inappropriate thought crossed her mind.

The Phantom Lady

Just like the head of the Parent Teacher Association at school . . .

'Naturally I don't mean to suggest this is your intention, but we have had incidents in the past of visitors and detainees conspiring to destroy evidence, so you are strictly advised not to discuss the case during your visit.'

This was the third time they'd been given this warning, either over the phone or in person.

'Moreover, if I determine you're discussing the case, I will terminate the visit immediately.'

The officer looked at the wall clock.

'You have fifteen minutes, starting now. Now, please send in number five-two.'

Five-two apparently referred to the second detainee in Detention Block Five.

'Wouldn't it be funny if Iwata-san had been the homeroom teacher of class 5-2?' Shiki whispered.

Ah, too bad. He taught 4-3 . . .

Just a minute, now was not the time to be joking around!

Was Shiki just naturally this eccentric, or was he trying to ease the tension? Kaede couldn't tell.

The detention officer made her way over to the corner desk, her heels clacking on the floor. Almost immediately, a rather haggard-looking Iwata came in. There was several days' worth of stubble on his chin.

Poor thing. They must be grilling him hard . . .

But the next instant, Iwata rushed towards the partition shouting, 'Kaede-sensei! Shiki! You've got to believe me; I didn't do it! I saw a man in his fifties in a suit stab him. I was trying to help him when a police officer—'

'That's enough!' yelled the officer, kicking her chair back to get to her feet.

What? No way! Is it over?

'Well, that was quick!' said Shiki, this time at full volume.

Not ten seconds had passed.

'Five-two-san, what do you think you're doing?' The detention officer's piercing glare took in Iwata from head to toe. It was the perfect illustration of the phrase *If looks could kill*.

'I-I'm sorry. I wasn't thinking.'

'If it happens again this visit will be terminated instantly!' she announced, shooting Kaede and Shiki similar death glares before returning to her seat.

Kaede let out her breath.

Try to take it easy, Iwata-sensei . . .

But at least they'd got some new information: Iwata had seen the real perpetrator – a man in his fifties in a suit.

But they couldn't risk any more mistakes. They'd need to proceed with caution.

'Iwata-senpai, we've brought some things for you,' said Shiki. As they'd planned, Shiki reached into his Boston bag

The Phantom Lady

and displayed the items from the Permitted Articles category that they'd had pre-approved.

'First, here's some cash. I'd lend you more, but the limit is thirty thousand yen.'

With that amount, Iwata would be able to purchase most of what he needed from the detention centre's shop.

'Thanks, Shiki. That's a great help.'

'Then some underwear and a sweatshirt and sweatpants. Fleece-lined to keep you warm.'

'That'll be a lifesaver. It's freezing in here.'

Iwata stroked his stubble with an expression of deep gratitude.

'And finally, one more thing from me,' said Shiki, digging into his bag once more.

Wait, what? He never mentioned this . . .

Ignoring the look of confusion on Kaede's face, Shiki produced a dirty old baseball and adjusted his grip on it.

'A fastball. Catch it.'

'Oh, you . . .'

'You must be bored in here. Might as well take a trip down memory lane.'

'Oh, you . . .' said Iwata again, placing a hand on the partition. 'You're so cheesy.'

His face crumpled, not into his usual smile, but into something odd and distorted. His eyes glistened.

The former pitcher–catcher duo nodded at each other, as

if confirming a baseball signal. After a beat, Shiki nudged Kaede to indicate it was her turn.

Now it's up to me.

Hurry but don't rush . . .

Kaede moistened her lips before delivering the lines she and Shiki had carefully rehearsed.

'By the way, Iwata-sensei, you're into mysteries, aren't you?'

Iwata's mouth fell open.

'No, I can't stand mysteries, well any novels at all really. The only thing I enjoy reading is *Cooking Papa*.'

Shiki cut in, drowning out Iwata's protests, 'Come on, you're really into them, aren't you?'

'Hey, what's with that weird look? . . . Oh . . .! Yes, right, right. Yes, of course.'

For a brief instant, Iwata's face crinkled up into one of his big smiles.

'Yeah, love mysteries! So, so bored in here. Nothing else to do!'

That's it. Keep that up!

Constrained as they were by all the strict rules, they were going to have to rely on indirect language to extract any information.

Iwata's text messages had contained the three words *woman*, *disappeared* and *find*.

The Phantom Lady

Who was this woman? How and where had she disappeared from? And if this woman was somehow connected with the case, they needed to know what she was wearing at the time. If they could skilfully extract this information from Iwata, it might provide clues to finding her.

'So, I've brought you two mystery novels by one of your favourite authors,' Kaede continued. She took one book from her bag and held it up to the partition. 'Hillary Waugh.'

'Ah, yes of course. That Hillary,' replied Iwata, making an awkward attempt to play along. 'Yeah, I do like that one. I've been meaning to read it again.'

'Yeah, this is one of his classics, *That Night it Rained*.'

Kaede glanced over at the supervisor. She was busy writing something at her desk, and didn't seem suspicious of them.

Iwata leaned in closer to the book and nodded at the two visitors. He'd picked up on their cue to steer the conversation towards the events of that rainy day.

'You recommended this one to me, Iwata-sensei, so I gave it a try. It's undeniably a masterpiece of police procedural fiction. It made me want to read another novel by Waugh.'

Slowly and deliberately, Kaede pulled out Hillary Waugh's most famous work, published in 1953. A cornerstone of classic police procedural mysteries, known to all mystery afficionados, Kaede announced the title, enunciating with care:

'*Last Seen Wearing.*'

Out of the corner of her eye, she thought she saw the detention officer get to her feet. But this was the moment to take a gamble.

'You're so good at recommending books, Iwata-sensei. Could you tell me a bit about the "plot" of this novel?'

5

Fortunately, they managed to reach the riverside walking path while there was still plenty of daylight. Looking down at the riverbank Kaede noticed that the grass seemed browner and more withered than it had two weeks earlier.

The meeting with Iwata had been productive. Walking alongside Shiki, Kaede opened her notebook to review the information she'd gleaned through the discussion of the 'plot' of *Last Seen Wearing*.

The 'woman' referred to in Iwata's texts was the same power-walker that Kaede herself had passed at this very spot. Iwata didn't know anything about her, they were visual acquaintances who exchanged brief greetings every Saturday morning. She was always dressed in a plain, monochrome hoodie.

The Phantom Lady

Then, despite witnessing the entire incident – from the moment the real assailant stabbed the victim and fled, to when Iwata had rushed over to help the victim – she had inexplicably 'disappeared' from the scene.

No wonder Iwata was desperate to find her. Her testimony would prove him innocent right away. Apparently, he had also asked the police to look for the 'power-walking woman'. However, they claimed that their inquiries had turned up nothing. They'd concluded that she didn't exist.

'It's hard to believe that these things still happen,' said Shiki in a low voice, walking alongside Kaede. 'It seems the police have already decided that Senpai is the culprit and they're not bothering to investigate any other leads.'

'You mean they're bluffing?'

'From what I've heard, such things used to be common practice.'

Kaede clenched her fists.

If that's the case, then we've no option but to find the power-walking woman . . .

She spotted a familiar elderly couple walking their dog towards them on the promenade. She nudged Shiki and ran over to them.

'Um, excuse me. I was jogging here two Saturdays ago. Do you happen to remember me?'

The woman with the elegant silver hair replied with a gracious smile.

'Of course we remember you. You were a new face around here, and such a lovely one at that. My husband wouldn't stop talking about you afterwards. Right, dear?'

'You shouldn't say such things,' her gentlemanly husband said, looking embarrassed. He addressed Kaede. 'You were with Iwata-sensei, weren't you?'

'That's right. We'd like to ask you about another regular here, a woman who power-walks. She came walking along here soon after we passed you. Do you happen to know her?'

'A power-walker?'

The couple exchanged a puzzled look.

'Could you describe her a bit more?' said the wife.

'She was wearing a dark-coloured hoodie. I think that day it was grey . . . She's probably in her thirties. And . . .'

Kaede cast her mind back to what had left the most vivid details.

'She had a very distinct way of walking. With her elbows bent at right angles, taking very brisk, purposeful steps.'

The couple looked at each other again.

'I'm afraid I don't recall anyone like that. Do you, dear?'

'No, sorry. I can't say that I do.'

The Irish setter playfully nuzzled Kaede's leg.

'Stop that!' the wife scolded the dog.

'I'm sorry we couldn't be of any help. Well, we should be going now.'

The Phantom Lady

No, wait a minute!

Kaede was about to ask Shiki if he had any questions for the couple, when she noticed he was hanging back, his body tensed as if ready for battle.

Surely not . . .

The elderly couple walked away.

'Hey, Shiki, don't tell me you're afraid of dogs.'

'Don't make fun of me,' he answered, his face pale and his tone defensive. 'I just don't trust creatures that can't understand human language. And you know, even in the world of mysteries dogs are often untrustworthy. Take the demon hound from *The Hound of the Baskervilles* – practically a monster . . .'

Kaede wanted to point out that there were plenty of cute, helpful dogs featured in mysteries, but she knew the conversation was likely to go on for ever, so she simply replied, 'Right. I get it.'

Just then, the young man in the track jacket and leggings came running into view.

What a stroke of luck . . .

'Excuse me,' Kaede called out, hoping that this time they would get some answers. But it turned out that he hadn't seen the 'power-walking woman' either, claiming he'd never noticed anyone with that distinctive walking style.

Despite her layers of warm clothing, a chill ran down Kaede's spine.

What on Earth . . . ?

As the sun set, both the riverbank and the promenade became deserted.

On the way to the nearest station, and even in the shopping area around the station, Kaede asked everyone she could find about the power-walking woman. Yet again, they came up with nothing.

Iwata saw her every week. Kaede was certain that she'd seen her too, and had even heard her speaking.

And yet it was as if she had never existed.

The police were likely to put in a request for an extension of Iwata's detention very soon, and unless Kaede and Shiki could locate this key witness it seemed very likely that he would be indicted. After that, a guilty verdict was almost inevitable. The circumstantial evidence pointed to Iwata as the perpetrator.

They couldn't afford to waste another moment.

6

The silence weighed heavy on the train ride back. And it wasn't only Kaede; Shiki also seemed too confused to gather his thoughts.

As Tokyo's dense skyline came into view through the train window, Kaede finally broke the silence.

'You know, there's a pattern in mystery novels where

everyone says, "I've never seen anyone like that, let alone met them." I guess you could call them "Phantom Lady" stories.'

Phantom Lady, Cornell Woolrich's 1942 classic crime novel (written under the pseudonym William Irish), was often considered a pioneer in this genre.

'I was just thinking the same thing,' Shiki admitted. 'If we analyse the pattern, we might just find a clue to the truth.'

'What other ones are there?' Kaede mused.

'Well, one of the most famous has to be Dickson Carr's short story, "Cabin B-13".'

'I don't know that one. But aren't you supposed to hate Dickson Carr's mysteries?'

'Well, I er . . .' Shiki sputtered, unusually flustered. 'It's probably because it isn't a novel. It's a radio drama script. You could say it's kind of in my wheelhouse.'

'OK, I get it. So, what's the story?'

'The protagonist is a woman who boards a luxury cruise ship with her newlywed husband. But then, once they're aboard, he disappears. When she asks the crew where her husband might have gone, nobody knows. Worse, they deny he ever boarded the ship at all, telling her, "You got on this ship by yourself. There was never anyone with you."'

'I remember that. I've read it.'

When it came to Dickson Carr, especially regarding her beloved detective, Dr Fell, Kaede couldn't let herself be outdone.

'You know that story's more famous for the unverified urban legend within it than for its actual plot? It's an episode that's been referenced in countless other novels.'

'How did that go again?' Shiki asked, his voice tinged with frustration.

'A mother and daughter are visiting Paris for the World Expo. The mother falls ill and stays in the hotel room while the daughter goes out to fetch a doctor. But when she returns several hours later, her mother is nowhere to be found. When she asks the hotel staff their response is totally unexpected – "We're sorry, mademoiselle, but you've been staying here by yourself." Everyone in the hotel tells her the same thing, leaving the daughter to return home heartbroken and alone.'

'I remember now,' said Shiki quickly, not liking to be outshone. 'The truth behind it was that the mother had contracted the plague on a stopover in India before arriving in Paris. She passed away while her daughter was out looking for a doctor. If word had got out during the World Expo, the city of Paris would have been thrown into chaos, and the hotel would have suffered a devastating blow to business. So the hotel management colluded with Parisian authorities. They secretly moved the mother's body elsewhere, and imposed a gag order on everyone involved, making it seem as if the incident never happened.'

'It's a well-crafted story that sounds quite plausible, doesn't it?' said Kaede.

'Speaking of the Phantom Lady genre,' said Shiki with sudden enthusiasm, 'there's another one. It's a TV series, but we shouldn't overlook the episode, "The Grey Village – Furuhata Catches a Cold" from the series *Furuhata Ninzaburo*. The detective's assistant meets a beautiful woman in a remote village and spends the whole night on an extended date with her, visiting various locations. However, come morning, she's vanished without a trace. All the villagers, and police officers too, claim that they never saw this woman, and that the man had been alone all night. Season Three of *Furuhata Ninzaburo* was notable for several episodes like that one. They challenged the established patterns of mystery storytelling, and that episode was one of the best.'

Kaede couldn't agree more. And now one of those patterns had manifested itself as a catastrophe for Iwata-sensei.

All those previous 'catastrophes' had been solved by genius detectives.

'Cabin B-13' by Dr Gideon Fell.

In *Furuhata Ninzaburo*, the eponymous Detective Furuhata himself.

But Kaede knew someone who was more than a match for those two.

7

Promising herself it would be her last, Kaede took another day of sick leave, and set out for her grandfather's house in Himonya.

As she carefully navigated the narrow garden path, taking care not to disturb the winter camellias, she could hear the voice of the physiotherapist – the one known as 'Soft-Serve Guy' because of his family's ice-cream shop – drifting across from the study window.

'Exhale as far as you can . . . now, this is the crucial moment.'

Crucial moment?

It sounded as if an intense rehabilitation session was underway.

According to Soft-Serve Guy, muscle strength could be developed at any age, as long as one's physical condition was carefully assessed, and appropriate training implemented.

Kaede entered the house and knocked on the study door at the end of the hallway.

'Is that Sanae or Kaede?' Grandfather asked from beyond the closed door.

'It's Kaede.'

The Phantom Lady

'Just a moment. All right, Soft-Serve-san, one more time.'

Wow. He's so motivated . . .

'Sorry to interrupt. Keep up the good work!' Kaede called out to them.

She went through the left side door into the living room, where the veteran home helper with the bob cut, 'Okappa-san', was stamping 'All done' in the care notebook.

'Thank you for always looking after my grandfather,' Kaede said.

'Oh no, not at all. He's been doing so well lately, it's hard to believe that incident with the otters ever happened.'

Okappa-san smiled.

'In fact, just today, he asked to try the Hasegawa Scale test again, and he got a perfect score.'

Still smiling broadly, she wiped a tear from her eye with her little finger.

The Hasegawa Scale, officially known as the Revised Hasegawa Dementia Scale, is a cognitive function test devised for simple dementia screening. It starts out with questions about one's birth date and current location, then tests memory by having subjects recall recently mentioned information or doing basic arithmetic. The maximum score is thirty, with anything below twenty suggesting possible dementia. For a Lewy Body Dementia patient such as Kaede's grandfather, it wasn't unusual to get astonishingly high scores. However, getting a perfect score repeatedly was truly remarkable.

Despite his Parkinson's-like symptoms, which had become more pronounced in the cold weather, and the decline in his spatial awareness, achieving a perfect score in a cognitive function test was a mark of Grandfather's extraordinary intellect.

Okappa-san slipped the notebook into her bag and bowed briefly before making her way towards the front door. Then Soft-Serve Guy with his close-cropped hair emerged from the study, turning to glance back and nod a farewell.

And in that fleeting moment, Kaede noticed something in his expression that unsettled her. It wasn't his usual gentle look.

How to describe it? It was almost like . . . yes . . .

If she had to express it in terms of an emotion, it would be 'hostility'.

'Hello, Kaede-sensei.'

Oh!

'Thank you,' she replied.

'He was in excellent form today again. Well then, I'll be on my way.'

The plastered-on smile hid any trace of emotion. She must have been imagining it. Perhaps he was just one of those people whose expressions seemed intense when they were serious.

The Phantom Lady

'Grandpa, are you OK now?'

'I'm still in the middle of my exercise but come on in.'

Entering the study, Kaede found her grandfather sitting in his recliner, extending and retracting a rubber exercise band above his head.

'Sorry to keep you waiting.'

'Don't worry about it. But don't overdo it, OK?'

Perhaps this was a cooldown exercise. When he finished with the exercise band, he took a towel and wiped the sweat from his face, then began to brush his hair.

It was heartening to see a little of his old sense of style returning. Just fixing his hair made him look five years younger. Finally, he ran a trembling hand through his locks and shook his head a couple of times. The way his fringe fell across the high bridge of his nose reminded Kaede of a certain someone . . .

'Grandpa, I'm sorry to jump straight in this way,' Kaede began, getting out her notebook, 'but today I need you to listen to my story without the use of a voice memo. There may be some gaps, but I'd still really appreciate your wisdom. It concerns a very special—'

She hesitated a moment.

'A very important well, um . . .'

She searched for the right words.

'The life of someone important to me is on the line.'

She recounted every single detail: the stabbing by the

river; the texts from Iwata; the call from the police; the visitors' room; and even her and Shiki's inquiries along the promenade.

'*Last Seen Wearing* – now that brings back memories,' said Grandfather. 'Now then . . .'

Clearly intrigued, he laced his fingers together, deep in thought.

'First of all, the key to this case lies with what the power-walking woman was carrying.'

'The hand towel, right?' responded Kaede as if she'd been waiting for her cue.

Grandfather gave her an enigmatic smile, and gestured in her direction, palm up, as if to say, 'Go ahead.'

'The hoodie she was wearing was plain, just a dark monochrome with nothing distinctive about it,' Kaede continued. 'The only really striking item she had on her was that loud-coloured hand towel wrapped around her drink bottle. So I really tried to dig into my memory, pushed myself to recall more details, and then it came to me. The character was green. And suddenly I remembered – it was a baby dinosaur by the name of Tiranonnon.'

'Tira—what now?' Grandfather chuckled.

'Tiranonnon. It's the lead character from a children's educational programme. It's cute because it uses a dinosaur eggshell for a house, like a hermit crab. And that's when I realized something about our power-walking woman.'

The Phantom Lady

Kaede studied her grandfather's expression carefully as she voiced her conclusion.

'She's a mother with a child in preschool or daycare.'

'Oh!' Grandfather murmured, then he clapped his hands. 'Brilliant! You must be right. If it was merchandise featuring some globally famous character then it wouldn't be unusual, but for someone to be using merchandise from a kids' educational programme suggests she must have a child who watches it. Now for convenience, let's refer to her as "Walking Mama".'

'That's a good name, Walking Mama.'

Matches Iwata-sensei's favourite, Cooking Papa . . .

'This narrows our puzzle down to three questions,' Grandfather declared. 'First, why, despite witnessing the whole incident, did Walking Mama leave without calling an ambulance? Second, why hasn't she come forward since that day? And third—'

Kaede already knew what the third question would be.

'Why does nobody besides you remember Walking Mama?'

'Right,' she said. 'That's the most puzzling part.'

'Well then, let's hear it.'

There it was . . .

'What tale can you weave from these threads, Kaede?'

Hmm . . .

She flicked through her notebook pages.

'I came up with two tales. Number One: Walking Mama was the wife or girlfriend of the man who fled after the stabbing. She ran away to protect the culprit and that's why she hasn't come forward.'

'I see,' Grandfather mused. 'At first glance it makes sense, but it doesn't adequately address question three. Why does everyone claim not to know her?'

Kaede had no response.

OK then, how about this?

'Number Two . . .'

Kaede began her second tale with a little more confidence.

'Iwata-sensei went to the river to run every Saturday morning. That means he only ever met Walking Mama on Saturday mornings. At the same time, Walking Mama only went for a walk there on Saturdays, meaning she wasn't a true regular on that promenade. She's not exactly "Walking Mama", more like "Part-time Walking Mama".'

For a moment, she thought she caught a sharp glint in her grandfather's eyes.

'And?'

'The fact that both my meeting with Walking Mama and the day of the incident fell on a Saturday would support this theory. No wonder the elderly couple with the dog and the young man in the track jacket couldn't remember her. To them, she was just a faint presence – someone they saw once a week at most. Barely memorable at all.'

'Not bad. Go on.'

Emboldened by her grandfather's unexpected words of encouragement, Kaede continued.

'So then, why did Walking Mama leave the scene of the crime? Sometimes the truth is disappointingly simple. She just didn't want to get mixed up in any trouble.'

'Seventy-five points,' declared Grandfather. 'Your insight that Walking Mama isn't a genuine walking mama is excellent. But ultimately that theory fails because –' he paused to take a sip of coffee from the cup on the side table – 'the same would go for Iwata-sensei: he's someone they only saw once a week, yet they all clearly recognized him, didn't they? Among people who walk or run every day, even if they only see someone once a week, they want to share a sense of kinship. And then, your reasoning for Walking Mama leaving the scene was a bit harsh, I thought. Sure, there are some people who prefer to avoid getting involved in any kind of trouble, but think about it – we're talking about a human life here. Wouldn't even the most conflict-averse person call an ambulance, and at least wait to explain the situation to the paramedics?'

Kaede had to admit he had a point. Although she had only exchanged a few words with Walking Mama, the woman hadn't come across as shy or nervous at all; rather, warm and friendly. And that was precisely why her disappearing from the scene of the crime the way she had felt so out of character.

'In short, both Tale One and Tale Two contain contradictions that can't be ignored. Which means of course—'

He raised a long forefinger.

'There exists another tale – Tale X – that will reveal the truth.'

The fierce wind that had been rattling the windows for the past few days had finally calmed down. Winter sunlight streamed in, illuminating Grandfather's dignified profile.

It was as if the curtain had just risen on a play. Sitting centre stage, Grandfather spoke that familiar line:

'Kaede, pass me a cigarette, would you?'

'I can see the whole picture now.'

Grandfather drew deeply on his Gauloise, the tip glowing as it softly crackled.

'Let's set aside Walking Mama for a moment and concentrate on the stabbing on the riverbank. This is purely hypothetical, but let's say the middle-aged man and his young victim were arguing over a drug deal. Given that no drugs were found on the victim, the middle-aged man was likely the dealer and the youth his customer.'

The Phantom Lady

Drugs?

The word came as a shock to Kaede.

'You're saying the young man was a drug addict?'

'Think back to how Iwata-sensei described the victim. He said that the young man's neck was drenched in sweat. Excessive sweating, even in the dead of winter, that's a tell-tale symptom of methamphetamine addiction.'

'Yes, I've heard of that. But isn't it unusual to conduct a drug deal in such an open location?'

'No, that's precisely why they chose it. The area under a large bridge is ideal for those kinds of transactions. Easy to arrange a meeting, good visibility and plenty of escape routes if anyone suspicious shows up. Hiding in plain sight, as they say. Do you remember that news story about marijuana being openly cultivated on the bank of the T— river? I don't believe it was a coincidence that a police officer showed up so conveniently right after this stabbing. They'd probably been patrolling the area in response to rumours of drug dealing around the bridges. The police aren't fools. While they may suspect Iwata-sensei, they're probably still keeping open the possibility of a drug deal gone wrong.'

That made sense. It explained why police had shown up without being called.

'Now, with that hypothesis in mind, let's consider the identity of Walking Mama.'

Finally, the crux of the matter . . .

Kaede leaned closer to be sure of catching every single word.

'Earlier I said that the key to this case lay with what Walking Mama was carrying.'

'The colourful hand towel.'

'Well, that's partly correct, but also partly incorrect. The crucial element is what was hidden inside that towel.'

'Eh?'

'It wasn't mineral water or a sports drink under there. It was a can of beer or chu-hi. She was an alcoholic who couldn't be a moment without a drink. In other words, this case is a story of two different addictions – drug addiction and alcoholism.'

'But that's . . . She seemed so—'

'You mean she didn't seem like an alcoholic? Think back to when you first met her. When she spoke to Iwata-sensei, didn't she cover her mouth with both hands?'

Ah!

The voice of recognition cried out inside her head.

'Why would she use both hands to cover her mouth rather than just the one? There's only one reason: to hide the smell of alcohol. I have to say, Kaede, I'd have expected you to pick up on that one by yourself.'

Grandfather's smile held a hint of mischief.

'After all, didn't you enjoy a can of beer the other day

The Phantom Lady

after giving up on your training? Surely the alcohol connection should have crossed your mind?'

Ugh. Wow, that's really embarrassing.

She had after all downed two whole cans of beer that day.

'But why was she walking so energetically?' Kaede protested. 'Power-walking with her elbows at right angles and her arms swinging that way?'

'She was likely putting on a show in front of Iwata-sensei. Maybe she even had a little crush on him.'

'Then what about the elderly couple with the dog and the man in the track jacket?'

'I'm sure they knew her, but not as the healthy Walking Mama. To them, she was a woman with an alcohol problem who often staggered along the promenade. The same goes for the people in the nearby shopping area. They probably all knew her as the local alcoholic, but knew nothing about any power-walker.'

Kaede still had doubts.

'Even if that's all true, why did she witness the whole incident but still leave the scene without calling an ambulance?'

'Because she had no choice. She had a very compelling reason.'

Grandfather took a long 'drink' of his Gauloise. The tip glowed bright.

'She was either in the middle of divorce mediation, or

recently divorced. Probably in a custody battle with the father of her child. Her alcohol dependency would have been the central issue. Unless she quit drinking she would lose custody. That's why every Saturday morning she was headed to a hospital that offered outpatient treatment for alcoholism.'

'I see. That explains why she was out walking on Saturday mornings.'

'On the day of the incident, she was on her way home from the hospital. Maybe she was heading home before picking up her child from daycare. However, she couldn't help buying some kind of alcohol, perhaps at a convenience store near the station, and ended up drinking as she walked. Alcoholism is a frightening disease – sometimes you can't even last a ten-minute walk home without a drink. And that was when she witnessed the stabbing.'

'And if she got involved, it would have been discovered that she'd been drinking.'

'There's likely another reason she didn't come forward later. The key is the torrential rain that fell right after the stabbing. This is again speculation, but perhaps she rushed home, and despite having been drinking, drove to pick up her child. That meant she was drink-driving, all the more reason she couldn't go to the police to testify.'

Admittedly it was just speculation, but at the same time plausible. Walking Mama would surely have come forward

The Phantom Lady

unless there was a risk of something serious such as being arrested for drink-driving.

It was time for the crucial question.

'Grandpa, how do we find her?'

'Simple. Search for a hospital offering outpatient treatment for alcoholism within three or four stops from the station nearest the riverwalk. Since she goes there by train, it'll be somewhere without parking, likely a small clinic.'

Rather reluctantly, Grandfather exhaled the last of his cigarette smoke.

'Next Saturday morning she'll be there.'

The Gauloise burned out.

'I can see her,' Grandfather said. 'Sitting in the waiting room. Such a kind face – she looks a bit like Sanae. Her child means everything to her. It's her reason for living. And when she thinks about Iwata-sensei, she's tortured with guilt.'

It was such a beautiful day outside. Kaede took her grandfather's hand and they sat side by side on the *engawa* veranda, just like they used to.

'Kaede, look!'

Grandfather pointed west, into the clear winter sky.

'Kaede? See those three clouds over there? Can you use those clouds to weave a tale?'

Unlike the past, there wasn't a single cloud in the sky. But Kaede began her tale anyway.

'The one on the left is you when you were young, Grandpa. The middle one is Dad when he was young. And the one on the right is Mum when she was young.'

The winter air turned each breath into a palpable reminder of loss. Every breath she drew, the chill of sorrow; every breath she expelled, a white cloud of grief.

She deeply regretted her choice to cast her parents as characters in her tale.

8

It was a weekend evening.

Shiki had invited Kaede to celebrate with him at a chain restaurant.

'Sorry for the sudden invitation,' Shiki said. 'My shift got cancelled. Well, cheers!'

It seemed he'd already downed a few beers before Kaede got there. His lightly flushed face made him look childish and a lot more than just two years her junior.

'*The night was young, and so was he.*'

The famous opening line of the mystery *Phantom Lady* flashed through Kaede's mind.

The Phantom Lady

'It's such great news about Iwata-senpai, isn't it? They found the woman at the clinic, and she agreed to testify. And that young kid who was in critical condition regained consciousness and can now give his own statement.'

As Kaede's grandfather had predicted, it turned out the stabbing had stemmed from a drug-related dispute. Iwata was scheduled to be released Monday morning.

'So, Kaede-sensei?' Shiki began, rather awkwardly. 'There's something I want to give to you. With a name that means maple, I'm going to guess your birthday is sometime in the autumn, so it's kinda late, but here's a present for you.'

He casually placed an unwrapped book on the table.

It was the collection of sci-fi short stories by Robert F. Young entitled *The Dandelion Girl*.

Kaede had never told Shiki the story of receiving this same book from her grandfather at her primary school graduation. It was pure coincidence.

'It's the only translated novel I really like. It's about a girl with dandelion-coloured hair who travels across time and space to meet the man she loves, despite the risk of ending up all alone in the world. I figured you probably already knew it, but this new Japanese translation came out and I thought you might like it. Nice cover design, don't you think?'

Looking at the familiar title, Kaede expected to feel joy,

but instead she felt a stinging behind her eyes. After thanking him, she posed a question, her voice trembling slightly.

'Shiki, what do you think is the saddest four-kanji character idiom in the Japanese language?'

'Huh?'

Caught off guard by the question, Shiki froze mid-motion, his fingers halfway through his hair.

She didn't wait for him to reply.

'I believe it's that phrase, *ten gai ko doku* – all alone in the world.'

'You see . . .'

The dam burst, and all her words and feelings finally poured out.

'Once Grandpa is gone, I'll be all alone in the world.'

'Oh, come on!' said Shiki with a rather strained smile. 'You're taking turns with your mother to care for him, aren't you?'

'No. Grandpa just believes that's how it is.'

Don't cry. Hold it together . . .

'On my mother's wedding day, she was already pregnant with me. They had planned to get married in a small chapel in the woods, her with her big belly and all.'

'Planned to?'

'Right. But the moment that Mum took Grandpa's arm to walk down the aisle, a man with a knife leaped out from behind a tree. He screamed, "Why did you abandon

The Phantom Lady

me?" and stabbed my mother in the chest before running away.'

A cold rain had begun to patter on the windows.

'They say that in an instant her white wedding dress turned crimson. Grandpa just sat there in shock, cradling her. Mum died a week later, but miraculously I managed to survive inside her.'

Shiki remained completely motionless.

'When I was in junior high school, Dad passed away from cancer. Right before he died, he told me the whole story of what happened to my mum. Ever since then I've been afraid of men, and I haven't been able to wear white any more.'

She glanced at the cover illustration of *The Dandelion Girl* – a girl in a white dress.

'Since my grandfather developed dementia, he sees not only visions of my mother, but also hallucinations of me covered in blood. But of course, it's not me in those visions – it's Mum when she was young. But how can I explain that to him?'

It was too much. Kaede's eyes blurred with tears.

'I'm sorry, Shiki. None of this has anything to do with you.'

'No, please tell me more.'

Shiki's expression was serious, his fingers laced together, elbows resting on the table.

'Where should I begin? Well, I've only ever talked back

to my darling grandpa twice in my life. The first was when my father's cancer came back. That was shortly before he died.'

It was time for Kaede to share the secret she had kept locked in her heart.

That day too there was a cold rain falling.

Kaede, dressed in her school uniform, sat in her father's hospital room. It was heavy with the smell of various medications.

'Ah, I'd almost forgotten – you're turning fifteen soon. Practically a grown-up,' her father had said, tears in his eyes at that simple thought.

Having already survived Stage IV cancer once, its recurrence now required a level of resignation and acceptance. That's how it was back then.

'What would you like for your birthday?'

Her father lay on the bed, his emaciated body covered in tubes, but the painkillers seemed to have allowed him to speak with more strength than of late.

Kaede started to say that she didn't want anything, that she just wanted him to get better, but then a thought crossed her mind. If she asked for something specific it might give him a reason to hold on until her birthday, so she requested a brand-name scarf.

The Phantom Lady

'Consider it done,' he said, then turned to his daughter with a resolute expression. 'That aside, there's something I need to tell you while I still can.'

He coughed before going on.

'It's about your mother, who you heard died of illness. I'm sorry this will be a heavy burden for you to carry, Kaede, but it can't stay hidden for ever. Eventually you're going to hear about it some way or other.'

And then her father began to tell her the story, beginning with how he and Kaede's mother had first met.

How he had met Sanae in the cancer ward when he was a patient there, and she was his nurse.

How Kaede's grandfather had strongly opposed their marriage at first, pessimistic about their having a future.

And then . . .

How on their wedding day, her mother had been stabbed to death by a stalker. And that the assailant had fled the scene and never been caught.

How in the emergency ward her mother had briefly regained consciousness and although no sound came out, her lips had formed the word 'baby'.

And finally . . .

How until her mother finally passed, her grandfather had made a daily pilgrimage to the guardian deity at the shrine in Himonya to perform the *o-hyakudo mairi* walking ritual.

Kaede waited for her tears to subside before asking, 'What's the *o-hyakudo mairi*?'

'It means praying to the gods one hundred times. It involves walking one hundred times between the shrine gate and the main hall. Your grandpa tried to keep it a secret but it seems someone in the neighbourhood saw him.'

Even as a junior high schooler Kaede was surprised that her normally logical grandfather had turned to divine intervention. But that made his actions all the more poignant.

But then if that was the case . . .

Kaede began to get angry. And this led her to blurt out some questions that she would have been better off never asking. Looking back now, it was possible she had wanted to distract herself from her father's illness and instead had taken out her frustrations on her grandfather.

'Why does Grandpa only care about Mum? Why doesn't he ever come to the hospital to visit you, Dad?'

Putting it into words only seemed to fuel her anger more, and her shoulders in their school uniform began to shake.

'Is it because you're not related by blood? Or because he was against your marriage? Or is it . . .'

She couldn't stop herself.

'Or is it because he's already given up? Is he afraid of seeing how thin you've got?'

'Kaede, stop it! Now!'

The Phantom Lady

Her father spoke with more force than he had been able to muster all day.

'I won't tolerate any badmouthing of your grandfather. This conversation is over.'

'But—'

'I'm a bit tired now, and I could do with a nap. I'll ask your Grandpa to get the scarf for you. Of course, I'll pay—'

'I don't want a scarf!' Kaede had yelled, running out of the hospital room.

Late that night, after the rain had stopped, her grandfather finally came home. Kaede was waiting for him in the entranceway, ready to unleash all her fury on him.

'Grandpa, you're so cruel!'

'What? Where did this come from all of a sudden?'

'Why do you never come to the hospital? I know you're busy being a school principal and all that, but it's just heartless of you. Maybe he's nothing to you, like a stranger, but he's my only father. And he has hardly any time left; he's running out of time . . .'

Grandfather stood in the entranceway to the house, stunned.

Kaede ignored his reaction, racing upstairs and letting her head collapse onto her desk.

It was the first time she had ever raised her voice at her beloved grandfather.

———

A few days later, the doctor told her that the next two or three days would be critical. Kaede's tears had long since run dry.

It was early evening, and wanting to avoid the awkwardness of facing her grandfather, Kaede made a deliberate detour on her way home from school, taking a road she never normally walked down. With the local fire station on her left, she ascended a gentle slope. Traditional old houses lined the right side of the street, while on the left the trees of Hachimangu Shrine stood lush and green.

She remembered climbing this slope many times as a child, holding her father's hand. The landscapes of the past and the present overlapped in her mind, like a traced drawing. The only difference was her slightly higher vantage point.

And of course, Dad isn't with me any more . . .

When she reached the top of the hill, the trees parted like a gateway to reveal an engraved stone pillar marking the side entrance to the guardian shrine.

She peeked into the grounds . . . to see her grandfather wearing a rather grubby white shirt. He was pacing backwards and forwards countless times between the torii gate and the shrine's main hall. His feet slapped the ground as he strode with fierce determination.

Kaede could sense in those footsteps his desperation and rage at the injustice of the world and his own powerlessness.

The Phantom Lady

Hidden behind a tree, she watched and felt ashamed that she'd raised her voice at him. Instead of the hospital, he'd been here all along, offering his hundred prayers to the gods.

After speaking to her father, she'd researched the *o-hyakudo mairi* ritual, and learned that it was a ritual walk performed to accumulate favour, and that it was imperative that it was done in secret.

Kaede poked her head out from behind her tree and watched her grandfather some more. Even from a distance she could tell that his expression was filled with fury.

'Damn it!' he shouted, words that seemed alien to the grandfather she knew. 'Damn it!' Over and over again.

He was crying with rage.

Her father's death came slightly earlier than the doctor had predicted. He passed later that night.

Whoa!

The sudden blare of a car horn outside the restaurant yanked Kaede back into the present. Shiki, on the other hand, didn't react, his gaze fixed downwards on the table.

'After learning the truth about my mother, I couldn't bear to read mysteries any more, even though I loved them so much. It took about three years before I was able to pick one up again.'

No, it was a full four years . . .

'At some point it hit me – mysteries are beautiful precisely because they are works of fiction, taking place in made-up worlds. And as I started reading again, I began to convince myself that what had happened to my mother was also something from a made-up world. Perhaps that's escapism. Maybe it's a twisted way of thinking. But you know . . .'

If you weave it, it's all a tale.

Everything that happens in the world is a story.

It's beautiful precisely because it's all made up – the real world, as well as mysteries, science fiction, even theatre.

'I thought maybe you would understand, Shiki. Even a little.'

Was he listening? She couldn't tell. He remained silent, his head down.

But Kaede kept on talking anyway.

The second time she had talked back to her grandfather . . . it was just the other day.

Summoning her courage, Kaede had managed to voice something she had been contemplating for a while.

The Phantom Lady

'Hey, Grandpa, there's something I'd like to discuss with you.'

'Yes?'

'Would you consider moving in with me? I've seen a nice property nearby – a bigger apartment.'

'I truly appreciate the thought,' Grandfather replied in a gentle voice, but Kaede could already hear the refusal in his tone.

'But then, I wouldn't be known as Master Himonya any more, would I?'

'Is that really—'

'I've told you before. The eighth Katsura Bunraku was known as Kuromon-cho. Hayashiya Hikoroku was Inari-cho, and—'

'Ko-san was called Meguro and Shincho was Yarai-cho. Yeah, I got it,' Kaede snapped back.

Grandfather's face briefly registered shock. Then an awkward silence filled the study.

Thanks to her grandfather's constant mention of these Showa-era *rakugo* storytellers, their names and location-based nicknames were ingrained in Kaede's memory. But it was the sharpness of Kaede's reaction that had seemed to surprise and slightly wound him.

Steeling herself, Kaede had pressed on.

'But, Grandpa, does it really matter what people call you?'

She'd almost added, 'You're just at home all day, anyway,' but managed to stop herself.

'I worry about you,' she said instead. 'I want to be able to take care of you, to be together.'

'I'm sorry, Kaede.'

A series of shadows crossed Grandfather's face. He seemed to be moved by his granddaughter's offer but at the same time pained at having to refuse.

'I feel bad, Kaede, but I really love it here in Himonya. I love the voices of the preschoolers, the sparrows that flit over from the bamboo grove in the park, and the cherry blossom petals that drift here on the breeze from the grounds of the shrine. I love this tiny garden always swarming with insects, and I love the lingering scent of my wife in the house, even though it gets fainter as the years pass. Perhaps that's why she's not in my hallucinations much any more, even though I long to see her. My only "son" – your father, who used to be my best drinking buddy – rarely shows up any more either. Still, there's the cherry tree he planted for me in the garden, and the chest of drawers that my wife used; her sewing machine; her dresser that you use these days too, Kaede. I watch you sitting there at that mirror and I feel perfectly content.'

Every word was a punch in the heart. He'd never told her that he'd been hoping for visions of her grandmother and her father to appear.

The Phantom Lady

'So then let me come and live here with you, Grandpa.'

'You should live in your own place, Kaede.'

His face was as serious as her father's had been back then.

'Old folks shouldn't steal precious time from the young. Thankfully, Sanae visits me every day. And when the time comes that I can't get around by myself any more, or if my mind completely goes, I'll move into a suitable facility. I've already made the arrangements, so there's no need for you to worry.'

Then Grandfather flashed her one of his smiles, the kind that in his younger days must have earned him the reputation of a charmer.

'Sorry for the long story. That's all,' said Kaede, wrapping it up on a cheerful note.

At which, Shiki, who had been silent the whole way through, finally spoke, his voice low.

'Sounds like one of those boring translations.'

'What?'

His face was completely concealed behind his long hair, but something was slowly dripping onto the tablecloth.

Shiki glanced up at the window, which was being pelted by the rain. Then he put his head back down, and with both hands roughly rubbed at his eyes.

'I'm sorry. I didn't know about any of that.'

'That's OK.'

'I just casually threw around words like "all alone in the world".'

'It's fine.'

'I didn't even know until recently that Iwata-senpai had no living family.'

Shiki's voice trembled as much as Kaede's own.

'And here I am still living off my parents.'

The sound of Shiki sniffling filled the now-empty restaurant.

'I've been skipping my job and focusing on acting.'

'What's wrong with that? You're such a wonderful performer, Shiki.'

'Hey, Kaede-sensei?'

Shiki suddenly looked up and met her eyes.

'Do you remember that famous line from *The Dandelion Girl*?'

'Of course.'

'*Day before yesterday I saw a rabbit* . . .' he began.

Kaede took it up.

'*And yesterday a deer* . . .'

'*And* . . .

Their eyes met as they finished the quotation in unison.

'. . . *today, you.*'

There was a beat and then they caught each other's eyes

again, and burst out laughing. Or in truth, they might have been crying their hearts out.

'I didn't think I was going to say this today,' Shiki mumbled.

Then –

'Kaede-sensei, it's not only the day before yesterday, yesterday and today. I've been in love with you since the first time we met.'

Chapter 6:
The Riddle of the Stalker

1

I'm not alone,
Together we are one.
But I'm still alone,
Desperate to become two.
Just thinking about it
Makes the day slip by.

Iwata invited Kaede and Shiki to his home for drinks to celebrate his acquittal, along with his class's victory in the school cross country competition.

'It's tradition for other people to make these kinds of arrangements for you,' Shiki pointed out.

'Shut up,' Iwata retorted, as he placed a dish of his homemade cooking on the low table in the tiny living room.

It's much better with the three of us here, Kaede thought, rather relieved.

The night of Shiki's sudden confession, he'd clarified, 'I'm not asking you to go out with me or anything. I just wanted you to know how I feel.'

Ever since, there had been an awkwardness between them, making Kaede uneasy to be alone with Shiki. Even now, sitting at the low table in Iwata's living room, she hadn't been able to meet his eyes even once. Shiki, too, seemed self-conscious, seeking refuge in his drink and likewise avoiding Kaede's gaze. Iwata seemed blissfully unaware of the tension in the room. Right now, he was explaining the art of making braised pork belly.

'The trick is to use the water you washed the rice in for the initial boiling,' he said with clear pride. 'It gets rid of the gamey smell of the meat.'

As not much of a cook herself, Kaede couldn't help being impressed. Steam rose from the succulent-looking pork, making Shiki's eyes widen.

'That looks amazing!'

'Right? And another trick is . . .'

As Iwata's recipe brag continued, Kaede gave Iwata's apartment a surreptitious once-over. It would be a lie to say she wasn't curious; after all this was her first time in a single man's apartment.

It was about twenty minutes' walk from Idogaya station on the Keikyu Line. The wooden building must have been over fifty years old, and the aged metal staircase had groaned

The Riddle of the Stalker

audibly under the weight of the three of them as they climbed up to his door.

'I'd like to move somewhere bigger and newer, but my landlady just doesn't want to let me go,' Iwata had explained, oddly cheerful.

Glancing over at a wall where bits of the interior plaster were chipping away, Kaede noticed several large-size message cards known as *yosegaki*, arranged in perfect rows.

Thank you, Gan-chan Sensei, from all of Year 2 Class 1

She knew that Iwata loved his nickname 'Gan-chan', derived from the alternative *on-yomi* reading of the 'Iwa' of Iwata.

Hope you get a girlfriend soon, Gan-chan! – from Year 5 Class 4

She smiled at the friendly teasing tone.

We love you, Gan-chan Sensei – Year 1 Class 3

Each message was written in the centre of the card in bold marker pen, and surrounded by concentric circles of endearingly clumsy signatures.

Kaede had her own treasured message card from her

homeroom class – from 'Harry' and the others – but so far only one. Having so many cards on his wall spoke volumes about Iwata's popularity at school.

But then her eye was caught by the message card at the far end. There was something different about that one. It was yellowed – clearly much older than the others – and the handwriting at its centre was far too sophisticated to have been written by a primary school pupil. When she realized why, Kaede felt a twinge of regret for having been so nosy.

Congratulations to our big brother on getting into university. Keep chasing your dreams, Gan-chan!

Beneath these words was the name of the orphanage where Iwata had grown up.

'When making gyoza filling, you need to chop the cabbage and the garlic chives roughly so they have a bit of texture. And the secret ingredient is miso . . .'

Iwata was still going on about his cooking.

'Senpai, this is really boring,' Shiki grumbled. 'Can't we just eat?'

Pork belly and gyoza – meat on top of meat – was the quintessential single man's home cooking menu, but Kaede found herself looking forward to it.

Her grandfather had always told her that you could learn a lot about a person by looking at their bookshelves. Kaede

The Riddle of the Stalker

glanced guiltily over at what appeared to be Iwata's makeshift bookshelf – a couple of plywood storage cubes. Beside the complete collection of *Cooking Papa* were heavily bookmarked study guides for the primary school teaching certification.

She understood the feeling of not being able to throw such things away. In Iwata's case, there must have been challenges and hardships she couldn't begin to imagine.

The next storage cube held an impressive array of DVDs, including the full series of The Avengers, Fast & Furious and The Terminator.

Noticing Kaede's wandering gaze, Shiki, who had finally managed to get some food, paused with his chopsticks in mid-air.

'Whoa! The Iwata Cinematic Collection – an impressive array you've got there!'

'What are you saying?'

'Well, I'm saying such a line-up of mindless action movies is quite the spectacle in its own right.'

'Are you taking the piss?'

Iwata glared at Shiki, his expression genuinely indignant.

'Listen, movies are best when they open with a bang,' he argued, 'have a ra-ta-tat-tat fight scene along the way, then end with a satisfying whoosh where everything is resolved.'

'Well, first of all, that's way too many sound effects. And second, way too narrow a point of view.'

'Oh, come on, aren't mysteries the same? Doesn't their appeal come from the way everything is all neatly wrapped up at the end?'

'Not necessarily. There's a particular subgenre of mysteries known as the "riddle story" which ends without any solution.'

For a moment, Kaede thought she caught Shiki glance her way.

Riddle stories . . .

A unique style that left the ending to the reader's imagination. A challenge for authors, because if poorly constructed there was a danger of ending up leaving the reader hanging. The Japanese idiom for that sense was 'a cut-tailed dragonfly'.

I wonder whether that's an actual species of dragonfly. I ought to google it later . . .

While she'd been lost in these thoughts, Shiki had launched into one of his lectures.

'Even though I can't stand translated mysteries, when it comes to riddle stories, it's impossible to ignore Frank R. Stockton's "The Lady, or the Tiger?" It's a piece of nineteenth-century classic literature – not exactly a mystery, so I don't think it'd hurt to give a few spoilers. But of course, if you don't want to hear it, Senpai, I'll stop there. Go ahead and make some more gyoza.'

'No need to be like that. Tell me what it's about . . .

The Riddle of the Stalker

although I think I'll make some more gyoza anyway,' said Iwata, heading for the kitchen.

Shiki raised his voice so Iwata would be able to hear.

'All right then, I'll take you right through to the ending,' he began in his rich baritone.

'Once upon a time, in a land far away, there was a young man who began a forbidden romance with a princess, the king's only daughter. When the king found out, the young man was subjected to a terrible trial. In the middle of a packed arena there were two doors, and he was forced to choose one of them. Behind one of the doors was the fairest maiden in the kingdom. If he chose that door, the king would pardon him, and he would take her as his bride. Behind the other door was the fiercest and hungriest tiger in the kingdom. The young man looks up in desperation at his lover, the princess, who is watching in the audience. Yes, the princess knew which door was which.'

'Interesting. And then?'

From the kitchen came the appetizing sizzle of water hitting the gyoza pan.

'The princess is torn by an unbearable dilemma,' Shiki continued. 'Needless to say, she doesn't want her lover to be devoured by a tiger. But at the same time, she can't stand the thought of him marrying a woman more beautiful than herself. The princess agonizes over the decision but then finally makes her choice. She subtly gestures to the door on the right. And so . . .'

After a dramatic pause, Shiki continued.

'Which came out of the opened door – the lady, or the tiger? The story ends by posing this question to the reader.'

'Huh? You call that a spoiler?'

Iwata tipped the gyoza rather too aggressively out onto a plate.

'What's that about? It's just weird, leaving things hanging like that. I mean, that wasn't even a spoiler. There's nothing to spoil!'

'And that's what makes it fascinating. Don't you see the appeal of this device?'

Still without making eye contact, Shiki steered the conversation towards Kaede.

'Kaede-sensei, I bet you know lots of mysteries inspired by that one.'

'Not that many, really. About the only one I can think of is "The Lady and the Tiger" by Jack Moffitt.'

Shiki, being more familiar with Japanese authors, picked up where Kaede left off.

'Then there's Reitaro Kada's "The Lady or the Watermelon".'

'What kind of choice is that?' Iwata chimed in. 'A watermelon? It's not even scary!'

'And Jiro Ikushima's "The Man or the Bear".'

The Riddle of the Stalker

'Lose-lose scenario, whichever comes out,' grumbled Iwata.

'Read them before you start criticizing,' Shiki retorted, sounding like the reasonable one for once. 'All of these spin-offs are well-regarded classics. It shows how captivating the original conundrum of "The Lady, or the Tiger?" was. Does the princess's love prevail, or does jealousy triumph? The lady, or the tiger? Doesn't it become more difficult to solve, the more you think about it?'

'No,' Iwata said. 'If you think about it rationally, you'll have the answer in a second.'

'Eh?'

'I can say with absolute certainty that it was the lady who came out of that door.'

'Huh? How can you be so sure? What's your reasoning?'

The look on Shiki's face said that he was expecting some nonsensical explanation.

'You've already decided that I can't think logically, haven't you?' Iwata complained, cracking open his can of chu-hi with a sharp pop. 'All right, here's my explanation. First, let me make sure of something. This arena was packed with spectators, right?'

'That's correct. I seem to remember in the story that there was a sizeable crowd outside the arena too, of people who hadn't managed to get seats.'

'And they all knew why the young man was being subjected to this trial?'

'Of course. They all came to see the tragic outcome of his love affair with the princess.'

'Then it follows that it must have been the lady who emerged from the door.'

'Why does it follow?'

'Patience. Don't rush me . . . The first thing to consider is the princess's state of mind. It's a mistake to limit it to two possibilities: love or jealousy. Human psychology isn't that simple. I'm convinced there was another factor.'

'And what's that?'

There was an oddly sombre look in Iwata's eyes.

'Self-preservation.'

After another swig of his chu-hi, he continued.

'At the moment of decision, the crowd would naturally be watching every move of not just the young man, but the princess too, as she is also a key player in the drama. The young man looks up at the princess; and she, after much deliberation, discreetly signals towards one of the doors. But here's the thing; in a crowd of that size, someone was bound to notice that gesture. After all, she's sitting right there among them.'

'I see. So that's what you mean,' said Shiki, catching on. He gave a knowing smile and nibbled on his thumbnail. 'Like how a catcher reads the batter's movements to

The Riddle of the Stalker

plan the next pitch. That's a very "you" point of view, Senpai.'

However, Kaede was dubious.

'Hold on, Iwata-sensei. I think there's probably a full translation online.'

She checked her phone.

'Yep, here it is. In the story it clearly states, *No one but her lover saw her. Every eye but his was fixed on the man in the arena.* So according to the author himself, shouldn't we accept that all the spectators were focused on the young man, and missed the princess's gesture completely?'

'No, that's not quite true.'

Rather surprisingly, it was Shiki who had spoken. He swirled his empty highball glass, making its one remaining ice cube clink. The rapidly shrinking ice was like the young man trapped in the glass fishbowl of that arena.

'Even if we accept Stockton's claim that all eyes were on the young man, wouldn't the spectators naturally follow his gaze when he looked up at the princess? They'd be curious about her reaction.'

Shiki looked down at the ice bucket as he added more ice to his glass. He smiled, managing to look simultaneously both feminine and childlike.

'You both just followed my gaze to the ice bucket, didn't you?' he said. 'When someone suddenly looks in a different direction, people are instinctively drawn to follow that gaze.

I did the same earlier when Kaede-sensei was looking at the bookshelf.'

He gestured towards the storage cube filled with DVDs.

Desperately trying to avoid direct eye contact, Kaede fixed her own gaze on the vicinity of Shiki's forehead.

'Yes, that makes sense, psychologically speaking,' she said. 'But then, why would Stockton deliberately create a contradiction by writing, *No one but her lover saw her. Every eye but his was fixed on the man in the arena*? Technically then, that was a lie.'

'Unless,' said Shiki, bringing his delicate, feminine fingers to rest on his sharp jawline, 'those lines weren't narration after all, but rather the princess's internal narrative. She must have thought, or likely wanted to believe "nobody has noticed my gesture"; "everyone's surely watching him". In other words, that passage was Stockton's devilish trap to mislead readers. It's as if he deliberately omitted phrases like "the princess believed that . . ." or "the princess desperately hoped that . . ." from this part of the text.'

No way . . .

Kaede gasped at the revelation.

'Narrative trickery.'

'Exactly. If Stockton deliberately designed the story so that readers would confuse perception with reality, "The Lady, or the Tiger?" isn't merely a riddle story, but arguably the world's first narrative mystery. If you read this section as the princess's perspective and analyse it carefully, there's only one conclusion.'

This was a completely new interpretation. To think that this story, famous for being both the original and quintessential riddle story, the nineteenth-century classic 'The Lady, or the Tiger?', was a narrative mystery with a trick embedded in the text.

'Shiki!' Iwata raised his voice impatiently. 'You've left me hanging here. I wasn't done explaining.'

'Sorry for the interruption out of left field. Senpai, please go on.'

'OK, for now we can agree that at least some of the spectators would have noticed the princess's gesture?'

Kaede and Shiki both nodded.

'More than a couple of spectators would have noticed the princess's covert signal. We might be talking about dozens or even hundreds of people catching on. Picture this: the princess points to the door with the tiger, leading to the young man being killed and eaten. Sure, the spectators might get their cruel spectacle, their bloodthirsty desires satisfied for a fleeting moment. But you know what? It wouldn't take long for the whispers to spread. "The princess went mad with jealousy and fed her lover to the tiger!" "I saw her give him a signal." "I saw it too!" "What a terrible woman."'

'And probably only a matter of time before total revolution,' Shiki agreed.

Iwata seemed happy with this nod of approval, and continued to expound his theory.

'The princess was an only child, you said? In other words, she will have to marry a prince or a nobleman and become queen someday. A woman in that position would never risk feeding her lover to a tiger. She'd lose the trust of the people completely. Powerful people always look out for themselves first. Logically, the princess could only point to the door with the lady behind it. That must be the ending that this . . . what's his name again? . . . Stocking?'

'I knew you were going to say that at least once,' said Shiki with a roll of his eyes. 'It's Stockton.'

'Right, right. This Stockton guy – that must be the ending he was thinking of.'

Wow, Iwata-sensei. You're beginning to sound a bit like Grandpa . . .

Kaede had to admit his logic was quite – no, very – compelling. 'The Lady, or the Tiger?' turned out to be a mystery where the 'truth' had been predetermined all along. She was impressed.

At the same time though she was bothered by something Iwata had said: 'Powerful people always look out for themselves first.' There was a bleakness to the phrase that didn't sound like Iwata at all. Perhaps in the past he'd been the victim of someone else's selfish actions.

'Well, Senpai, I've gained new respect for you,' said Shiki,

The Riddle of the Stalker

setting down his chopsticks to applaud Iwata. Although if I may add something . . . There's absolutely no need for the princess to feed the man to the tiger right away. She could easily wait until he married the beautiful woman and then quietly command her servants to take him out.'

'Seriously?' said Iwata with a look of exasperation. 'Why do you always insist on going down the darkest route? Nobody wants to see a young man get eaten by a tiger. There's no satisfying whoosh of an ending there.'

'But that's not the point of the story. It's—'

'This is why mystery fans are such a pain. Right, mystery talk is banned for the rest of today. Eat more! And go and read *Cooking Papa*.'

Kaede caught Shiki's eye, and burst out laughing. It was the first time they had made eye contact all evening.

Kaede appreciated that Iwata had prepared garlic-free gyoza, probably taking into account that she'd be travelling home on the train and wouldn't want to inconvenience other passengers. By the time the perfectly salted edamame were all eaten, Kaede was also out of the lighter alcoholic drink that Iwata had got in for her.

'I guess I should be going,' she said, starting to get to her feet. But Iwata jumped up to stop her.

'Please stay a little longer. Hey, Shiki, let's go and get some more alcohol.'

'Eh? Do I have to go too?' Shiki moaned, but he stood up immediately and put on his jacket, possibly relieved not to be left alone with Kaede.

'OK then, just a little longer,' Kaede agreed. 'I'll pay you back later.'

'My treat!' said Iwata and Shiki together.

Glaring at each other, the two left to go shopping. Kaede listened to the sound of their footsteps descending the metal staircase, a rhythmic clanking in perfect unison.

They really do have that pitcher–catcher synchronicity.

Smiling, Kaede stood up and went towards the kitchen to get a start on the dishes. That was when she noticed something odd. On the bottom shelf of the storage cube, below all the DVDs, there was one single item prominently displayed. Judging by the absence of dust around it, it must have been placed there quite recently.

It was a baseball resting on top of three bats, arranged to point in alternate directions.

That must be the ball that Shiki brought him at the detention centre . . .

It had become Iwata's treasured possession.

Although she knew she shouldn't, she peered again at the old, yellowed card on the wall.

In that instant a lingering question was finally answered

The Riddle of the Stalker

for her. It concerned the reason that Iwata took an hour-long train ride every Saturday morning just to run along one specific riverbank. There was no doubt that it was an excellent spot for jogging, but if his sole purpose was to go for a pleasant run, then there must have been plenty of suitable locations closer to home.

Why there?

Well, now she knew the reason. Or, she should say, had stumbled upon the reason.

The name of the children's home written on the congratulations card began with the name of the town where it was located. It was the same area as that riverbank promenade.

Every week Iwata-sensei would go for a run along the riverside area he'd known since childhood. Then he probably retrieved his belongings from the train station locker and went to visit the younger children at the orphanage.

And then probably . . .

. . . No, for sure.

He brings them homemade sweets. What he brings to school on a Monday must be what's left over . . .

Her eyes drifted to Iwata's apron, hanging by the sink. It was old and hand-sewn, its seams so frayed it was about to fall apart. As she'd guessed, the words 'Gan-chan, our big brother' were embroidered onto it.

Nicknames tended to stick with you, no matter how

many years pass. Even now, the staff and the children of the orphanage probably called him 'Gan-chan'.

Iwata wasn't 'all alone in the world' at all. He had lots of little brothers and sisters.

And me too. I'm not alone either. I have my Grandpa.
And . . . And . . .

Maybe it was the alcohol, but Kaede could feel her face growing warm. She picked up her glass. There was nothing but melting ice left in it, but she brought it to her lips anyway and let the cold water pour down her dry throat.

Just then her phone vibrated violently on the table.

Checking what I want? At this point as long as it's alcohol I'll drink anything.

But the caller ID was 'public call box'.

Must be one of the two guys. They've forgotten their phones.

She swiped to answer.

'Look, I'll let you choose which brand to get,' she said right away. 'I don't know much about those kinds of drinks.'

Was it Iwata or Shiki?

Shiki or Iwata?

But the person on the other end said nothing.

Surely not . . .

She was instantly sober, and cold sweat began to run down her neck. She ran to the window, opening the curtain a crack to peer outside.

'Hello.'

The Riddle of the Stalker

It was the first time she'd ever heard the voice of the 'other party', but it sounded altered, no doubt run through a voice changer. It was a mechanical voice like the ones she often heard on video sites, that made neither age nor gender possible to determine.

'Kaede-sensei?'

She remained silent, her eyes fixed on the dark, one-way street in front of Iwata's apartment. Somehow her intuition told her that the caller was close by.

'Sorry to keep you waiting.'

Iwata, Shiki, where are you . . . ?

The five-metre-wide road was sparsely lit, and without moonlight it was wrapped in almost total darkness.

No – there was one spot of light.

'You must have been waiting to hear from me, Kaede-sensei.'

About a hundred metres away, just by a small park, was a phone box, faintly glowing like some kind of mirage.

She recalled a recent news article about how, thanks to the spread of mobile phones, phone boxes were close to extinction. To Kaede, this phone box was like a sinister structure from another world, or perhaps a giant creature from prehistoric times, its skin tough and metallic.

There he was. There was the person who had been making silent calls to her almost daily for months.

'Hey, are you listening to me?'

The tone had changed completely.

'You'd better not ignore me.'

Who knew a robotic voice could be this terrifying when filled with anger?

'Um . . . I . . .'

Despite Iwata and Shiki's warnings not to engage with the caller, she found herself responding.

Sorry, I can't ignore him . . . I'm scared . . .

'I'm not ignoring you. It's just that I don't know who you are, so—'

'You don't know who I am?'

A note of disbelief.

'Right. And so I'd like you to stop calling this number.'

'I'll kill you.'

Somehow the literal meaning of the phrase didn't register right away.

'I'm sorry, what did you just—'

'I'll kill you if you keep saying such heartless things.'

Her heart began to thud in her chest.

'Are you listening to me, Kaede-sensei?'

'. . . Yes.'

Her voice had turned hoarse with terror.

Please! Iwata-sensei, Shiki, come back quickly . . .

'There's no need to worry. All the preparations are complete. This call was just to let you know.'

They hung up.

The Riddle of the Stalker

From the phone box in the distance a vague shadow emerged, slowly, deliberately turning to wave in Kaede's direction, before melting back into the pitch darkness of the night. They seemed confident that at this distance and with the absence of light, neither their build, gender or age would be possible to determine.

2

I wonder what people think when they look at me.
What do they assume about my behaviour?
Do I seem too intense to them?
But that's just a misunderstanding on their part.
You would understand
I'm not that intense at all.

The next day, just after noon, Kaede's feet automatically led her in the direction of her grandfather's house.

As she passed by the guardian shrine, a sudden gust of wind stirred up the trees. She instinctively pulled her coat collar tighter.

The persistent chill she felt was not simply due to the sudden cold snap. As she'd walked from the station, she felt a creeping sense of being followed, causing her to check constantly over her shoulder.

In the end she'd found herself unable to tell Iwata and

Shiki about the phone box incident. She didn't want to be admonished for ignoring their advice not to engage with the caller. But more than that, she hadn't wanted to spoil the pleasant atmosphere.

Since then, in addition to the persistent silent calls, there was this new unpleasant sensation of being followed, which only intensified with each passing day. Kaede had tried to find ways of coping with the situation by herself. Today she was wearing the running shoes she'd bought for the school cross country training, hoping to be able to escape quickly if necessary. The shoes didn't match her coat at all, but it was a small sacrifice.

She'd also come up with a plan to deal with the phone calls. Since the stalker was using a public phone or a number without an ID, all she had to do was set her phone to reject those kinds of calls completely. For the past few days this had allowed her to breathe a little more easily.

However, as a homeroom teacher responsible for over thirty primary school children, she couldn't maintain that set-up indefinitely. The rule that all communication with teachers should go through the school was just a formality. Parents would call her mobile about some urgent matter, sometimes not realizing they were calling from a withheld number. In the case that a child was involved in some kind of accident, or a bullying incident, Kaede wanted to be sure she could be reached.

The Riddle of the Stalker

One time, Iwata had dragged her to her nearest police station, but as she'd expected, ultimately there was no concrete evidence of harm, and no way to identify the caller, so the police hadn't been able to help her.

She didn't want to cause her grandfather any unnecessary worry, but she had mentioned her concerns to him a few times, even though she knew that as someone who never left his house, there was nothing he could do for her. Yet it brought her a sense of calm when he assured her that she was probably worrying unnecessarily.

'Grandpa, I'm here!'

She almost tripped over the entrance step as she pulled off her shoes and hurried down the hallway towards the study. However, she stopped when she heard a rattling sound coming from the living room on the left.

There was a jagged feeling of unease in her chest.

He must be unwell . . .

She opened the door to find the veteran caregiver, Okappa-san, adding corn starch to a cup of green tea and stirring vigorously.

'I'm so sorry,' said Kaede. 'It's well past your scheduled hours, isn't it?'

'I'm fine,' Okappa-san replied with a smile, but Kaede couldn't help noticing there were beads of sweat on her forehead. 'I don't have a shift scheduled after this one. But more importantly, today he's not feeling very well.'

Ah, I was right after all . . .

Kaede felt rather dejected. He'd been doing so much better lately.

Patients with Lewy Body Dementia can experience extreme fluctuations in their condition, almost as if they become a totally different person, sometimes between the morning and afternoon, and even at times within the space of just an hour. When the Parkinson's-like symptoms are particularly severe, the muscles throughout the body become rigid, making it difficult for them to swallow properly. Occasionally food or drink can enter the lungs instead of the oesophagus, potentially leading to aspiration pneumonia – a life-threatening condition.

The speech therapy and throat muscle massage were supposed to help prevent such occurrences. But if her grandfather, who could normally consume food and drink without trouble, needed specially thickened tea in order to swallow, it was a sign that his condition was deteriorating.

Kaede thanked and bowed to Okappa-san, before taking the teacup and knocking gently on the study door.

'Grandpa, may I come in?'

'Uhh.' A small sound came from within, neither a clear yes or a no.

She forced a smile and opened the door. Her grandfather

was sitting in his recliner as usual, but his upper body was leaning heavily to the right.

Pisa syndrome . . .

A wave of dread washed over Kaede.

Pisa syndrome referred to a condition where a person's torso leaned to one side, reminiscent of the famous leaning tower. Grandfather's spatial awareness had dropped drastically, leading him to believe that he was in fact sitting up straight.

'Here's some warm tea. It's been thickened though.'

Without changing his expression, Grandfather shook his head slightly. This lack of expressiveness, also known as 'mask-like' face, was another characteristic of DLB patients.

Kaede wasn't even sure he recognized her. Nevertheless, she made up her mind to tell him everything about the previous day's events. She knew it might cause him worry, but she believed that in the case of her grandfather, it was beneficial to give him something to occupy his mind.

When she talked about the brand-new theory that 'The Lady, or the Tiger?' might in fact be a mystery with a predetermined answer, she thought she caught a faint smile on Grandfather's face, but perhaps it was just her imagination.

Talking of tigers . . .

She recalled how during a severe bout of hallucinations he'd told her about a blue tiger entering the study. It was undeniable – her grandfather was a dementia patient, and the stark reality cast a shadow over her heart. As if to shake this off, her speech naturally quickened.

When she recounted how her caller in the phone box had progressed from silent calls to giving her mysterious messages about preparations being complete, she thought she saw anger flicker in Grandfather's eyes, but again it could have been another trick of her mind.

Grandfather's head bobbed in a way that could either have been nods of understanding, or simply him nodding off to sleep.

What if . . . What if Grandpa stays like this?

Although generally the condition of Lewy Body Dementia patients didn't tend to deteriorate abruptly, instead fluctuating over months, weeks, or days, Kaede couldn't help but let despair take over. Carers looking after a DLB patient during a bad spell often experienced this creeping fretfulness and frustration as if grains of sand were constantly trickling, unstoppable, through their fingers. There was always the chance that the illness would advance irreversibly, leaving no way back to meaningful communication.

The doorbell chimed, followed immediately by the voice of 'Doting Father' – the speech therapist.

The Riddle of the Stalker

The golden light of dusk had begun to stream in, illuminating Grandfather's frozen face.

Oh no, perhaps I pushed him too hard . . .

Glancing at the clock on the chest of drawers she realized she'd been talking non-stop for a whole hour.

'Grandpa, I'll put away some of your winter clothes, and then I'll head home.'

Briefly she thought she saw him move a hand, perhaps in a gesture of thanks, or then again, maybe it was just a tremor caused by his Parkinson's-like symptoms.

She carefully folded several winter coats and sweaters before opening the chest drawer. Although she was worried it might be packed full, she was pleased to see there was exactly enough space for these clothes.

That's the spirit . . .

She knew it was important to appreciate even the little things. Not everything in life was bad. All that was happening right now was, in its own way, exactly as it should be.

It was too early to get out most of his spring clothes, but she did pick one item: a cardigan that was Grandfather's favourite.

The cherry blossoms around here were spectacular. Soon they'd be able to sit together just like the old days, and admire the blossoms in the shrine grounds.

Kaede picked up the hairbrush from the dresser in the

corner of the study and quickly tidied her hair, forcing herself to smile at her reflection in the mirror.

A knock at the door was followed by Doting Father's hesitant voice.

'Er . . . is it all right if I come in?'

His warm gentle voice was touching.

'Yes, of course,' Kaede called out.

'Are those your shoes at the door? They're really nice running shoes.'

'Oh no, not really.'

'I bet they'd look good on my daughter too. What do you think, Himonya-san?'

Doting Father was trying to make Grandfather laugh, but today there was no response.

Of course, there was always a way to handle things whenever a patient wasn't in good shape. Undaunted, Doting Father patted his own freshly shaven head, and with his customary cheerfulness asked, 'Well then, what shall we do today?'

Kaede had to admire the man's professionalism.

She bowed to Doting Father and rather reluctantly took her leave.

The Riddle of the Stalker

Seeing Kaede emerge from the house, the man deliberately concealed himself in the shadow of the fence.

'Kaede-sensei,' he murmured to himself.

Then, taking the usual precautions not to be seen, he began once again to follow her.

3

By the time Kaede got home to her apartment in Gumyoji, night had already fallen. She unlocked the building entrance and leaned wearily against the wall while waiting for the lift. She had the sense that her own physical condition was somehow linked with her grandfather's deterioration.

I'll take a nice long soak in the bath tonight, she thought as she stepped out of the lift. But then she noticed a strange conical object hanging from the door handle of her apartment. A scream rose up in her throat but she managed to stifle it.

Wait, what? What is . . . what the hell is that?

She cautiously approached with only the light from the lift behind her, and saw . . . a bouquet of black roses, hanging upside down from the door handle. The bouquet was wrapped in a white lacy fabric which contrasted sharply with the dark flowers. With the doorknob looking like a head at the top and the blooms spreading out downwards it bore an unsettling resemblance to a bride in her wedding dress. If she let the darker side of her imagination run wild, she saw a body hanging from a noose.

A doll made of black roses. Meanwhile there was Kaede dressed in her black coat that day. Was it just a coincidence?

And what about the words of the caller from the phone box? 'All the preparations are complete.' What had they meant by that?

She quickly glanced around the hallway but there was no sign of anyone. She was painfully aware that this was no luxury apartment building with a round-the-clock security guard. The auto-lock system on the front entrance door to the building was pretty much just for show. Anyone determined enough could easily find their way in. For this reason, Kaede had got her landlord's permission to install a double lock on her own door.

Which meant . . .

Whoever delivered the bouquet had come up to her door and then left . . . or . . .

Oh god . . .

Or they were still somewhere very close by.

Turning around again was going to take real courage. She slipped her hand into her pocket and gripped her phone like a weapon. Then with a deep breath she spun around.

The Riddle of the Stalker

There was nobody there.

She realized her whole body had broken out into a sweat.

But then something about black roses clicked in her mind. She pulled out her phone and hurriedly googled the language of flowers.

It was as she had thought – two possible interpretations came up:

'You are forever mine.'

And –

'Hatred.'

A breeze swept down the hallway, making the bouquet sway. The light from the lift and the glow of her phone lit the 'head'of the arrangement from different angles.

4

I want to see you smile,
I want to see you cry,
I want to see you angry
From close enough to feel your breath.

There was no way Kaede was going to sleep at home that night. Fortunately, it was the middle of a long holiday weekend, and when she called her old university friend, Misaki, to ask to stay with her, she was met with an immediate positive response.

'Perfect timing. I just opened a bottle of expensive wine. No need to explain, just get over here!'

Kaede could tell that Misaki was pretending to be drunk just to put her at ease. She hadn't wanted to worry her friend by telling her about the stalker, but she knew that Misaki had sensed something was troubling her. She appreciated her friend's choice not to pry. Instead, she showed her concern through playful demands of 'Drink up!' or 'Come on, I have enough camembert here to open a cheese shop.'

Kaede was touched by Misaki's thoughtfulness. She hoped it was the start of a real friendship.

The next morning Kaede headed straight over to her grandfather's house.

Of course, she wanted to tell him about the incident with the bouquet, but more than that she was concerned about his health.

She made her way up the concrete path that had once been paving stones, and reached for the front door.

'Grandp—'

The Riddle of the Stalker

A soft piece of fabric suddenly covered her mouth, preventing her from finishing the word. Almost simultaneously she was grabbed from behind with a crushing force. Against her back she felt the kind of heat that only a male body could transmit, and along with it, a familiar scent.

'Sorry to keep you waiting, Kaede-sensei.'

Damp lips brushed her earlobe and hot breath tickled her deep inside her ear. An overwhelming pressure squeezed her chest, causing her to gasp.

'That's it. Don't speak. Don't move.'

The sing-song tone reminded her of a children's game, playful yet also menacing.

'If you understand, nod your head slowly. If you don't do what I say, I'll kill you.'

Unlike before, Kaede instantly grasped the meaning of the phrase. Although frozen with terror, she somehow managed to move her head.

The rigid iron bar around her chest loosened its grip for a moment. But then right away, she felt a sharp pinprick at the nape of her neck.

'Chloroform is such a movie cliché. This method is much more reliable.'

Finally, she felt the cloth removed from her mouth.

Now!

She opened her mouth to scream for help, but the words wouldn't come.

What??

How do I form an 'h' for help again?

The realization struck her that her tongue was numb and completely immobile.

No . . . it wasn't just her tongue. Both upper and lower jaws were numb too.

Wrong again . . . it was her entire body.

She heard something clatter to the ground.

The last thing Kaede saw through her narrowing field of vision was a syringe rolling across the concrete.

5

Was this dream or reality?

'Ah–eh–ee–oo, eh–oh–ah–oh'

From somewhere far away she could hear her grandfather's voice. He was practising his vocal exercises.

'Ah–eh–ee–oo, eh–oh–ah–oh'

Thank goodness, his voice sounds strong today. Grandpa must be better.

Kaede tried to sigh her relief but she found herself unable to exhale properly.

What was this? The weird tightness in her chest?

'Kah–keh–kee–koo, keh–koh–kah–koh'

Had she been asleep? Her eyelids felt heavy.

No – too heavy.

The Riddle of the Stalker

She tried desperately to open her eyes, but it was as if something was blocking them, preventing her lids from moving.

'Kah–keh–kee–koo, keh–koh–kah–koh'

She couldn't move her hands. Or her feet.

'Sah–seh–shee–soo, seh–soh–sah–soh'

Her right cheek was pressed against a floor that was cold and slightly soft.

Her nose picked up two distinct smells. The first was the artificial soap scent of the antibacterial spray used on her grandfather's wood carpet.

In an instant, like jolting awake from a dream of falling off a cliff, Kaede grasped the situation.

She was blindfolded, gagged, and her mouth was sealed shut with duct tape. Her wrists tied behind her back and her legs bound together at the knees and the ankles. She was sprawled on her grandfather's living-room floor.

And that other smell . . .

It was a faint fragrance she'd caught somewhere before, not at all unpleasant, but its identity was masked by the strong scent of the antibacterial spray.

'Your enunciation has made remarkable improvements since yesterday. Have you been chatting with somebody?'

From the next-door study came the voice of Doting Father.

'Not exactly, but I think I might be able to make it through all the "r" sounds today,' her grandfather replied.

'Now, let's not overdo it,' Doting Father gently admonished him. 'We'll leave pronunciation practice there for now. Let me give you a throat massage.'

Kaede heard the snap of rubber gloves being pulled on.

Where did he go? The man who attacked me?

Maybe she had woken up earlier than he'd anticipated. But obviously she had no idea when he might return. And when he did come back it was possible he'd kill her right away.

If only I could somehow let those two know I'm here . . .

Telling herself to stay calm, she began to assess the situation.

Her vision was completely obscured by the blindfold. Her coat had been removed and through her black sweater and fitted trousers she felt the cold floor along her right side. But there was also something rigid cutting into her side at intervals.

When she realized what this was, despair washed over her. It wasn't just her hands and feet that were tied together. She was completely bound with rope from head to toe . . . Which meant that rolling over would be practically impossible.

The only tool left at her disposal was her voice. She'd read in some mystery novel that, given enough time, it was possible to remove a gag or duct tape from your mouth.

Hurry but don't rush . . .

Her tongue had regained some mobility, so she began to use it to moisten the gag that dug painfully into her mouth.

'How does your throat feel now?' came the voice of Doting Father from the next-door study.

'Ah, that felt wonderful,' Grandfather replied. 'Like I've been brought back to life. Is time up already?'

'No, we still have about ten minutes.'

Kaede prayed that the speech therapist would stay as long as possible.

The study where the two men were talking had two doors. One opened into the hallway, and the other led directly into the living room where Kaede currently lay. If Doting Father took the former route, he would leave the house without ever realizing she was there.

'Shall I make you some tea? I hear from the helper that you can manage it without thickener today.'

'No, let's skip the tea. Instead, could you indulge this old man for a while, and listen to his story?'

'Of course. As I always say, conversation is the best therapy.'

And then, the most surprising words reached Kaede's ears.

'Actually, my granddaughter has a stalker.'

'What?'

Doting Father sounded completely caught off guard.

'By your granddaughter, you mean Kaede-sensei?'

'That's right. It started with silent phone calls, but lately she's being followed.'

'Well, I may be speaking out of turn, but this kind of behaviour tends to escalate over time. I think she should go to the police as soon as possible.'

'She's already talked to them, it seems, but since she has no idea who might be behind it, and there's no concrete evidence of any harm done, the police told her there's nothing they can do.'

'Hmm, I can understand what they're saying, but how frustrating! Just bureaucratic excuses.'

'Then I thought, maybe if I could uncover the identity of the stalker by logic, and also provide some concrete evidence of harassment, then surely the police would be forced to act?'

'I see. But is that even possible?'

'Well, who knows if it will work? But would you mind listening to my ideas as a kind of thought experiment?' Grandfather suggested.

'I'm intrigued.'

'Let's start by referring to this stalker as "X". Their gender is almost certainly male, especially as, when Kaede's

The Riddle of the Stalker

friend Iwata-sensei chased after him, he was too quick on his feet to be caught. What do you think?'

'He must be a man,' Doting Father agreed. 'We're talking about someone targeting a beautiful woman.'

'Furthermore, Kaede says that she has absolutely no idea who X might be. There's nobody among her friends or colleagues who fits the profile. Of course, we can't rule that out completely, but let's assume for the sake of this exercise that X is someone outside those circles. Does that sound good so far?'

'Makes sense. If the stalker was a friend or someone at work, she'd surely have noticed something by now.'

'But then, if that's the case, it brings up another important question.'

'Another question? Hmm.'

'Can't you see the problem?'

'No, I'm sorry. I can't begin to imagine.'

'The question is: how does X know Kaede's phone number?'

'Ah! Now that you mention it, that is strange.'

'In this day and age, a young woman's contact information is the ultimate in personal data. And yet X was able to obtain those details with remarkable ease. So – how did he manage that?'

'Oh, come on, Himonya-san. Don't keep me in suspense. Just tell me.'

'There is only one place where Kaede's contact information is written in bold and displayed in plain sight. X was able to look at it and memorize it easily. And that place is . . . well, look. Posted right there on the wall is a list of emergency contacts. Somewhere in the vicinity of a person like me, a patient who requires home nursing care, there's always a written note or a board with emergency contacts listed. In other words, X must be one of the people who has access to this house.'

As she listened to the conversation coming from the study door, Kaede's heart began to race. She was shocked by the revelation that the stalker could be someone who regularly visited her grandfather's home.

As she worked her mouth, the gag began to loosen, little by little.

Grandfather began to speak again, and once more Kaede strained to listen.

'You seem surprised,' Grandfather remarked.

'Of course I am! I have a weak heart. Please don't shock me like that.'

The Riddle of the Stalker

'Well then, please do take a moment to calm yourself and then consider this. Based on the pieces of information I've given you, Doting Father-san, what kind of tale would you weave?'

'What do you mean by "tale"?'

'Well, put simply, can you deduce the identity of X?'

'Hmm. I'm not sure I should say this . . .'

'Don't hold back.'

'Let me preface this by saying this is just my foolish thinking. X is a man, we've decided? But Okappa-san and the other home helpers, and even the care manager who drops by occasionally, are all women. Therefore, when we look at the men who have access to this house, the list becomes very short.'

'That's good. Far from foolish – it's very logical. You are too self-deprecating.'

'To be precise, there are only two men – the speech therapist (me), and the physical therapist. In other words, Doting Father and Soft-Serve Guy.'

'That's correct.'

'But narrowing it down any further than that is beyond my capabilities.'

'I'm sure that's not true. But I understand your hesitation, so I'll take it from here. First, X is someone who is quick on his feet. Forgive my bluntness, but you are a man over sixty with a heart condition, and not someone I would call athletic. On the other hand, Soft-Serve Guy is solidly built and helps out in the family business. I hear those milk tanks are extremely heavy.'

'Then that means—'

'Moreover, being a physical therapist is a very physically demanding job. It's not unusual to have to support the full weight of heavier patients. Thus, the identity of X becomes self-evident.'

'People can turn out to be not what they seem, can't they? Although I hate to speak ill of others.'

'I understand. But I asked for your opinion, so there's no need to feel guilty at all,' Grandfather reassured Doting Father.

Kaede had broken out in a cold sweat. And then, like a lightning bolt it hit her – that other scent.

It's vanilla!

Though faint, it was unmistakeably the scent that had tickled her nose when she'd met him before. Even in her current dire situation, an image flashed through her mind of the man who smelled of vanilla from Ellery Queen's famous work, *The Tragedy of Y*.

How could it be? That serious-looking Soft-Serve Guy is my stalker?

The Riddle of the Stalker

But considering his extraordinary speed, and the strength with which he'd seized her, it made perfect sense.

But what if he turned up here right now? Kaede felt a surge of terror at the mere thought.

'Actually, there's another reason I was suspicious of Soft-Serve Guy,' Grandfather continued from the next room.

'Oh, if you don't mind, please share.'

'At first glance he seems very honest, but he told me a blatant lie.'

'What kind of lie?'

'Well, you know all about the bell crickets that live in my garden and make such beautiful sounds, don't you? Well, he once asked me if he could record their calls on his mobile phone.'

'Yes, of course. You let me record them with an IC recorder before.'

'But here's the thing: I was recently given a gift of an encyclopaedia of insects by some children who came to visit me. I read that the sound of bell crickets is too high-frequency to be captured by a mobile phone. You need either a directional linear PCM recorder or a high-performance IC recorder like yours, and even then, you have to be close to a cricket to get a clear sound.'

'Wow, I didn't know that.'

'Yet he claimed he was using the crickets' call as his ringtone – a bald-faced lie. And if he's lying there must be some reason for it. Can you think what that might be?'

'Hmm . . . perhaps to get you to let your guard down, Himonya-san?'

'That's one possibility.'

'But as I said before, shouldn't we report him to the police right away before his stalking escalates any further?'

'No, that won't be necessary, Doting Father-san.'

'What do you mean?'

'From the limited information available, I initially reached the same conclusion as you. But then when I looked at it from another perspective and continued to analyse the data, ultimately I arrived at an entirely different conclusion.'

'A different conclusion?'

'Yes. Let's start by examining why he would lie about recording the crickets. After all, I don't think there's much benefit in his trying to trick me or win my favour. If you really think about it, the disadvantages of being caught in a lie would seem far greater.'

'That makes sense. Once you know someone's a liar it's hard to trust them at all after that.'

'Then how about this theory? He was unable to find a cricket anywhere in the grass or bushes. Though I could see them clearly, for some reason he was unable to get anywhere

The Riddle of the Stalker

close to one. Yet, to put my mind at ease, he pretended that he'd been able to record them.'

'Which means . . . so you're saying that the crickets were—'

'Exactly. Those crickets were my hallucination. Yes, he did lie – but that lie was rooted in his inherent kindness.'

'Ah, I see . . . But what is this alternative conclusion you arrived at?'

'Let me explain. But first, may I ask you a small favour?'

'Right now, of all moments! What is it?'

'Sorry . . . Pass me a cigarette, would you?'

'A cigarette? I didn't know you smoked.'

'On rare occasions. Look – they're there in the dresser drawer. The blue box marked "Gauloises". There should be a lighter with them . . . Right . . . Yes, I'm sorry but I would appreciate it if you could light one for me.'

There was the sound of Grandfather exhaling smoke.

'Thank you. Sorry about that.'

'No problem at all. Now, you were saying . . . ?'

'What I was saying? . . . Hmm, what was it again?'

'Don't tease me. You mentioned reaching a different conclusion about the identity of the stalker.'

'Oh, that's right. First, although Kaede herself doesn't seem to have noticed, let's look into the concrete harm that she has suffered through X's criminal acts. Most stalkers typically covet items belonging to their target.'

Grandfather exhaled again.

'X is no exception. In broad daylight, he brazenly stole a certain item related to Kaede.'

'I see. Well, that certainly sounds like the action of a stalker. But how does that lead you to a different conclusion?'

'Well, let's not get ahead of ourselves. When Kaede visited me yesterday, she was sorting out winter clothes. She put away several items of clothing in that chest of drawers over there, and took out this red cardigan for me. What do you think? Does it suit me? I know it's supposed to be fresh spring wear, but I'm worried it might be a little too flashy.'

'It suits you very well. I'm quite envious.'

'That's good to hear . . . No, hold on . . . This isn't a good idea.'

'What's the matter?'

'I was just thinking what a shame it would be if this lovely cardigan stank of cigarette smoke.'

'Look, I apologize if I'm getting the wrong idea, but are you purposely trying to make me anxious?' Doting Father asked.

'No, that's just your imagination.' (Exhale.) 'Now, where was I? Ah yes, the winter clothes. Kaede seemed pleased to find that there was plenty of space in the drawer to store them. But you never find a perfect empty space to

The Riddle of the Stalker

store bulky clothes just like that. That means that until very recently, something else must have been stored there.'

'Something else? Knowing you, Himonya-san, probably some old books.'

'Unfortunately, not. That "something else" was multiple picture frames containing photos of Kaede. For us DLB patients looking at photos of people or landscapes can often trigger hallucinations. That's why Kaede, concerned for my well-being, had put away all the photos and then completely forgotten about them. Oh, Doting Father-san, are you all right for time?'

'No, no. This is getting interesting. Since we've come this far, I'd like to hear the whole thing.'

'I'm glad to hear that. Now, it's not only inanimate objects such as photographs that stalkers desire, is it? They often want organic, physical materials from the person they're fixated on – for instance, fingernail clippings, a water bottle with their saliva on it, or perhaps a lock of their hair – don't they?'

'Why are you asking me?'

Grandfather took a long draw on his cigarette.

'Pardon me. No, I just meant to check if you were following the flow of my story up to this point.'

'I'm following it perfectly. As always, I'm impressed by your storytelling skills.'

'Thank you. Now there's a dresser specifically for Kaede

over there. She usually fixes her hair in the mirror before heading home. The other day I noticed something rather peculiar. Several days after Kaede visited me here, I took a magnifying glass and examined her hairbrush. Strangely enough, there was not a single hair left behind on it. Of course, one time might have just been coincidence – it's possible that no stray hairs come out when someone brushes their hair – but no matter how many times I checked, the result was always the same. The home helpers do a wonderful job of keeping my personal items clean, but they certainly wouldn't extend their services to Kaede's dresser. Which leads me to the conclusion that X must have been stealing the hair from Kaede's brush.'

'Ah I see. So, you're saying that Soft-Serve Guy has been stealing Kaede-sensei's hair?'

'Let's not be too hasty.'

'Why do you say that?'

'First off, we deduced that X is someone athletic enough to outrun a male teacher in his twenties who jogs regularly. In other words, somebody who has considerable sporting experience.'

'That's why it has to be Soft-Serve Guy.'

'Not necessarily. Talking of fast runners – I've long suspected that you, Doting Father-san, have something of a track and field background.'

'What?'

The Riddle of the Stalker

'I think it was back in the autumn when you gave me a compliment. Do you remember? Because of the breadth of my knowledge across various fields, you likened me to a decathlon champion? Come on, don't tell me you've forgotten?'

'I remember. But you see, I only brought up the decathlon as an example. I don't think it was a stretch using that as an analogy. Just because I said the word doesn't mean that I have track and field experience.'

'No, that's not the issue. It was the pronunciation.'

'What? Pronunciation?'

'Yes.'

'Are you feeling all right? You're beginning to sound incoherent.'

'Then let me do some vocal exercises in front of a professional. Will you listen?'

'As you like.'

'Decathlon, decathlon, decathlon, deca—'

'All right! How long are you planning to keep this up? I've no idea what you're trying to convey. Although I must admit your enunciation is pretty good today.'

'Ask the average person to say the word "decathlon" and they would pronounce it with an extra "a" sound between the h and the l. Decath-a-lon. But you pronounce it correctly. Maybe it's because you're a speech therapist; or perhaps it's a word you're extremely familiar with.'

'Huh. So then how come you pronounce it correctly?'

'My knowledge all comes from books.'

'Well, what a coincidence. My own knowledge is from books too. It's simply a well-known fact that decathlon is pronounced that way. I have zero experience in track and field.'

'Fair enough. That's quite possible. So let me ask instead; why does your breath smell of vanilla today?'

'What?'

'It's because you're drinking protein shakes. I've heard that the vanilla flavour is very popular.'

'I don't know anything about protein shakes. I just love ice cream, especially vanilla. Even though I'm a diabetic I end up eating it every day – twice sometimes.'

'That's the first time you've mentioned it. If you're so fond of vanilla ice cream, wouldn't the topic naturally have come up when we were talking about Soft-Serve Guy?'

'Theoretically, I suppose, but I must have forgotten to mention it.'

'Let's move on to the next one.'

'There's more?'

'Yesterday when Kaede was here you asked her, "Are those your shoes at the door? They're really nice running shoes."'

'I said that because that's what I thought.'

The Riddle of the Stalker

'But why did you call them "running shoes"? Usually when people see that style of shoes, they refer to them as "trainers".'

'That's . . . er . . .'

'If you're going to hesitate, allow me to explain. Ordinary people without an athletic background can't distinguish that easily between trainers and running shoes. In fact, even Iwata-sensei, who's a runner himself, initially mistook Kaede's shoes for regular trainers. Yet you, with just one glimpse of Kaede's shoes in the entryway, referred to them as running shoes. It suggests to me that you're still an active runner.'

'So, what if I am?'

'What do you mean?'

'Let's say I am an experienced athlete and still keep in decent shape, that doesn't clear the physical therapist of suspicion. Compare our ages, build and appearance objectively. Wouldn't the young, energetic physical therapist still be the most suspicious?'

'No. He's not X.'

'Oh, please! How can you be so sure?'

'I collected fingerprints from the hairbrush multiple times. It's not widely known, but it is surprisingly easy to take fingerprints just using items found in a dresser. Put some foundation onto a cotton bud and gently dab it on the hairbrush handle. Then you carefully place clear sticky tape over it, and voilà, the fingerprints appear.'

'Well, I'm sorry I just don't get it. What's the significance of a fingerprint on a hairbrush? Are you trying to tell me that you found my fingerprints?'

'Quite the opposite.'

'The opposite?'

'No matter how many times I tried, over many days, the only fingerprints I found on that hairbrush were Kaede's. The physical therapist always works on me barehanded, so if he touched the brush, he would have left prints. Which means that X is someone who always wears gloves when he visits.'

'Like I do?'

'Yes. Kaede's stalker, X, is you.'

Snap, snap.

Snap, snap.

In the ensuing silence, Kaede heard the repeated sound of a pair of thin rubber gloves being pinched and snapped.

She couldn't believe it. The person who had been stalking her was none other than that kindly Doting Father.

The shock at the revelation that her hair had been stolen, and the utter terror at discovering her stalker was

The Riddle of the Stalker

an acquaintance old enough to be her father, were like two invisible ropes constricting her heart.

But worse than that, there was a more immediate fear that began to creep into her mind.

How was her grandfather so calm and composed after revealing directly to the stalker that he knew his identity? If Doting Father were to retaliate physically, neither Grandfather nor she would stand a chance.

Her only hope was to somehow escape and call for help.

If she could somehow cut one of the ropes binding her, then at least she might be able to roll over. Then she could roll down the hallway to the front door . . .

No, that won't work . . .

Here in this room was Grandfather's bed, and beside it, an emergency button to connect to medical services. If she could just press that button . . . but no, she realized it would be impossible to reach that high.

Of course, the toilet!

If she could somehow get there, she'd be able to reach the emergency button even from the floor. And the toilet was directly across the hallway from the living room where she was. Even though she was blindfolded, she knew exactly which way to go.

Keeping an ear open to the conversation in the study, Kaede began to rub her right side against the floor in the hope of fraying the ropes.

'Hmm, only a mystery enthusiast would come up with such a convoluted solution,' Doting Father was saying. 'Is it your love for a whodunnit with an unexpected culprit that's leading you to cast me as the villain in this story?'

'I see what you mean, but it is pure coincidence things have turned out this way,' Grandfather responded. 'This is no attempt to frame you.'

'Although it might appear logical on the surface, your line of reasoning has its flaws.'

'Does it now?'

'All you've done is prove that a speech therapist removed hair from Kaede's brush. It happens that I'm meticulous about cleanliness. I immediately dispose of any trash so as to reduce the burden on your family members. I expect gratitude, not accusations of being a stalker.'

'Then why wasn't there any hair in the nearby rubbish bin? Not a single hair in the large waste bins in the living room, or the corner of the kitchen. Where did it all go?'

'Maybe you threw it all away?'

'I see. That's where you're going with this?'

'In any case, the absence of hair and fingerprints doesn't prove anything. It may just be that there weren't any stray hairs lately. And to claim that your speech therapist touched

The Riddle of the Stalker

the hairbrush because there *weren't* any fingerprints – well, that's just far-fetched. The lack of my fingerprints on it would imply to most people that I *didn't* touch it.'

'Hmm. The game gets interesting, Doting Father-san.'

'Yes, I'm enjoying it too, Himonya-san.'

Grandfather exhaled loudly.

'Ugh, no more cigarettes for me. Please wet the butt and properly dispose of it in the rubbish bin *this time.*'

'Well, I object to your phrasing, but understood.'

'Now then, there's one thing I intentionally avoided mentioning earlier.'

'So that's how we're playing it?'

'Are you familiar with the term "glove prints"? Ah, it seems from your expression that you aren't. While you won't find clear patterns as with fingerprints, the presence or absence of gloves can be easily proven. But really, there's no need to go through such complicated procedures – if the police were to search your home, they'd doubtless turn up both Kaede's hair and photographs. Oh, and I almost forgot something important. Earlier you said, "Once you know someone's a liar it's hard to trust them at all after that." But you're the liar. You once claimed that your daughter was delighted when you played the recording of the crickets for her. That was a lie.'

'Wait a moment! That wasn't a mobile phone I used to record them on. It was a state-of-the-art IC recorder that can capture any insect sounds. You even mentioned that earlier. It was Soft-Serve Guy who lied, not me.'

'No, you're lying.'

'I don't understand.'

'According to that insect encyclopaedia the children gave me, crickets never chirp in groups. They make their call individually, alone in separate patches of grass. But I found three crickets perched together on the same leaf. That's impossible. Those crickets were hallucinations. Soft-Serve Guy's lie was out of kindness. But your lie is different – a dirty lie to cover up your true identity. That IC recorder was for eavesdropping on Kaede. I bet it's full of recordings of her voice. What's more, you're not even a doting father. You don't have a daughter. When you bragged about your daughter's beautiful hair, you were really complimenting Kaede's.'

'Who the hell do you think you are?'

'Just an old man with dementia.'

Doting Father's – or rather, X's – tone had changed completely.

Careful, Grandpa!

Desperately, Kaede rubbed her side against the floor, but the ropes were stubbornly solid. If only she had those fake

The Riddle of the Stalker

gel nails like so many young women of her generation, they might have helped . . . Ironically, the gag was finally loosening, and her tongue could almost reach the duct tape covering her mouth. But she knew that shouting would be a bad move right now.

That physical strength . . .

The sensation of being so brutally restrained outside in the garden suddenly flooded back.

'Are we still playing our game, Himonya-san?'

'I think it's almost game over. Is there anything you'd like to ask me?'

'How I'm doing. I think I've cleverly evaded capture up to now, even if I do say so myself.'

'Ha ha. No, you haven't. You made a major blunder earlier.'

'Earlier?'

'Remember when I told you that my granddaughter has a stalker? Normally people would ask who. Questions such as "Who's she being stalked by?" "Does she know him?" "Is it a friend?" "Someone from her workplace?" The first thing anyone would be interested in is the identity of the stalker. But you skipped all that and went straight to suggesting calling the police. That was a gigantic misstep, a serious blunder on your part. It would never occur to anyone to recommend police involvement without knowing the details of the case. Which means, of course, that you, better than anyone, already know the full details.'

'I see. Indeed, it might be about time to end this game.'

'Typically, I'd ask for a cigarette right about now, but since it's about time, I'll hold off for now.'

'What are you talking about? It's about time for what?'

'Calm down and listen. It's a rare opportunity we have here. As this game nears its climax, let me speculate about X's motives. The other day, you called Kaede from a public phone box and you told her, "There's no need to worry. All the preparations are complete." What exactly have you been preparing? Stalkers' distorted romantic feelings sometimes lead to tragic outcomes such as murder-suicide, but thankfully that doesn't seem to be the case here. Your threat to Kaede, "I'll kill you if you keep saying such heartless things" suggests you don't actually intend to kill her. Which leads me to suppose these are preparations for a wedding. I wouldn't be surprised if right now in your home, Kaede's hair and photos were on display, and a wedding dress hanging in the middle of the room. You're planning to confine her to your home and live together for ever. That's your definition of marriage.'

'Very impressive, Himonya-san. But what a waste for you to die here in such a cramped room.'

The Riddle of the Stalker

'Sorry, do you mean in the near future, or are you saying right now?'

'What if it's the latter?'

'I'd advise against it. I mentioned before that it was about time. What I meant was that the police are going to arrive at any minute.'

'What the—?'

Kaede heard the sound of a chair clattering to the floor. X must have jumped to his feet.

Thank goodness Grandpa's always one step ahead . . .

They were going to be saved. And with that thought, the last bit of adrenaline drained from her body. No need to waste any excess energy. She calmed her breathing and waited for the police to arrive.

Lifting her head slightly, she continued to listen to the conversation in the study.

'When did you call the police?'

'Right before you got here. They should be here at any moment, although they seem to be running a little late.'

'But there's no phone in this room. How did you manage to call?'

'Sanae happened to be here. When I told her you were X she was quite shocked. I asked her to call the police right away.'

'. . . Sanae?'

'Don't you know her? My daughter. She drops by from time to time.'

Oh no.
This can't be happening.
It was all so brilliantly calculated.
Grandpa, stop. This is heartbreaking.
Mum – Mum is . . .

'As a parent I shouldn't say this, but ever since childhood Sanae has always been a cheerful child, bright like a sunflower. She loves singing for people. The living room next door has been remodelled to be barrier free, but it used to be a traditional Japanese-style room with dividing fusuma sliding doors. Whenever family was over, Sanae would hide on the other side of the doors and whisper to me, "Daddy,

The Riddle of the Stalker

I'm behind here. Open the fusuma really slowly." And then the intro to an *enka* song would start playing on a cassette deck behind the doors. I'd open the doors as if they were a curtain on a stage, and announce, "Ladies and Gentlemen, thank you for your patience. And now, five-year-old Sanae will perform 'Tsugaru Kaikyo Fuyugeshiki'." Her song was always received with cheers and thunderous applause. Ha ha. I wonder how many times I got roped into playing the role of stage hand. For some reason, the song was always the same one: "Tsugaru Kaikyo Fuyugeshiki". Of course, when Sanae got married she sang that – hmm, I don't recall if she sang it at the wedding reception . . . Now did she or not . . . ? Huh? What's the matter? Why the strange face?'

'I'm laughing.'

'Why?'

'Why? Because this is just too funny. It turns out that the odds of this game were stacked in my favour from the beginning.'

'What are you on about?'

'Too bad, Himonya-san. Your mind seems razor-sharp, but in the end you're just a senile old fool.'

'Senile old—'

'Since you pride yourself on being so logical, allow me a logical rebuttal of your argument. You already pointed out to me that Kaede's contact information is posted over there on a memo. If that's the case then why isn't Sanae's information written there too? She's your daughter, after all, and supposedly she visits this house quite frequently. Then why are there no contact details for this precious daughter? Does it not seem more puzzling to you than the absence of fingerprints on a hairbrush?'

'I hadn't thought of that.'

'You seem to have forgotten, but I set you a trap during today's pronunciation exercises. I asked you if you'd been chatting with someone, and you replied, "Not exactly," which neatly sidestepped my question. But right before I entered this room, I clearly heard you talking to someone – someone who no longer exists. In fact, you were asking your daughter's ghost to call the police for you. Hilarious, isn't it?'

'Wait – I hate to admit it, but it is possible that I was talking to a vision of Sanae. But you're wrong when you say she no longer exists. The fact is, Sanae is still very much alive.'

'Oh, wow, this is too much. My stomach hurts. Could you cut it out? I can't keep it up any longer. I've been trying so hard to keep a straight face this whole time.'

'What are you talking about?'

'Let me make it crystal clear for you. Sanae is no longer in this world. Twenty-seven years ago, on the day of her wedding, I killed her with my own hands, that traitorous

The Riddle of the Stalker

betrayer of a woman. And that's why, regrettably for you, the police won't be coming.'

Kaede let out a soundless scream.

'*Mum!*'

And then, as if to admonish herself for feeling faint,

'*Dad!*'

At the same moment, there was a dreadful thud from the study. She imagined her grandfather's arm had slipped from its armrest and collided with the study wall.

Abandoning all reason, Kaede continued to scream into the tiny space behind the duct tape.

'*Mum! Dad! The killer . . . the killer's right here!*'

'Hey, don't get all wobbly on me now. We can't end this game without you hearing my side of the story. Recently Kaede has started to look so much like Sanae. They call that a "spitting image", don't they? Now the resemblance is that close, I just can't control myself. Yes, I even feel hatred for her. You know it's all Kaede's fault. Please forgive me for dropping the honorific "sensei" but she is my fiancée after all . . . Huh? What's that? I can't hear you. You look all deflated now that you've lost the game. Ah, you want to know where Kaede is right now. I'll tell you – she's currently lying unconscious on the floor in the next room. As long as she stays quiet, I plan to take good care of her. Ultimately, she does love me. So, feel free to go ahead and die in peace, Himonya-san.'

Snap, snap.

The sound of latex gloves once again.

Kaede was so filled with rage that she couldn't even cry.

I won't forgive him. I can't forgive him.

There was no time to make it to the panic button in the toilet.

It was her last chance – she had to scream for help.

Kaede stretched her tongue through the gap in the loosened gag and desperately tried to peel the tape off her mouth.

'Now, let's try another vocal exercise. This is simply language rehabilitation, so no one will think twice about the glove marks around your mouth. First, I'll place each of my index fingers into the corners of your mouth . . . That's it.

The Riddle of the Stalker

Ready? Let's begin. "Ah–eh–ee–oo, eh–oh–ah–oh." What's wrong? There's no sound coming out. Shall we try changing the chant? "Sa–na–e, Sa–na–e." Oh dear, is that not working either? Where's all that energy you had before? Let's change the chant again. "Ka–e–de, Ka–e–de." Oh my, my, you're not doing well at all, are you? Shall we move on to a throat massage? Ugh, there's so much drool. I'll have to change these gloves.'

(Snap, snap)

A corner of the duct tape over Kaede's upper lip was finally beginning to peel away.

Just a little more . . .
A little bit more . . .
(Snap, snap)
(Snap!)

'Now then, let me take a look at your throat. Oh my, it's already tense again, even though I just massaged it for you. This time I'll apply a bit more pressure, so bear with me. What's wrong? It's just for a moment.'

A section of the tape tore away.

Kaede took a deep breath and screamed through the tiny gap.

'Help! Someone!'

But right at that instant, warm fingers covered her mouth from above.

'Be quiet, Kaede-sensei. It's me, Shiki.'

Long, soft hair brushed her cheek as her blindfold and gag were removed.

'Sh-Shiki! Grandpa—'

'Your grandfather's fine. Don't underestimate him.'

There was a loud crash of a body or a chair falling . . . followed by a shrill cry – X's voice.

'Ow, that hurts! My arm . . . it's breaking!'

'A Japanese jujutsu technique popular in Victorian England. Holmes used to call it "Baritsu". Whether he had mastered this arm lock is uncertain though.'

'Quit it, old man! You'll regret this later!'

'Don't bother trying to escape. I've got you completely pinned. On days like today when I'm in good health my old skills come in handy. And lately I've been practising arm-wrestling with the physical therapist, Soft-Serve Guy. Of course he goes easy on me, but the other day I managed to beat him for the first time. He was quite frustrated about it.'

I see . . . I get it now.

That time Soft-Serve Guy came out of the study with a hint of hostility in his expression – it was nothing more than frustration at having lost to Grandpa.

'Enough with the chat. Let me go. Or do you want to die?'

'The more you struggle, the more it's going to hurt. Now, Iwata-sensei, how did it go?'

Along with the loud shattering of a window, Kaede heard Iwata's voice.

'Great! It's all been recorded.'

'Good. What a blessing to know how to use a high-performance IC recorder.'

Shiki sighed and ran his fingers through his hair.

'I told him it'd be fine to come in through the front door, but he didn't listen.'

X's tone had shifted to one of pleading.

'P-please stop.'

'No, that's not an option. First, you need to listen carefully to my explanation.'

Grandfather's voice was surprisingly steady, despite still having X's arm in a lock.

'I also suspected that Sanae might be a product of my hallucinations, so each time Kaede visited, I'd say things like, "You just missed Sanae again today," and observe her reaction. When I saw her forced smile, I realized the truth. And the absence of her phone number on the contact list suggested to me that something horrifying might have happened in the past. I might even speculate that X had been stalking two generations of "Dandelion Girls". But you know, human beings are ultimately fragile creatures.'

'Stop rambling, will you, and let me go!'

'Today as always, I believed Sanae would come. When she appeared and I asked her to call the police, I had the feeling that this would finally settle things. It's sad to say, but having considered the possibility that she was a hallucination, I had already asked Shiki-san and Iwata-sensei to come over. Now, as for the issue of whether Sanae exists . . .'

For a moment, Grandfather stumbled over his words. Traces of tears were in his eyes.

'. . . Whether Sanae exists or not, it would seem there is no room for debate. It seems that right now I am presented

The Riddle of the Stalker

with two potential tales to weave. The first is the tale of breaking your arm right here and now.'

'Tales? Who the hell do you think you are, old man? Just go ahead and try!'

X's attempt at bravado through his pain seemed to fall on deaf ears.

'The second tale is about the power of will, and not being swayed by hatred. My intellect is already diminishing daily. To break your arm would mean I'm no longer myself.'

His voice didn't waver as he spoke the next words.

'I can't bring myself to break it.'

He continued in his resolute tone.

'And I won't break it.'

What a strong person her grandfather was. Out of sheer willpower he had managed to banish his personal grievances, to chase them away like swirling purple smoke.

For a moment it felt as if Grandfather's grip had loosened, and X might manage to break free. Shiki half rose, ready to spring into the study. But . . . there was another shriek from X.

'Ow, ow! You stop too! You know I'm well over sixty!'

Iwata was apparently punching him.

'What gives you the right to say that?' Iwata demanded, his voice trembling with tears as he struck X. 'This one's for Grandpa!'

'Help me!'

'And this one – it's for someone I love deeply.'

Iwata-sensei!

A few moments later, Shiki called out to his former catcher in the study.

'Hey, Senpai, that's enough. There's such a thing as a citizen's arrest, but if you take it any further you could be charged with assault.'

And at last, the sound of police and ambulance sirens signalled the end of the game.

X surrendered, still muttering curses.

Then . . . 'Sanae?' The tone of Grandfather's voice was much softer than before.

'I'm sorry for opposing your marriage. Please, both of you, there's no need to bow. Please.'

He seemed to be seeing visions, interwoven with old memories.

'Sanae tells me you like a drink . . .'

His voice grew even softer.

'My dear, remember that bottle of Scotch we picked up

The Riddle of the Stalker

in Baker Street on our honeymoon? Where did we put it . . . ?'

Kaede instantly understood. Right now, it wasn't only her own young parents her grandfather was chatting with, but his late wife was there too.

'No, don't get up. I'll do it. There's an art to mixing it just right. Hey, don't look so worried. I'm not here to pick a fight, and anyway who am I to come between two people in love? You know, back in the day when we got married, we faced lots of opposition at first.'

It was the first time Kaede had heard that story.

6

Kaede woke up in bed to Shiki's face right in hers.

'Did you manage to get some sleep?' he asked with a childlike grin that could have made anyone relax. 'They wanted to keep you in hospital overnight just in case.'

'How's Grandpa?'

'Sound asleep in the next room. He must be wiped out.'

The steady beep of a heart monitor filled the room. It was eerily quiet in the emergency ward at night.

'I wonder if Iwata-sensei's OK?'

Shiki lowered his voice.

'He's at the police station giving a statement. That guy's pretty tight with law enforcement these days.'

Kaede pulled her arms out from under the covers, arching her back and stretching her body, before letting her head drop back on the pillow.

'Hey, Shiki, I need to ask you something.'

'What is it?'

'How did the two of you know where to find me?'

Shiki scratched the tip of his nose thoughtfully.

'You remember when someone was staring at you on the riverbank? After that I discussed it with Iwata and we decided to confer with your grandfather too. We devised a plan to take turns keeping an eye on you. On weekdays it was me, and on weekends Iwata.'

'So, the creepy feeling I've had lately of being followed—'

'Was probably our fault, yes. But I practised tailing people when my theatre company was putting on a detective drama, so I was pretty confident I wouldn't be spotted. If you ever felt anything, blame Iwata.'

He chuckled.

'Yesterday I was tailing you from Himonya to Gumyoji, but before you got there, the stalker had already left you a bouquet of flowers.'

The wail of an ambulance siren sliced through the silence of the hospital ward, eventually fading away, replaced by the sounds of a stretcher being wheeled through the corridor, accompanied by racing footsteps.

The Riddle of the Stalker

'Listen, Kaede-sensei,' Shiki began, his expression serious. 'I genuinely believe that jobs in the medical and education fields, such as yours or my senpai's, are sacred professions. Maybe it's because I'm an actor, which some might see as a frivolous job, but I want you to know I really respect the work you do. That doesn't mean that I see myself as inferior or anything; I think everyone has their own role to play.'

'Yes,' said Kaede quietly.

'That's why this case is so troubling. Something really felt off about it.'

Shiki glanced towards the door, beyond which the commotion had not yet subsided.

'We've been speaking with some of the other carers and home helpers, and it revealed something totally astounding and horrifying. It turns out that the stalker was impersonating a speech therapist.'

'What?'

'When home care for elderly patients is first set up, there's generally a care manager who leads the team. This team will consist of physical therapists, speech therapists and home helpers. What is less commonly known is that these professionals are employed from various separate agencies, meaning they generally meet for the first time at the patient's home.

'He exploited a blind spot,' Shiki continued. 'First, he called the care management office, pretending to be your grandfather, and explained that, as rehabilitation costs were piling up, he was going to have to cancel his speech therapy sessions. Then he turned up at your grandfather's house, claiming to be the replacement for the previous speech therapist, who had been transferred. All these care workers are so incredibly busy that occasionally these communication gaps do occur, although of course not usually with any malicious intent, unlike what happened here.'

Kaede gripped the edge of her pillow, her gaze drifting beyond the hospital ward window. What were people thinking about out there, under the myriad lights of the city night? There were always those who concocted vile schemes beyond the comprehension of ordinary folks.

Perhaps the visions that her grandfather saw were more beautiful than the real world.

7

The first time I took your picture,
You didn't notice, did you?
A 'two-shot' of you and me.
You didn't notice, did you?

(It refers to an ultrasound photo, of course.)

Kaede gently closed the little diary she always carried with her, one that could instantly calm her soul with just one glance. On the cover, in the elegant calligraphy she had inherited from Grandfather, Kaede's mother had written, 'To You in my belly, From Sanae.'

Soft sunlight flooded the garden where the buds on the cherry tree planted by Kaede's father had started to burst open.

From his seat on the *engawa* veranda, Grandfather began to speak with pride.

'Sanae came to visit yesterday. She was delighted to hear that our cherry blossoms were blooming before the shrine's.'

Sitting beside him, Kaede turned her head as she choked back tears of relief.

There seemed to be truth in the theory that negative memories faded when self-defence instincts kicked in. Grandfather seemed to recall every detail of the recent incident, but his memories of Sanae's death were totally erased. He still believed that she was the one who had called the police.

Or maybe not, Kaede reconsidered. Possibly her grandfather was aware of everything, but was pretending not to remember, trying to spare her the worry.

She glanced at Grandfather's profile, where its many wrinkles formed soft curves. Today he was in remarkably fine spirits, busy devouring a castella cake that appeared to be a gift from someone. He wasn't even taking a sip of coffee to wash it down.

'You know, it's not only Sanae who's been dropping by; I've seen quite a lot of Iwata-sensei lately too,' he remarked.

'Eh?' That was the first she'd heard of it.

'He came around bowing so deeply I thought his head was going to scrape the floor, begging me to teach him about mystery writing, starting at the basics. And right then, that adorable trio of students came by to borrow books. "Whoa, Gan-chan-sensei," they said, "what are you doing here?" They laughed at him, and he looked quite embarrassed. Anyway, I'm starting off by getting him to read Poe.'

'I see. So that castella cake—'

'Yes, Iwata-sensei made it. But how did he know I had a sweet tooth? Everything he brings is so intensely sugary.' He gave Kaede a playful wink. 'I think that man might have some deductive skills after all.'

Kaede closed her eyes for a moment. Given the tangible existence of the homemade cake, she knew that Iwata's visits weren't a figment of her grandfather's imagination. She could picture the teacher's face crumpling into a smile as he borrowed a copy of the world's first modern detective story, Edgar Allan Poe's 'The Murders in the Rue Morgue'.

She knew the murder mystery lectures were just a pretext – the truth was Iwata was worried about her

The Riddle of the Stalker

grandfather's health. And she was sure her grandfather was perfectly aware of this.

Oh no . . .

She'd been lost in thoughts of Iwata, and forgotten her main purpose for visiting today.

'Grandpa, could you take a look at this? It's an anonymous letter,' she said, seeking his approval before opening the envelope with its neatly written address.

Grandfather put on his reading glasses and his mouth curved into a sweet smile at the sight of the postmark.

'It's from Madonna-sensei,' he said.

He took his time reading, then carefully folded the letter, his hands trembling slightly.

'She's become the adviser to the swimming club. She says she can't wait for summer to come around.'

Even though she'd never met the young woman, Kaede couldn't help being happy for her. She decided not to ask which island school she was teaching at. It was good to retain some mystery.

She had more good news to share.

'And I must tell you, I stopped by Haruno izakaya earlier. It's still closed of course, but there were messages to the owner from her regular customers posted all over. Things like "Can't wait for you to open again" and "Looking forward to trying your new stew recipes". There were so many notes.'

'That's just what I want to tell her, too,' said Grandfather, tossing a crumb of castella to a sparrow that had just flown in from the bamboo grove. The bird pecked at the cake and then flew off in the direction of Haruno, like a carrier pigeon conveying a message.

Conveying a message . . .

Kaede finally made up her mind to bring up the topic she'd wanted to discuss all along.

'Hey, Grandpa?'

'Yes?'

'I . . .'

Tears streamed down her cheeks. She had no idea where they'd come from.

'I think . . . for the first time ever, I may have fallen in love with someone.'

Grandfather's face gradually transformed, like a scene in slow motion. It was a smile more radiant than any Kaede had seen in years. He was instantly ten years younger.

'I see.'

He paused a moment, then repeated the phrase, savouring it.

'I see.'

His gaze drifted back to the cherry blossom buds.

'Well, this is quite a challenging case, isn't it?' he remarked, the charming smile still lighting up his face.

He rubbed the high bridge of his nose.

The Riddle of the Stalker

'They are both such fine young men. "The Lady, or the Tiger?" . . . In your place, Kaede, I'd be deeply conflicted. But am I the right person to hear such an important story?'

'I really want you to hear it, Grandpa. I want your advice.'

'I see,' he said once again, beaming with delight.

And then . . . as she had predicted . . . he uttered that familiar phrase.

'Kaede, pass me a cigarette, would you?'